THE MISSING MINX

Nadine Price, the beautiful new barmaid at the Riverside Hotel in Larne, revelled in stealing young men from their sweethearts, playing them off against each other and discarding them. When the community was seething with anger, she vanished. Various people were suspected of murder, but the police were convinced that Nadine had bolted and the case was closed. However, the village was still a hotbed of suspicion and ex-Superintendent 'Tubby' Greene was persuaded to visit Larne, in a very private capacity, to see what could be done . . .

RICHARD GOYNE

THE MISSING MINX

Complete and Unabridged

LINFORD
Leicester

First Linford Edition
published 1998

British Library CIP Data

Goyne, Richard
    The missing minx.—Large print ed.—
Linford mystery library
    1. Detective and mystery stories
    2. Large type books
    I. Title
823.9′14 [F]

ISBN 0–7089–5389–1

Published by
F. A. Thorpe (Publishing) Ltd.
Anstey, Leicestershire

Set by Words & Graphics Ltd.
Anstey, Leicestershire
Printed and bound in Great Britain by
T. J. International Ltd., Padstow, Cornwall

This book is printed on acid-free paper

1

The big, fat florid man who was trimming the hedge in front of the red-brick villa was in a vile temper. He cursed the clippers for their bluntness; he cursed the privet hedge for its toughness; he cursed the sun for trying to fry him through his flimsy, wide-open shirt; and he cursed the cigarettes he was chain-smoking for not being impervious to sweat. Now and then, too, he peered expectantly into the open doorway of the house as though he were only waiting for his housekeeper to appear and he would curse her with the rest of his troubles — particularly if there was lamb again for lunch.

At the root of all this ill-humour, however, there was a black, impenetrable hatred of himself. Ex-Superintendent Frank Aloysius Greene — 'Tubby' Greene to his intimates — had hated himself in varying degrees ever since his unwilling retirement from Scotland Yard and the

Metropolitan Police two years ago. This self-hatred became unbearable on hot days when the lawns or the hedges needed urgent attention, and Mrs. Chard was deaf to his ingenious excuses for further procrastination.

Bitter thoughts chased one another through his mind now, in a sort of rhythm with the savage clop-clop of the devilish contraption in his plump, sore hands. What in the name of reason had induced him to retire to the country? He would certainly go permanently off his rocker if he remained much longer in this damned backwater of Herefordshire with that housekeeper of his. Mrs. Chard and her lamb! Tough lamb at that. A decent meal of it on Sunday, but he'd had to gulp down his beer at the Bell Inn and rush for lunch prompt at one o'clock to enjoy it hot. So, inevitably, indigestion. And on Monday there'd been cold lamb with boiled potatoes — in the steam and smell of washday! Tuesday it'd been chopped lamb, tasting like bits of rubber in a medley of chopped-up other things. Today, Wednesday, it was dam' certain to be minced lamb, and —

Failing with six savage assaults to sever a piece of stalk in the hedge, the Super — as he was known to other than his intimates — flung down the clippers in a gesture of blind, frustrated fury.

'Damn and blast the blitherin' bloody — !'

'Mr. Greene, *please!*' Mrs. Chard had chosen this worst of all moments to appear in the front doorway. 'You should be gentle with those clippers,' she admonished him.

'Gentle!' he roared. 'The darned thing don't even bend these stalks if you treat it like a human being. It's — '

'It's hot mince cakes for lunch,' she informed him. 'The last of the lamb. So if you want your usual pint at the Bell Inn it's high time you were making in that direction.'

She disappeared, leaving a somewhat mollified employer to pick up the clippers and feel slightly ashamed of himself. He was reflecting that it was decent of the old bird to remember his pint, when he heard the sound of a car turning into the Avenue, and cocked a selective ear.

3

It was not, he decided by the sound of it, one of the few cars that belonged to the Avenue. When it came round the bend he took a look at it, and, remembering his antiquated Austin Seven in the garage, glowered with envious hostility. The Super detested 'all these flash modern cars', and he dubbed the new and expensive saloon approaching him now as more like a boat on wheels than most of its contemporaries. Then, to his astonishment, he saw that the monstrosity was slowing down and drawing to the kerb with the obvious intention of stopping in front of his house.

'Blimey,' he muttered incredulously, 'I've got a caller.'

The gleaming car stopped. The near-side front door opened and a clean-shaven, handsome giant of a man, in the uniform of a police sergeant, squeezed himself out on to the pavement and straightened up. The Super's florid face and its several chins creased into a pattern of smiles.

'Jim Dolly, by crikey!' he cried, flinging the clippers away and making a dash for

4

the front gate. '*Sergeant* Jim Dolly, by all that's wonderful!' He gripped the newcomer's hand and pumped it hard. 'Last time I saw you, Jim, you was a ruddy p.c. How're you getting on over at Wynchester? How's the wife? How's Grandma? How's the family?'

Jim Dolly laughed as he gently but firmly freed his hand.

'Yes, sir,' he said. 'I've got my stripes at last, thanks to you. The family's fine. We miss Drawbridge quite a bit, on and off; and we miss you most of the time, Mr. Greene.' He stepped to one side and drew himself to attention. 'I've brought a gentleman to see you,' he announced. 'Colonel Fielding, the Chief Constable of Levenshire — ex-Superintendent Greene.'

The Super glanced keenly at the tall, grey, immaculately dressed man who had followed the sergeant from the car. The newcomer looked a typical Army officer, except for the small, neat beard he had apparently acquired since his retirement from that service.

'Colonel Fielding,' the Super recalled,

offering a guardedly friendly hand. 'Let's see, sir, you must be the father of Inspector Fielding, Sergeant Dolly's new boss over at Wynchester?'

The colonel nodded and smiled.

'That's right, Superintendent. I paid my son a surprise visit this morning; that's one reason I'm here now.'

The Super pulled out a vast handkerchief and wiped his face.

'Come inside, gentlemen,' he invited them. 'I dare say we can all do with a drink.'

He led the way into the front room of the house: a room that was a perpetual battleground between Mrs. Chard and himself. He grunted disgustedly when he saw that she had been tidying it out of all recognition again, while he had been agonizing over the front hedge. Colonel Fielding glanced approvingly, however, at the well-worn, comfortable furniture, and the collection of photographs and other trophies and souvenirs of the Super's long service in the Force.

'By jove, this radiogram is a beauty!' he exclaimed. 'A presentation from your colleagues at the Yard, I see.'

'Never listen to anything except the news,' the Super snorted from the cocktail cabinet. 'Get too much of the Hardings, the Pickles and the Lyons in my newspapers, without having 'em on the radio as well. Make yourselves comfortable, gentlemen. Yours is a beer, Jim, eh? What about you, Colonel?'

'The same for me, please,' Fielding pleaded, dropping heavily into one of the armchairs in front of the fireplace. 'Gad, what a summer this has been. Mid-September and no end to it yet.'

The Super nodded heartfelt agreement as he handed round tankards and bottles of beer, and established himself in the other armchair.

'Summer in Drawbridge is Purgatory personified,' he grumbled. 'Nothing has happened here since the Draper murders, and that business lost us our most lively inhabitant — Jim Dolly there.'

Colonel Fielding laughed.

'Jim Dolly owes his promotion to your influence, Super, after your brilliant work on that Draper case, and he knows it.'

7

'Jim's superiors,' the Super chuckled, 'didn't take so kindly to the meddling of an old pensioner from the Yard.'

'Well, Super, perhaps we can do something to relieve your present boredom.' Fielding drank from his tankard and set it aside. He looked suddenly a badly worried man. 'You will have read about the Price mystery over at Larne, of course.'

The Super nodded.

'Gold-digging barmaid disappeared from the Riverside Hotel there eight weeks ago. In the same night there was another disappearance and a suicide in the district. The natives won't have it that the barmaid wasn't murdered in the locality. The police won't have it that she was. I suppose, Colonel, she actually *did* do a bunk, or didn't she?'

Colonel Fielding frowned.

'The police are convinced the girl has left the country. Officially, our investigations in Larne and district are at an end, in that connection. But, as you suggested, the local people won't have it that way.'

'Nadine Price,' he went on gravely, 'played havoc with the hitherto peaceful life of that village, Greene. She left Larne a hot-bed of suspicion and strife, and local feeling, instead of dying down since our investigations ceased, has boiled up into something quite frightening. No one, it seems, will be satisfied until the girl's body has been found and her killer convicted. This state of affairs has provoked a number of alarming incidents which haven't got into the papers; and, frankly, we are apprehensive of even more serious trouble. I was talking about it to my son in Wynchester this morning, and Dolly, who has an illimitable faith in your gifts, Super, made an interesting suggestion. Tell him, Sergeant.'

Sergeant Dolly looked mildly embarrassed.

'Well, Mr. Greene, there's this disturbing situation over at Larne, and the police can't do anything about it. So I took the liberty of suggesting you might visit the village, in a private capacity, of course, and look into things for yourself.'

The Super grinned delightedly.

'Your faith in the old pensioner is

certainly illimitable, son,' he agreed. 'But what d'you expect me to do? Dole out sedatives to the natives? Or pull a Sherlock Holmes and prove the cops a lot of dunderheads?' He turned suddenly to the chief constable. 'Aren't you satisfied, sir, that your conclusions on this case *are* the right ones?'

Colonel Fielding chose his words with care.

'I believe that Nadine Price is alive, and that sooner or later she will be found. In the meantime the people of Larne, and in the neighbouring village of Colwin, are literally at each other's throats. Anything may happen. We might even find ourselves with a real murder on our hands. Officially, I can do nothing. Unofficially . . . well, it seems just possible that an experienced investigator like yourself, coming fresh to the whole baffling business, starting from scratch and working quite privately and independently . . . '

He stopped, frowning with self-disapproval. The Super's small eyes

10

gleamed as he leaned forward accusingly in his chair.

'You used the word 'baffling', Colonel. Does that mean you think it possible I *might* find something your people have missed?'

Colonel Fielding sighed.

'I want to be absolutely sure that the police *have* missed nothing, Greene, particularly in view of the possibilities of the present dangerous situation.'

The Super nodded.

'Fair enough,' he said, settling back in his chair again. 'I'm your man, if there's anything I can do. Between ourselves, I don't like this business any more 'n you do, going on what I've read in the papers. Too many loose ends. Too much coincidence. And there's that open grave to be explained. However, let's start from scratch, as you suggest. You tell me the whole story as if I'd never heard of Nadine Price or Larne, either. Then we'll see . . . '

He folded his arms, shut his eyes and waited.

2

Colonel Fielding stretched his long legs and rested his head on the back of his chair. The strong sunlight, playing on his lined and troubled face, was cruelly revealing.

'I'm going to take it,' he began quietly, 'that you do not know these two villages, Larne and Colwin, or their setting. The country there is rather wild, but warm and lovely — fifty miles the other side of Wynchester. Larne stands on one side of the River Eve, Colwin on the other. The surrounding mountains seem to isolate them almost completely. Larne is a picturesque village, an exciting mixture of the old and the new, rather like a miniature Windermere, as I see it. Colwin is a smaller community, old and rather ugly. The contrast between the two villages, in fact, is quite startling. However, until recently the only cause of ill-feeling between them has been

12

that Larne is in England and Colwin is in Wales. Just there the river is the border.'

The Super grinned.

'I get you, Colonel. The pubs and cafés in Larne do a roaring trade on Sundays. In Colwin the pubs shut on the Sabbath.'

'That,' the chief constable agreed with a faint smile, 'is the essence of it. But there are only two pubs in the picture. Colwin has the Welsh Harp, a rough-and-ready establishment that matches the village — and a landlord, Hughie Grant, who matches his pub. Across the river, the Riverside Hotel is a go-ahead, comparatively palatial affair. Apart from its bar trade, it caters extensively for anglers and holidaymakers, and owns the best stretch of fishing for miles. The present proprietor is one Gabriel Laval. He's French, of course; came over in the last war and joined up with the Free French; made several trips back to France in connection with the Resistance. Quite a colourful character. He didn't go home after the war, but got himself naturalized and married an English girl. His wife died just before he came to Larne four years ago and bought and modernized the Riverside Hotel. Laval is making a fortune there, and he's none too scrupulous in his methods.

'Ten months ago he advertised for a barmaid to attract and exploit a certain type of custom. Nadine Price turned up, literally out of nowhere, and got the job. She admitted she had never worked as a barmaid before, and Laval stated quite blandly that he engaged her without asking questions about her past or even requiring references. In his own words to Inspector Griffiths, 'She brought her references with her.' Meaning, of course, her physical charms and personality.'

The Super grunted.

'Did she sleep with him as part of the contract?'

Fielding shot him a searching look.

'I'm hanged if I know, if that's important,' he confessed. 'But Laval volunteered the information that it was purely business so far as he was concerned. He said it was bad policy for a publican to foul his own nest, and even worse to hang a reserve ticket on an attractive barmaid. Anyway, the girl was a sensation from the word Go. Her fame spread like wildfire. Male admirers came to Larne from miles around, like bees to a honeypot; and Nadine saw that they spent their money freely in the hotel and on herself. But, as you must know she wasn't content with imported admirers. She played havoc with the young men locally — both married and single. She seems to have indulged an insatiable passion for seducing young men from their sweethearts and wives, and dropping them when she had caused the maximum of trouble. You can imagine the local feeling she stirred up against herself. Two local parsons organized a deputation to demand her dismissal. Laval and Nadine laughed in their faces. And so it went on. Nadine appears to have received threatening anonymous letters and telephone calls, too, and to have boasted about them.

'Then, suddenly, she got herself engaged to Denis Pugh, the only son of one of the wealthiest farmers in the district.

This attachment landed young Pugh in for a lot of trouble with other young men who had considered themselves in the running, and with his family; but the general idea does seem to have been that the beautiful Nadine was determined on making a very successful marriage and turning respectable.

'Not a bit of it!' Colonel Fielding laughed derisively. 'Nadine was merely pulling off a super-jilt. Just when she'd got Denis Pugh completely and hopelessly enslaved, she threw him over and got engaged to a young chap from the other side of the river — Michael Amber. And this is where things began to get really grim. Michael Amber is a finely-built handsome ex-commando, immensely popular with both sexes. He's in charge of the forestry on Lord Belford's estate — which, incidentally, takes in the two villages. He lives alone in a cottage just outside Colwin. The night that Nadine announced her engagement to Amber, young Pugh got tight and forced him into a fight. According to Sergeant Evans, my local man, Pugh might have got himself killed in that affray if the ex-commando hadn't exercised remarkable self-restraint. And that affair seems to have scared even Nadine . . .

'Eight weeks ago today, at ten o'clock in the morning, Gabriel Laval sent for Sergeant Evans and reported that Nadine had cleared out in the night. This was approximately three weeks after the fight between Amber and Pugh; three weeks during which Pugh had kept himself drunk, and continued his threats to kill Nadine before he'd let anyone else have her. Nadine took with her, on her flight from Larne, all her best clothes and the jewellery and other presents she had acquired during her stay there; and she left behind not a single clue to her origin, her background or her immediate plans. She just vanished. And here I might mention an interesting point: Nadine Price never had a picture of herself, and never allowed anyone to take a snapshot of her during her time in Larne. So, of course, we were unable to publish a photograph of her during our search for her; and the detailed description we circulated was damned unsatisfactory in itself because there was nothing in the shape of a physical peculiarity we could pick on.

'Laval himself was now a bit frightened, too. He still insisted he knew nothing about the girl's past. But he did confide to Inspector Griffiths that he had been on the point of sending her packing; not on account of her gold-digging activities, but because he suspected she might be mixed up in blackmail. All he could, or would, say in explanation of this, however, was that she had been receiving mysterious sums of money which he knew were not presents from her admirers. When he had tackled her about them she had merely laughed in his face. So Laval had determined, according to his story, to take no chances.

'Well, much in the way of sensation filled that day following Nadine's disappearance. During the morning a grave, open and recently dug, was found in some woods behind Colwin, three hundred yards from Michael Amber's cottage. A cloche hat belonging to Nadine was found in the grave. Nearby was a spade, which the grave-digger had borrowed for the purpose from a tool-shed at the house of a woman resident of Colwin — Miss Evelyn Radford, of whom more anon. No fingerprints that mattered were found on the spade; the grave-digger used gloves in handling it.

'Neither Michael Amber nor Denis Pugh could produce an alibi for the previous night that was worthy of the name. Young Pugh patronized the Colwin pub in the evening; when he left it he was drunk and muttering his usual threats directed at Nadine and Michael Amber. Pugh says he crossed the river by the bridge, wandered off into the forest on the north of Larne and fell into a drunken sleep. He awoke at dawn and crept home and to his bed — for all of which there is no confirmation whatever.

'Michael Amber admitted to having had a tiff with Nadine two nights previously, during a walk after closing time. The reason for the tiff was, apparently, that on several occasions she had left the hotel at night saying she was going to meet him, when in fact she had done nothing of the sort. She had denied this, and apparently she was lying. On the night of her disappearance, Amber says, he stayed in his cottage — where she could find him if she wanted to. He drank a bottle of whisky, fell asleep, and didn't budge until the alarm clock wakened him at six next morning. There is no confirmation of this story, either, because no one seems to have passed his cottage that night, or even to have seen a light in a window of it.'

Colonel Fielding paused in his narrative to start a cigarette going; and through half-open eyes the Super noticed that his long, sensitive hands were none too steady in the progress.

'This,' Fielding continued at length, 'brings us to what the police are convinced is another story altogether. It was introduced by two discoveries made in Colwin on this day following Nadine's disappearance, immediately after the finding of the open grave, Nadine's hat, and the borrowed spade. As I have said, the spade was identified as belonging to Miss Evelyn Radford, whose house was not far away from the grave. When inquiries were made there Miss Radford's dead body was discovered in her kitchen. She had died late the previous night, from drinking cocoa which had contained cyanide.

'Miss Radford had rented her house and grounds from Lord Belford. She had let a cottage in a corner of the grounds to a man known locally as Robert Charlton, with whom she had been more than friendly. Inquiries at this furnished cottage resulted in another startling discovery: Robert Charlton had disappeared in the night.'

Colonel Fielding pulled himself upright in his chair and crushed out the end of his cigarette.

'I want to emphasize that no two people in Larne and Colwin had been, on the face of it, more *disinterested* in Nadine Price than Evelyn Radford and Robert Charlton. The latter had only once called at the Riverside Hotel since Nadine's arrival there, and he had never been seen with her in the locality. As for

Miss Radford, she had never patronized either of the two pubs, and during all the years she had lived alone in Colwin she had kept herself very much to herself.

'Miss Radford was a rather plain spinster of forty-six. She came of a very old Cumberland family, and for all her life until 1939 she lived on the family estate in Cumberland. From 1933–1939 she kept house for her wealthy bachelor brother, who, by all accounts, led her a pretty miserable existence. He was notoriously a drunkard and a seducer of women, but, none the less, popular with most of the 'county' families, and particularly the sporting element. I'm not going into the details of the case. David Radford, the brother, sacked his estate manager, Stanley Weaver, for no better reason, apparently, than that young Weaver was in love with Evelyn Radford and wanted to marry her. Weaver left the district and disappeared. A few mornings later David Radford, in his cups in an inn in the district, said his sister had been poisoning his food. A week after that he was found, one morning, lying dead in the grounds behind the family mansion; a sporting-gun, the cause of his death, was found at his side.

'The coroner's jury brought in a verdict of accidental death. Such evidence as there was supported the theory that the deceased — the worse for drink, and out with his gun after poachers on the night in question — had accidentally shot himself. This did not prevent a considerable section of local opinion from branding Evelyn Radford a murderess, while another not inconsiderable section preferred to have it that Stanley Weaver had returned and shot his late employer.

'At all events, Evelyn Radford, who now inherited the estate, did not go to her lover. She sold up the estate and came down to Colwin, where she spent the last fifteen years of her life. She lived a solitary spinster existence there, all alone except for a daily woman. She never entertained. Reading and painting seem to have been her main occupations, apart from housework. She attended church regularly, gave liberally to charity, and was generally esteemed and respected. Local people, it seems, had even come to virtually forget her unhappy past.

'This brings us to the advent of Robert Charlton in Larne and Colwin, just over ten months ago. He came to Larne for a day's fishing about a fortnight before the arrival of Nadine. So did a lot of other amateur anglers. Charlton gave Laval to understand that he was a bachelor of independent means, and was looking for a furnished cottage. Laval promised to look out for one. When Charlton returned, three weeks later, Nadine was already installed at the Riverside Hotel as barmaid. It was she who, briefed by Laval, told Charlton that Miss Evelyn Radford had a furnished cottage she might be induced to let. Charlton went to see the lady, and a week later took possession of the cottage.

'Robert Charlton arrived at Colwin a complete mystery, as far as local people were concerned; he remained a complete mystery until he vanished on the night of Nadine's disappearance. But it seems clear enough that he did not remain a complete mystery to Evelyn Radford. They very quickly became close friends; and then, more than friends. They were always being seen about together, on country walks, and at her house and his cottage. Charlton seems even to have lost interest in fishing on her account. And evidence from certain quarters — notably Miss Radford's daily woman — is emphatic that they were lovers, and were making plans to be married. Yet, in fairness, I must admit that Miss Radford never gave anyone a clue to who or what this fellow Charlton was. And not even in the Welsh Harp, which Charlton patronized for an hour or so each day, is anything known about him — except that he was in the last war; and he appears to have let that slip out by accident.

'Well, there it is.' Colonel Fielding made a gesture of finality. 'Charlton cleared out at the same time as Nadine, and we haven't a clue to how he went, or where he went. And on that same night Evelyn Radford drank cyanide in her kitchen. The coroner's jury returned an open verdict. But all the evidence available is to the effect that she was alone in her house when she herself prepared and drank that fatal cup of cocoa. If you ask me where she obtained the cyanide — if she did obtain it — there is an answer of sorts. It seems that the unhappy woman was known to have attempted suicide years previously in Cumberland; and it is possible that she obtained cyanide then, for a second attempt, and had the stuff with her when she came to Colwin.'

Colonel Fielding got stiffly to his feet and set his back to the fireplace.

'I'm nearly through, thank God,' he said fervently. 'We have searched Larne and Colwin and for miles around, without turning up a vestige of a clue to suggest foul play in any of these mysteries. Nadine Price and Robert Charlton have vanished completely. In the former case we have good reason, I believe, for assuming she is no longer in this country. Among thousands of reports that she had been seen, from all parts of the British Isles, we received one from a member of the crew of a Weymouth-Jersey steamer. This man swears he saw a woman answering to Nadine's description aboard his boat when it left Weymouth two nights after her disappearance from Larne. A stewardess took note of her, too, but much more casually. This seaman noticed her particularly because she was alone, because she spent a good part of the night on deck, and because of her striking appearance. He was able to describe the clothes, and even the jewellery she was wearing, in such detail that Gabriel Laval identified each item. He saw the girl leave the steamer at Jersey, and that's the last we know of her. Widespread inquiries in Jersey got us nowhere; and that fact itself strikes me as significant. We believe she went on from Jersey to France; and that journey would have presented little difficulty even if she had no passport. It is simple enough, as we know very well, to arrange such a passage if you have money enough to bribe someone who has a boat and knows the ropes.

'Finally, Superintendent, I want to

emphasize how comparatively easy it was for Nadine Price and Robert Charlton to disappear as they have done. They are the sort of people who *can* vanish into the blue. Neither had left even a police record behind; we should have found such records through their fingerprints, of course, had they existed. As far as we know, these two people had a perfect right to disappear if they wanted to.

'The police have been forced to the conclusion that Nadine Price is one story, as I have said, and that Robert Charlton and Evelyn Radford are another. Nadine Price seems to have cleared out because she found Larne too hot for her, though she may have had other reasons as well. Robert Charlton cleared out for reasons of his own; and one can only assume that Evelyn Radford — a spinster of forty-six — decided to end it all when she found herself left high and dry after the one passionate romance of her chequered life. I can assure you, Super, there is no question of Charlton having been after her money.'

He paused to light another cigarette,

and then wound up his story.

'You can imagine the fantastic stories the local people have made up out of this material. You can imagine the impossible conditions under which the police have had to pursue their investigations. Dozens of local people were literally at each other's throats over Nadine when she disappeared; and local opinion is stronger now than even it was that some person or persons belonging to Larne or Colwin murdered her as an act of vengeance, and buried her body somewhere in the locality. Certain irresponsible people are still organizing searches, in defiance of the police. Local feeling has been frighteningly indignant and hostile since our investigations in the district ceased and our conclusions became public property. The way it looks, there will never be peace until the body of Nadine Price is found and her killer named and convicted. It's a fantastic, ghastly situation.'

The Super nodded sympathetically.

'How do the locals connect the disappearance of Robert Charlton and

Miss Radford's suicide with the other mystery, sir?' he asked.

Colonel Fielding laughed bitterly.

'In a dozen ways, most of 'em completely crazy. The favourite seems to be that Miss Radford and Charlton saw or overheard too much of the murder plan, and had to be silenced. Charlton took to his heels in terror and got away; Miss Radford wasn't so lucky. There seems no limit to the frenzied imaginings of these people, or their determination to find a murderer among themselves.'

He returned to his chair. There followed a long and rather painful silence, during which the Super seemed lost in thought. Suddenly, he opened his eyes, sniffed, stared incredulously at the clock on the mantelpiece, and jumped to his feet.

'Excuse me, gentlemen.' He hurried out of the room, closing the door carefully behind him. Three minutes later he was back and looking smugly pleased with himself. 'My lunch,' he explained, sitting down again. 'I've told my house-keeper to put it out to grass for a while. Now,

Colonel Fielding, there are just a few questions. First, about this suicide of Miss Radford's. You say — on the authority of fingerprints, I guess — she prepared the cocoa drink for herself. She'd have found the cocoa in a tin, and so on.' He paused. 'You've no idea where she found the cyanide?'

The chief constable started at the unexpected question; then, frowning, he shook his head.

'There was no sign of any sort of container for the poison, if that's what you mean. But the stove was alight, and she was a fanatically tidy person, so she may have thrown it on the fire. It's possible, of course, but hardly probable, that she had the cyanide contained in capsule form.'

The Super shook his head on the latter suggestion, and dismissed it with a wave of a podgy hand.

'You did say,' he went on, 'that the lady was keen on painting, didn't you?'

Colonel Fielding flushed.

'I did,' he agreed, 'but I can't for the life of me see — '

31

'And her will,' the Super persisted. 'Who gets it all?'

Fielding laughed impatiently.

'I thought I'd put you off that scent,' he replied. 'Miss Radford left the whole of her worldly wealth to charity.'

The Super nodded.

'Just one thing more, Colonel. You did also say that this chap Charlton went right off his fishin' when he took this furnished cottage and got tied up with his landlady?'

'I did.' The chief constable almost shouted the words in his bewilderment and indignation. 'But, good God, what *has* all this to do with — '

The Super silenced him with another wave of a hand, and sank into a further period of cogitation. Finally, he jerked himself upright in his chair and thumped the arms decisively.

'Right, sir. You want me to go over to Larne, in a private capacity, and sniff around and see if anything can be done about anything; that's the size of it? Well now, there's a lot of snags there, you know. Just sniffin' around and askin' questions and advertising myself as a busybody won't get me nowhere. The locals, as I see them, will just freeze solid against me. A more likely plan would be for me to go as a solicitor representing Miss Radford's relatives; but from what you say about the will I take it she hadn't any who'd reasonably want to be represented?'

'She had none at all in this country,' Fielding told him, 'and only very distant relatives abroad.'

'Right.' This seemed to please the Super immensely. 'Then the only thing is for me to go over there, in a purely private capacity, as my celebrated self. Ex-Superintendent 'Tubby' Greene. I'm on a motorin' tour of the Southern Marches, and, after reading about all the goings-on in Larne I just naturally looked in in passin'. I just get myself known in a quiet way, and interest myself in the feelings and opinions of the people; maybe I don't think too much of the police handling of this business; maybe the people will talk to me more freely than they would to the cops.'

He chuckled. 'They might even want to make 'Tubby' Greene a champion of their cause, Colonel. No, don't get alarmed. I won't start anything to make matters worse. What do you think about the idea, Jim?'

Sergeant Dolly laughed.

'Well, sir, to be frank, that was roughly the idea I'd got in mind when I suggested Colonel Fielding might see you. There seems to be a hardening wall of hostility between the people and the police, and if anyone could slip through it you could.'

Colonel Fielding was a man of quick decisions.

'It's worth trying, Super,' he said emphatically. 'Go ahead and see what you can do. You certainly seem to have got something in your mind about this business that is definitely not in mine; and almost anything is worth a go in the present situation. I should have called in the Yard long ago, if we had turned up anything to substantiate the suggestion that there had been foul play . . . '

The Super grinned reassuringly.

'You got yourself something better

than the Yard, Colonel.' He turned again to the sergeant. 'You still got that nice young chap Henry Baxter lodging with you, Jim?'

'Yes, sir. Henry's quite one of the family now, and we hadn't the heart to suggest parting with him when we moved to Wynchester. He's got the whole top floor of our house to himself, for sleeping quarters, sitting-room and laboratory.'

'Good. Do you think he'd like a holiday with me at Larne?'

Colonel Fielding looked apprehensive again.

'Excuse me,' he said, 'but may I ask who — ?'

Jim Dolly took the question at a nod from the Super.

'Henry Baxter is a young man of twenty-six, sir. He took his B.Sc. when he was nineteen, and was going on for something still bigger when the doctors ordered him to live quietly in the country for his health . . . His mother died just then, leaving him plenty of cash, so he came to lodge with us when we were here in Drawbridge about three years ago. He's a very nice chap, as Mr. Greene knows, and he's mad on chemistry.' He turned to the Super. 'He's been mad on forensic stuff since you got him to do that chemical analysis for you during the Draper case, sir; and the books he's bought and digested on criminology — '

'Books!' the Super scoffed. 'I'll give him something better than books. Don't suppose he's ever been to Larne?'

'Henry's worse than you, sir, for staying put.'

'Right. Then, Colonel Fielding, if it's agreeable to you I'll take Henry along as — yes, I've got it! He can be a young writer who's doin' my memoirs for me. He'll come in useful in a lot of ways. I'll telephone the Riverside Hotel and book rooms for us right away. You go home, Jim, and tell Henry to get packin'. I'll be along in my Old Wreck about three o'clock, and we'll go on together from there. Henry still got that posh roadster of his, by the way?'

'The Chesterfield, sir? Yes, and still nurses it like a baby, though he never goes anywhere much with it except when the family wants an outing.'

'Henry and I will travel in state in the Chesterfield, then,' the Super decided. 'We don't want to advertise the miserly pensions we ex-cops get, not in a fashionable place like Larne — eh, Colonel?'

Colonel Fielding looked relieved and grateful as he got to his feet and held out his hand.

'I'm damned glad I came here this morning, Super,' he said warmly. 'I've lost a lot of sleep over this business. I don't like leaving a case with a question mark at the end of it any more than anyone else would in my position, but — '

'Don't worry.' The Super smiled. 'This case has a whole row of question marks tagged on to it; and that's the way I like things. Just brief your local men, and tell 'em to take a discreetly dim view of old meddlers like myself.'

Fielding grinned.

'I understand, Super. I shall be hearing from you when — ?'

'Probably when I've found a body or two,' the Super retorted, ushering his visitors to the door.

A minute later he was waving good-bye to them, and feeling ready for lamb in any condition . . .

3

'Well, there you are, Henry,' the Super said blandly at five o'clock that afternoon. 'That's the chief constable's version of the business pretty well word for word. Now we both know what we're up against.'

The Super was sprawled on a chair on the terrace of a road-side café at which he and Henry Baxter had stopped for tea on their way to Larne. The long gleaming bonnet of Henry's powerful roadster, parked in front of the café, was just visible at one end of the terrace. In front of them, in the far distance, a misty line of mountains marked the edge of the country for which they were making. Behind them the hot blue sky was faintly tinged with gold.

Henry Baxter had listened spellbound to the Super's performance, his elbows on the table between them, his small chin cupped in his hands, his prominent ears twitching spasmodically with excitement, his eyes wide and bright as an owl's behind thick steel-rimmed lenses. His hair was so fair and he took himself and life so seriously that from a distance he was often mistaken for an old man. At the moment, to the Super, he looked like a fiercely absorbed youth of fifteen.

'Well, sir,' Henry said in his small yet compelling voice, 'it all sounds most frightfully complicated. What do *you* make of it?'

The Super produced a packet of cigarettes that was even more crushed than it had been that morning. He searched laboriously among the tissue and silver paper inside, produced a bedraggled Players and stuck it into a corner of his mouth. When he had lit it he smoked in silence for a minute or two until on the windless terrace, he and Henry were enveloped in a vast cloud of tobacco smoke.

'Cases is like stories, son,' he confided at length. 'You can work so hard at them that the time comes when you get plain addled. Then you send for a chap with half your brains, and, coming fresh to the job, he gets the whole thing pat before you can say Jack Robinson.'

Henry stared at his idol incredulously.

'That never happened to you, sir, surely?'

'*Shush*, Henry.'

'Well, anyway, you do think that Colonel Fielding is addled over this case, Mr. Greene.'

The Super looked quite shocked.

'I don't mean I've only got half his brains,' he explained hurriedly, 'and I didn't mean you to apply the rest of them remarks literally, Henry. Let's say the colonel has worked too hard at this case, and he's none too happy about it.'

'No more are you, sir?'

The Super shrugged.

'I've got a sympathetic nature, Henry, if that's what you mean.'

Henry smiled.

'Just where do you sympathize with Colonel Fielding most, sir?'

The Super chuckled.

'That was nicely put, Henry.' He blew a stream of smoke towards the roof and peered into it for inspiration. 'Well, it's like this,' he continued. 'Some of the characters in this business don't look quite the same colour to me as they do to the colonel. This chap Gabriel Laval, the proprietor of the Riverside Hotel at Larne, for instance. He told the police he took on this barmaid, Nadine Price, without seeing a reference or knowing anything about her. That was the act of a fool, Henry. Yet in almost the same breath, apparently, Laval said he was too good a business man to foul his own nest by sleeping with the girl, or hanging a reserved card on a barmaid so much in demand. Those, son, are the sentiments of a wise man. See what I mean?'

'Certainly, sir,' Henry responded promptly. 'You can't see Laval as both a wise man and a fool. But,' and his freckled face lit up again, 'you could see a liar with either one of those other qualities.'

The Super nodded approvingly.

'I always said you got an exceptional brain, Henry. You're going to need one, anyway, if you want to keep pace with me. Yes, well then, there's this Nadine

Price herself. Why did she come to Larne a mystery woman if she hadn't a past to hide? And if she came to Larne a mystery woman with a past to hide, why did she go all out to make herself the talk of the district and the best-hated person in it — in record time, too?

'Then, on the other side of the river,' he continued, 'there's a good deal I find as clear as mud in Miss Evelyn Radford and that chap Robert Charlton; a good deal that Colonel Fielding seems to think don't matter — if he's thought about it at all. I don't like the way Miss Radford appears to have shaped as a middle-aged spinster in the throes of the one real, belated romance of her life — if you except the one years before in Cumberland that doesn't seem to have amounted to much. And I don't like this Charlton's fishing habits.'

Henry grinned — an expression which made him look incredibly cynical.

'You're not being very explanatory, Mr. Greene, are you?'

'My experience of spinsters,' the Super resumed, 'is quite considerable, Henry, and it amounts to this. Spinsters, when they land a man, don't keep him as secret as Miss Radford appears to have kept Robert Charlton's secrets. On the other hand, Robert Charlton was an angler, apparently, and I've had considerable experience of anglers. I've known anglers give up their women for angling; I've never known a fisherman, not a real fisherman, give up his fishin' for a woman. See what I mean?'

'I'm trying to keep up with you,' Henry replied.

'Good. Keep tryin', son, and you'll get used to me in time. Maybe you've spotted already my main objection to the police conclusions on this business?'

'I think so, Mr. Greene, chiefly because of the sceptical way in which you related part of Colonel Fielding's story just now. His view is that the Charlton-Radford story is one thing and the Nadine Price business is another story altogether; that Nadine and Charlton disappearing on the same night, eight weeks ago, was sheer coincidence. You don't agree with any of that, do you, sir?'

'No, Henry, I don't. Not on the face of things as I see them. The colonel's case is, of course, that Nadine and Charlton came to Larne quite independently, and never went near each other during their stay in the district; so why shouldn't their clearing out the same night have been coincidental? But there's another way of looking at that, son. Nadine and Charlton were both mystery people determined to keep themselves mystery people so far as the inhabitants of Larne and district were concerned. They arrived in Larne at approximately the same time. Now, Charlton came to Larne the first two times as an angler, looking for some decent fishing and a furnished cottage. He found the fishing from the Riverside Hotel. On his second angling visit to Larne he met Nadine for the first time, and, briefed by Laval, she put him on to Miss Radford's cottage. Charlton took the cottage, and from that moment, apparently, he never went near Nadine or the Riverside Hotel. He never even went back to say he was comfortable at the cottage and thank you. He gave up fishing so that he could keep away from Nadine and the Riverside Hotel, you might say; and for the same reason he patronized the inferior pub in Colwin. Yet the timetables of the separate affairs of these two people, Nadine and Charlton, coincide so remarkably that they both disappeared from the district during the same night, nobody saw either of 'em go, and they were both able to defy successfully a nation-wide search for them afterwards. What's more: during the same night somebody borrowed a spade from Charlton's landlady-love to dig a grave that was discovered next morning with Nadine's hat in it. All that, Henry, adds up to a hell of a lot of coincidence as I see it.'

Henry nodded.

'Or a hell of a lot of something else, Mr. Greene.'

'Exactly. And that shows us the relative importance, I think, of that open grave. Who dug it and why?'

'But surely, sir, that was the work of — ' . . .

'No, Henry, we're asking questions

right now. We'll find the answers when we get over to Larne. And while we're at it, here are some more questions to complete our list for the moment. Why *do* the local people still persist in searching for the body of Nadine Price when the police have asserted she has fled the country? Why *are* they still hostile to the police after all this time?'

'But Colonel Fielding was most emphatic on that score,' Henry protested. 'After all, sir, this mass-suspicion is no new thing. It's a sort of mass-hysteria, isn't it, and — '

'Eight weeks is a long time for that sort of thing,' the Super said sternly. 'And where there's smoke there's fire.'

Henry took his point and stared at him.

'You mean that people in Larne and Colwin know more than they've told the police? They don't *want* the police to find out the whole truth?'

The Super shook his head.

'Now you're fighting on two fronts, Henry.' He turned his head slowly and nodded at the line of distant mountains.

'That's where all the answers are,' he said, pushing back his chair. 'It's time we were on our way. You go out and sit in the car while I pay the bill and do a spot of telephoning.'

He led the way into the restaurant where he settled their account with the solitary waitress on duty. Henry was busy with a duster when he joined him in front of the café. The Super crossed the road to a telephone kiosk. Ten minutes later he returned to the car and squeezed himself into the front seat.

'You know, Henry,' he said, as they drove on towards the mountains, 'you've got brains for this sort of thing all right. We'll make a criminologist out of you yet.'

Henry laughed happily as he slid his small hands caressingly over the driving wheel.

'I've been trying to work out why you brought me with you today, sir,' he confessed.

'Have you!' the Super snorted. 'Then I'll take back what I said about your brains. How d'you expect me to play

48

Sherlock Holmes without a Watson to listen to me? Besides, I like to talk to you, son, and see from that freckled face of yours how clever you think I am. However, you stick to your drivin' for a bit. That's another reason I brought you.'

Two minutes later he was breathing so evenly and heavily that Henry thought he was asleep. He seemed to remain so until an hour later when they had climbed between the mountains and were on the point of descending to the plain beyond. Then, suddenly and violently, he sat up and commanded Henry to stop the car. He climbed out, walked round the bonnet to the off-side of the road and beckoned.

'Here it is, Henry. Come and look for yourself.'

The scene below them was awe-inspiring: a vast sweep of flattish, richly-timbered country that, practically encircled by mountains, looked indeed a world apart.

The Super pointed to a winding silver thread that cut across the scene from corner to corner.

'That's the River Eve, son. All the country on the north of it is Wales; this side of it we're in good old England. Now, where . . . Yes, there they are, those two villages on that bend in the river. There's the bridge connecting them. Couldn't see things better from a ruddy aeroplane, could we.'

There was no mistaking which village was which. Larne was a large and picturesque community, with narrow, winding streets and an old church at its heart, and modern residences lining the river and bejewelling the forest behind the village. Farther still behind it Belford Castle stood out nobly on its own steep hill rising out of an ocean of trees. The Riverside Hotel was plainly visible in its considerable grounds by the river, its name picked out in silver letters across its frontage.

Colwin, the comparative small village on the other side of the river, seemed nakedly exposed in contrast, against an almost black background of trees. It looked old, shabby and neglected, yet somehow defiant of its elegant neighbour across the river.

The Super studied every visible detail of the scene like a general surveying a potential battleground; and then he grunted and tapped Henry on the shoulder.

'Seems a pity, don't it,' he said, 'that down there among all that prettiness and beauty there's so much ugliness. All my life, Henry, I've been livin' with ugliness; thrivin' on it, scorin' off it. Maybe that's why I can't appreciate the country like I ought to.'

Henry looked up and smiled encouragingly.

'You'll learn, Mr. Greene,' he promised.

The Super led the way back to the car.

'That's the trouble, son,' he growled as they climbed in and slowly began the descent. 'You have to retire to find out how much you've missed. And then it's too late. Look at me, now. Talk about the beauties of nature! I can't even a-bear the sight of my own garden.'

'No?' Henry looked old and wise for

a moment. 'Yet you've been weeding all your life, sir, and making a fine job of it, too. Where would the flowers be if it wasn't for the weeders?'

The Super turned to stare at him incredulously.

'Why, Henry,' he cried, 'you're a ruddy philosopher! That's the first time I've been called a weeder! Come to think of it, you're bein' good for my morale as well as the other things.' He added grimly after a pause, 'We've got quite a bit of weeding to do down in Larne, son, if I'm any judge.'

4

The sky was on fire when the Chesterfield slid silently into Larne. The sunset illuminated the cobbled streets, the cottages and shops, the ancient parish church in its topsy-turvy churchyard, as firelight illuminates a room full of old furniture. The main street was crowded; the shops were closing and people were hurrying over belated errands. But even in his first cursory appraisal of the scene, the Super spotted what was wrong with it: the absence of those friendly, gossiping groups of young people to be found in every village at that hour of the day.

The riverside scene, below the church, was impressive for two reasons. The tree-lined promenade, the comfortable public benches, the tables and chairs outside a small café, would not have disgraced the Côte d'Azur; but it was empty and deserted, as the broad, gently-flowing river was deserted, and this desolation was emphasized by the peaceless din from the village above it.

Henry turned the big car sharply to take the gently-rising private road to the Riverside Hotel. The building itself, high above the river, was a fine old country mansion that had somehow managed to retain much of its dignity despite the drastic alterations which had been made to transform it into a conspicuous hotel. Here again was desolation: the ornamental gardens were as empty as a museum after closing time; two large, expensive cars looked lost on the edge of a vast expanse of drive and a vaster parking space behind it; and the long frontage of the hotel gave the impression of a large, go-ahead establishment wide open to a patronage that had dried up quite suddenly.

'You know, Henry,' the Super remarked as he climbed out of the car, 'this place would look more homely and hopeful if there was a bit of litter lyin' around. Much as I hate litter.'

They climbed a flight of stone steps and passed into the entrance hall of the hotel. It was empty, too. The Super rang twice before a tall skeleton of a man in porter's uniform appeared, noticed their luggage and went off again. He returned in the wake of a large, brisk woman of middle age. She was darkly handsome, and smartly dressed in black; but there was something vaguely hostile in her manner as she went behind the reception counter to attend to the newcomers.

'Greene and Baxter are the names, I believe,' she said in a husky voice with a French inflection. She turned to a rack of keys, selected two and beckoned the aged porter. 'John, take these gentlemen up to Nineteen and Twenty. Dinner,' she informed the new guests abruptly, 'is half-past seven.'

She bustled away at once. The porter picked up the newcomers' two suitcases and led the way up the red-carpeted staircase to the first landing, and along a winding passage to two facing rooms at the end of it. He opened the two doors and set down the cases between them.

'Thank you, sir,' he said, as he pocketed the Super's tip. 'I'm afraid we haven't got many in at the moment.' He gave the Super a curious look, as though wondering what he and his younger companion were doing there, and ambled away. The Super watched him out of sight and grunted.

'You know, Henry,' he said, 'somehow I can't see that old chap fittin' into the picture here when this place is crowded. However, let's freshen up and take a look around.'

He picked up his battered case and went into Room 20. It was a long, narrow room, luxuriously appointed, with its own private bathroom. Its one window overlooked the river and Colwin beyond. Close to, Colwin looked more nakedly ugly and defiant than ever. The village inn and the chapel stood facing each other just beyond the bridge, and the Super found it difficult to decide which looked the more unfriendly. Behind the village great patches of trees patterned the miles of desolate country stretching as far as the line of mountains that formed the wall of this shut-away world; and it was over there, the Super reflected grimly, that tomorrow he and Henry would begin their search for something the police had missed — or something that, if Colonel Fielding was right, did not exist.

The Super stood for a moment longer by the open window, listening to the sounds from the village behind the hotel. You could tell even from the spasmodic sounds of motor sirens, he decided, that Larne was a community suffering from nerves.

After a wash and brush-up, he collected Henry and went down to find the bar and a drink. They passed the entrance to the dining-room in their search, and peeped inside. It was a huge, elegantly-furnished apartment richly carpeted in crimson, and with a wall of big windows overlooking the River Eve.

They found the bar behind the dining-room; and this was even larger than the latter apartment. The walls were of imitation oak-panelling; the floor was of polished oak lavishly bestrewn with gaily-coloured rubber mats. The place was furnished in the main as a lounge bar, but there was accommodation for

57

all tastes. One corner was devoted to darts; another held a grand piano and a radiogram; a third, shaped like an annexe, contained a bar billiards table, and other tables devoted to skittles, quoits, shove-ha'penny and cards.

There were only two people in the room at the moment: the barmaid and a solitary customer. The former was a plump, painted blonde of indefinite age; she was polishing glasses, and, after a cursory glance, she greeted the newcomers with a cold, disdainful stare. The Super felt very old and very fat as he appraised her in turn.

The solitary customer was a big man sitting at one of the round tables near the counter. His head and shoulders were hidden by the newspaper he was reading. A pint tankard of beer stood in front of him.

'Well, Henry,' the Super began as they moved towards the counter, 'what'll it be?' He heard the sudden, sharp rustling of a newspaper, but his back was towards the customer responsible for it. 'All right,' he went on, beaming at the barmaid, 'a pint tankard of bitter for me, and a half for my friend. You know, miss, we expected to find a full house here, with this grand weather lastin' so long. Blackpool is chock-a-block, they tell me. Are we the only guests you've got?'

The barmaid snatched up the pound note he had laid on the counter and turned to the till. It was not until she had planted his change in front of him that she deigned to answer his question.

'You're not the only guests, sir,' she snapped in a hideously affected Cockney voice, 'and it's too early for the bar trade, see.'

The Super saw, picked up the two drinks and led the way to a nearby table where he perched himself gingerly on a leather-and-chromium chair. Out of the corner of his eye he saw the solitary customer watching him intently over his newspaper. He saw also that he was a man of thirty or so, with a full, handsome face and a clipped grey moustache.

The Super raised his tankard to Henry. 'Here's to a nice quiet time, son,' he said. 'Signs are certainly propitious, eh?' He laughed, produced his crushed Players box and searched for the last cigarette contained therein.

At the sound of the laugh the solitary customer pushed back his chair and emptied his tankard.

'Another pint, please, Janet,' he ordered, in a deep, cultured voice.

'*Certainly*, Major!' the barmaid gushed. 'P'raps you'd like me to fetch the dinner menu now as well . . .'

'It doesn't matter, thanks.'

Slow footsteps crossed the polished floor a moment later, and the big man stopped in front of the Super.

'Excuse me, sir,' he began politely, 'but have I not the pleasure of addressing Superintendent Greene of Scotland Yard?'

There was an audible gasp from behind the counter as the Super shook out the match in his hand and appraised the newcomer.

'*Ex*-Superintendent Greene, sir,' he corrected. 'I've been out of harness a couple of years. You have the advantage of me . . .'

The big man smiled.

'May I?' He drew up a chair and sat down. 'I happened to see your name in the hotel register when I came in. It awakened a memory. I recognized you the moment you spoke just now. My name is Valentine — Major Hugh Valentine. My father was Major-General Valentine, V.C. You were mixed up with a rather serious case that crossed his line of territory during the last war, Mr. Greene. He pointed you out to me during the hearing *in camera* at the Old Bailey. I heard you give evidence.' He grinned. 'I also heard you laugh, after the hearing, as I heard you laugh a moment ago.'

The Super's face creased into multiple smiles as he held out a podgy hand.

'General Valentine!' he cried. 'Of course, I remember your famous father, Major. A mighty tragic blow it was when he got killed in that air crash in '43. But Scotland's your home country, ain't it?' he went on, half seriously. 'Haven't you got enough fish up there without coming to this part of the world in September?'

Major Valentine carefully trimmed the

ash from his cigar before he replied.

'Yes, our estates up there have taken up a great deal of my time since my father's death, Mr. Greene, but I like to get off on my own sometimes. I've got a furnished house here on the other side of the river, and a motor-boat I find rather fun. It's a bit late for fishing, of course.' He gave the Super a searching look that somehow contrived to include Henry Baxter; and he glanced briefly in the direction of the bar before he asked anxiously, 'Are you sure you're not here in an official capacity, sir?'

The Super looked innocently taken aback.

'But, my dear Major, I told you . . . ' he began, and seemed suddenly to cotton on. 'I see what you mean. No, sir, I've finished being a cop. This young gentleman here is Henry Baxter, a writer. Sorry to take so long to introduce you, Henry. You see, Major, Henry's doin' my memoirs, and we're touring the Southern Marches to combine sight-seein' with literary composition or whatever it is. Besides,' he added darkly, 'I understood that business you referred to was officially closed.'

Major Valentine looked vaguely relieved.

'I understand it is,' he agreed. 'But seeing you gave me rather a shock none the less. I only arrived here after that mysterious business had broken into the headlines; and I almost changed my mind about coming here when I'd read 'em. You see, like you, sir, I've had my fill of excitement. I came here for peace and quiet — on doctor's orders as a matter of fact.'

The Super nodded sympathetically.

'I suppose that business emptied this hotel, Major?'

Valentine shrugged.

'It cleared out most of the staff as well,' he confided. 'Gabriel Laval, the proprietor, has to do his own cooking just now. All the same, Mr. Greene, I'm sure you'll be comfortable. I eat here myself.'

Prompted by the Super, he went on to talk about his famous father. He confessed, rather shyly, that he also had won the coveted Victoria Cross in the last war, while serving as a commando. He had left his mother and a small son in Scotland, he added; and then his reticence hinted that that was about as far as he wished to go with his own affairs.

The dinner-gong sounded from the hall. Valentine got up from his chair and held out his hand again.

'Come and see me tomorrow, if you feel like it,' he urged. 'You cross the bridge and walk back this way along the river path to find my place, The Retreat. Frankly,' he confessed, 'I'd be glad of your company any time you like. Larne is a bit lonely for strangers like myself.'

'We'll certainly look you up,' the Super promised.

Three minutes later, when they followed the major into the dining-room, they found him eating alone at a corner table — behind his newspaper again.

There were seven other diners in the room. The waitress was the receptionist plus a white apron. The food and wine were excellent, and the Super seemed to lose interest in his surroundings as he indulged his inner man to the full. It was not until they had reached the coffee stage, and Major Valentine waved to them as he left the room, that he woke up again.

'Nice chap, Valentine,' he said warmly to Henry. 'Son of a grand father. Glad we met him. Well now, let's have another look in the bar and then take a stroll.'

They found the lounge bar brilliantly illuminated and quite busy. The Super brought liqueurs and a fresh packet of Players to the table they had occupied earlier, and sat down to take leisurely stock of their somewhat changed surroundings.

Janet, the barmaid, was apparently very efficient at her job and very free-and-easy with her customers. The Super noticed, too, from her frequent glances in his direction, that she had acquired a new, if clandestine, interest in himself.

The customers were an interesting study. Most of them were obviously young men from the locality, who had 'poshed up' for their evening's entertainment. But there was a smattering of men and women who had apparently come to Larne by car; they kept themselves very much to themselves, and did not associate with any of the 'locals'. Even the barmaid seemed acutely aware that her customers came from two very different worlds, for she had a separate language and demeanour for each.

There was nothing actively hostile in the atmosphere of the bar, however; it was merely divided and somehow artificial. There was an air of alertness, of expectancy among the motorists; and, in contrast, the 'locals' behaved exaggeratedly like natives who, while tolerating this invasion of their territory, were determined to give nothing of themselves or their secrets — if they had any — away.

Yet, the Super reflected on the strength of what Colonel Fielding had told him, it must have been very different when Nadine Price held court here.

Then, in his individual inspection of these young and not-so-young men from the farms and the shops in the locality, he noticed a young giant who was standing in the middle of the long bar and steadily consuming pint after pint of beer from a battered tankard. He was fair-haired, clean-shaven and strikingly handsome; and he had certainly not 'poshed up' for the evening. He was wearing a working shirt wide open at the neck, a pair of shabby corduroy trousers, and mud-stained rubber boots. Janet ogled him brazenly when she served him, but he scarcely noticed her. He drank with a constant succession of friends, who came to chat with him before passing on into various 'schools' in the bar; but his thoughts seemed to be miles away. Most of the time he stood with his massive arms wide apart, leaning heavily on the counter, his gaze fixed on the clock high up on the wall in front of him.

The Super had his keen, unimpaired sense of hearing to thank for the fact that he overheard two of the young giant's drinking friends address him as 'Mike' and 'Michael' respectively, and he was thus able to identify him, without much hazard, as Michael Amber, the woodman to whom Nadine Price had been engaged at the time of her disapperance.

He felt an odd apprehension as he went on watching him; and he had an uncanny feeling that others in the bar were watching him apprehensively too.

Then, just after half-past eight by the wall clock, when the atmosphere of the place was becoming mildly hilarious, and more and more motorists and their womenfolk were arriving, the door of the main entrance opened and a tall, dark-haired young man came in alone. He was immaculately dressed and very pale, and he paused on the threshold as though looking for someone. Janet saw him and stood suddenly motionless, a glass in one hand and a bottle in the other. All over the bar men turned to stare at the newcomer; and there was a hush the more impressive because it was gradual.

Then one of the 'locals' called, 'Hello, Denis!' The young giant at the bar stiffened perceptibly, and slowly turned his head. He and the newcomer stared at each other for a long moment. Then the latter sniggered and turned to join a group of young men who were standing nearby; and Michael Amber emptied his tankard and walked quietly out of the bar.

The tension around him relaxed so promptly that the Super felt instinctively that the little piece of drama he had witnessed was a regular occurrence. The 'locals' had been waiting for it, and they were mightily relieved that nothing more sensational had happened. Denis Pugh, the young man whom Nadine Price had thrown over for Michael Amber, was laughing and chatting with his friends, indeed, as though nothing untoward had happened at all.

The Super emptied his tiny glass and pushed back his chair.

'Come on, Henry,' he growled, 'let's go for that stroll.'

Outside, the drive and the car park were full to capacity.

The din from the bar followed them as they walked down to the deserted promenade, above which the village brooded in silence.

'Well, Henry,' the Super said as they

reached the bridge, 'what did you make of that little episode?'

Henry said in a small, rather shaken voice:

'Those two must be the chaps Nadine Price was engaged to, surely. I noticed Amber, a fine-looking fellow, minutes before it happened. Why did he have to wait there all that time, just to snigger at Denis Pugh?'

'He didn't snigger at Denis Pugh,' the Super said grimly. 'That's the whole point.'

He did not elucidate, however. They crossed the bridge slowly and in silence. Uncannily, they could still just hear the din from the bar in the Riverside Hotel when they stopped at the far end of the bridge, on the threshold of Colwin.

The windows of the chapel were illuminated, but the front doors were closed. Not a glimmer of light showed from the heavily-curtained windows of the Welsh Harp facing the chapel. Ahead of them stretched the narrow winding main street of the village — dark and deserted.

Then, without warning, a burst of sound came from the chapel, as violent as it was unexpected. Lusty Welsh voices, like an army of incensed militant musicians, assaulted the stillness of the night with the first verse of a hymn sung in their own language, accompanied by an even more violent blare of organ music. Fantastically, it sounded like the dark spirit of the village screaming defiance at the two intruders who had come to probe its secrets.

'Choir practice,' the Super grunted, and turned towards the closed front door of the inn. He paused with his hand on the latch; then he quietly lifted the latch and opened the door.

They heard a murmuring of voices as they stepped inside; then suddenly a deep voice warned, 'Look out, this is them,' and the murmuring ceased.

The Super left Henry to close the door. He found himself standing at one end of a long, low-ceiled, stone-floored bar. The landlord — a little wizened man in his shirtsleeves — was standing behind the counter at the far end of the room, with four customers in front of him. Three of them looked typical sons of the soil. The fourth, who had just been served with a pint, was Michael Amber.

The Super braved five pairs of hostile eyes as he walked to the bar and nodded pleasantly.

'A pint tankard and a half-pint, please,' he ordered, and nodded at the young woodman. 'It'll have to be good if it's better than the stuff we got at the Riverside just now, eh?'

There was a startled silence as Michael Amber stared at him levelly; and then his handsome face relaxed into a cautious smile as he appreciated the humour of the situation.

'You saw me at the Riverside, sir,' he said tentatively.

The Super nodded again.

'I've got in the habit of noticin' people, son,' he explained blandly. 'I've been a copper all my life until two years ago. Can't get out of the habit now I'm a decrepit old pensioner.'

Michael Amber nodded, still smiling faintly.

72

'I saw you too, sir. Janet pointed you out to me. You're Superintendent Greene of Scotland Yard.'

The Super's eyes widened, and then he laughed.

'Say, that's something I didn't notice, so I may be sheddin' the objectionable habit after all. Well, you and Janet are both wrong, son. I'm *ex*-Superintendent Greene, and no connection whatever with Scotland Yard — as I've explained to one gentleman already this evening.'

The ruse worked. Amber's clear grey eyes lit up.

'Janet told me about that too, sir,' he said. 'It was Major Valentine who recognized you, wasn't it? He's a toff is the major. I was in his mob during the war,' he went on proudly, 'though I didn't know him personally.'

'I knew his father slightly,' the Super explained. 'The major saw me once at the Old Bailey.' He chuckled. 'Nobody'll ever see me there again, gentlemen, unless it's in the dock.'

Gradually the hostility around him was melting, but the landlord and the three

73

typical sons of the soil were still looking to Amber for a lead. Amber held out a massive fist.

'My name is Amber, sir,' he said, his eyes narrowing a fraction. 'Michael Amber, if that means anything to you.'

There was a dead silence charged with possibilities; and then the Super reached for the proffered hand.

'It might do, Mike,' he said cheerfully, 'if I like your company. And if you remember I'm no longer a copper. My friend here don't look enough like a copper for me to have to worry about explainin' him, eh?'

The five men stared at a blushing Henry and burst out laughing . . .

Half an hour later the Super and Henry began to retrace their steps across the bridge. Henry said in an awed tone of voice:

'You were simply terrific, Mr. Greene! Especially when you said you didn't even read the papers any more. But God help you, sir, if they rumble you. Aren't you running a terrible risk by — ?'

'Listen,' the Super commanded, and

stopped in his tracks.

They listened. Another burst of singing was coming from the chapel in Colwin. They heard a wave of cheery laughter as the door of the Welsh Harp opened and closed, and somebody went off in the other direction. Then, faintly but uncannily clear, the din from the Riverside Hotel came to them again across the moonlit water.

'Colonel Fielding was right, son,' the Super growled. 'It's ugly.'

He moved on towards Larne, gingerly caressing the hand that Michael Amber had shaken with a strength that had made him flinch — a hand that still ached a little from a grip that might have meant friendliness or warning.

5

The entrance hall of the Riverside Hotel was empty when they walked in, but the din from the bar was deafening.

'Can't be far short of closing-time, Henry,' the Super remarked. 'Maybe you'd better hit the hay — '

'*Messieurs! Messieurs!*' a loud, very masculine voice interrupted. 'One little moment if you please!'

A dark-haired man of medium build bustled out of the reception office and hastened to join them at the foot of the staircase. He was clean-shaven and swarthily handsome, with thick lips and fiercely dark eyes. He was immaculately dressed in a black coat and vest and striped trousers and a large diamond glistened on the little finger of his left hand as he embraced the newcomers by gesticulation and beamed at the Super.

'You are Mr. Greene and Mr. Baxter, yes?' he went on gushingly. 'I am desolate

I was unable to receive you in person this evening. Please follow me to my private room at once, gentlemen, and join me in a little drink.'

He turned and led the way back through the tiny reception office into a small, lavishly-furnished room behind it, where warmth was provided by an elaborate electric fire, and illumination by shaded electric wall candles. A thick purple carpet covered the floor. A massive, glass-topped desk occupied the centre of the room; and most of the space on the far side of the fire was occupied by a large divan littered with silken cushions of diverse colours; but there was still ample room for three smallish, comfortable-looking armchairs.

'Now then, *messieurs*,' Gabriel Laval commanded, 'try a couple of these chairs and tell me what I may have the honour of bringing you from the bar.' He glanced at the divan behind him and hurriedly moved the position of a silver cushion a few inches before he beamed again at his guests. 'I have an excellent liqueur brandy — '

'Do me splendidly,' the Super agreed, 'but my young friend touches nothing stronger than beer.'

Laval bowed and hurried away. The Super glanced around him again, noting three gilt-framed nude studies on the walls, a television, a radiogram, a clock sunk into the wall, and other expensive fittings.

'Does himself well, Henry,' he muttered. He got up, moved to the divan and lifted the silver cushion Laval had moved, revealing a broken string of imitation pearls. He picked them up and examined them before he returned to his chair. 'Must have been quite a wrestling match to have broken a string like that,' he said.

The Frenchman returned with three drinks on a tray. He closed the door behind him and, taking a large brandy for himself, sank heavily into the vacant armchair.

'You will have seen already, gentlemen, how it is with me just now. It is the end of the season, and most of my staff have left me. I am reduced to being my own *chef*, on top of my other troubles.' He waved despondently and gave the Super a searching look. 'You two gentlemen, I understand, are taking advantage of the unusual weather, yes? You want a quiet holiday? Perhaps you come looking for salmon; it is rather late for that, and the water — '

'Good health, Mr. Laval,' the Super interrupted, tasting his drink and giving the Frenchman a level look. 'I think you know who I am.'

Laval stopped his glass half-way to his lips and frowned sharply; but after a moment's hesitation he capitulated with a charming smile and another gesture.

'You know how it is, *messieurs*. One of my regular customers, the excellent Major Valentine, recognized you in the bar; and my new barmaid is rather talkative. You are, I was given to understand, Superintendent Greene of Scotland Yard.'

The Super nodded.

'Don't worry, Mr. Laval. My friend and I are on a motoring tour, and he's combining business with pleasure by squeezing out of me the necessary material for my memoirs.'

Laval sighed exaggeratedly with relief.

'Then your presence here has nothing to do with the distressing business that — '

'Nice brandy this,' the Super said, tasting his liqueur again. 'Oh, I'm not saying I'm not interested in the queer goings-on here lately, Mr. Laval. But it's purely academic, if you know what I mean. I happened to run into Colonel Fielding in Wynchester today, and he sort of whetted my curiosity. But the case is officially closed, I understand.'

'The case is closed,' Laval said emphatically, 'and the police are right in their conclusions — about the disappearance of my barmaid, which is all that concerns me. She left here suddenly because she had made the place too hot for her.'

'Left with that chap Charlton?' the Super suggested gently, staring into his glass.

The Frenchman's eyes darkened as he reached for a cigarette from the silver box on the desk — perhaps, Henry Baxter thought, to gain himself a little time.

'Monsieur Greene,' Laval said coldly at length, 'I can assure you the gentleman you mention had nothing to do with my barmaid, Nadine Price.'

'Then,' the Super chuckled, 'he must have been about the only male in these two communities who — '

'That may be so,' Laval said sharply. 'Also, I know nothing of the man myself — except he came twice for the fishing, and I was able to put him on to a furnished cottage which he took. After that no, he never came here again.'

'So he came here fishing,' the Super reflected. 'Was he much good at it, Mr. Laval?'

Laval laughed scornfully.

'He was a putrid exhibition. My water was ashamed of him. Perhaps,' with a smile that bared his fine teeth, 'that was why he did not come again after he got the cottage.'

'All the same,' the Super persisted, 'it seems a very strange coincidence, Charlton and your barmaid disappearin' the same night from an isolated spot like this. And the same night somebody digs a grave, apparently for Nadine Price; and that lady, Miss Radford, commits suicide.'

'Monsieur Greene,' the Frenchman replied confidently, 'whatever happen in Colwin that night — I mean the Charlton-Radford affair — was something quite different from my barmaid's disappearance. If you had been through the last war as I was, you would know that stranger coincidences happen there than — '

'Did you run across Nadine Price during the last war?' the Super suggested.

Laval was taken completely off-guard. He started so violently that he spilled some of his drink; and some of the colour went out of his face as he stared at the Super. Before he could speak, however, the latter waved his hand apologetically.

'Sorry,' he said. 'It just occurred to me, because I understand you took on this girl without references. Mind you,' he went on blandly, 'I'm not well briefed on this business. I don't bother much with the newspapers, and Colonel Fielding only gave me a general survey of the case when I saw him. All the same,' he grinned, 'when an old bloodhound sniffs the scent of a baffling business like this! So you had no inkling of what this girl was up to when she cleared out that night? She didn't get a telephone call or anything like that to alarm her?'

'There was no telephone call for her that night, sir. I am sure of this because I question the staff myself.'

'Then, next morning,' the Super sympathized, 'it was all over the place: a double disappearance, a suicide and that open grave. Did your guests get scared and leave you, Mr. Laval?'

'Most of them,' the Frenchman confessed bitterly, 'but it was more because of what happen in Colwin, and the ridiculous panic that swep' through both villages. I could have filled my place with reporters, but I refuse them all. For one thing, my place had had enough unpleasant publicity . . . '

'I suppose your staff got scared, too?'

Laval was not to be caught napping a second time.

'My staff,' he answered cautiously, 'were naturally perturbed, like everyone else concerned. But their circumstances were difficult. Most of them were already looking for situations for the winter months, and many hotel proprietors are chary of engaging staff from establishments that figure unpleasantly in the news. However, I could sympathize. I let all go at once who wished to go; I even helped some of them out of my own pocket. Fortunately, I was able to lay my hands on a receptionist who would work also as waitress, and my new barmaid; and the porter you saw today, who worked here before my time, was willing to come back — though he lives in the locality and won't sleep in.' He smiled unexpectedly. 'So we do our best, m'sieur, and we shall make you as comfortable as possible.'

'I'm sure you will,' the Super said warmly. 'As for the cooking, I haven't enjoyed a dinner like tonight's for longer'n I can remember.'

'Thank you.' Laval looked pleased. He smiled again. 'I am sure, in the circumstances, you will understand my cautious approach to you just now. I want my business to live down this thing as quickly as possible. I was only thinking today it is about time Miss Price's room was cleared of her belongings, and — '

The Super emptied his glass.

'It's still as it was the night she cleared out, eh?'

'Exactly, Mr. Greene. I have kept it locked, and — '

'Mind if we look in there, as a matter of curiosity, on our way to bed?'

Laval hesitated as the three of them rose.

'Not at all,' he said. 'I'll get the key and take you up myself.'

The bar was quiet when they came back into the hall; the noise was all coming from the drive and the car park now. Laval led them up to the third and top floor, by way of the stairs. Here, at the end of a long, carpeted corridor, he unlocked and threw open a door.

'Some of these are emergency guest rooms,' he explained as he switched on the light and stepped aside for the Super to pass. 'I let the staff use them when they are vacant.'

The Super's eyebrows went up, nevertheless, as he entered a room as expensively furnished as his own, and with a bathroom attached.

The place was untidy, and strewn with the clothes and other belongings Nadine Price had left behind her. He crossed to the uncurtained window and saw that it had the same outlook as his own. After a cursory inspection, he rejoined Laval and Henry outside the door.

'A pretty hurried departure,' he remarked, and turned to switch off the light and manipulate the key which he returned to the proprietor. 'Thanks for indulging my curiosity, Mr. Laval.'

Laval accompanied them down to the first-floor landing where he bade them goodnight and promised them tea in bed at half-past seven. The Super led the way to Henry's room, where he threw open the door and went inside.

'Just want to see how you're accommodated, son,' he said as Henry followed him and closed the door. He looked

86

around and grinned. 'Nothing to choose between all three rooms, eh, Henry: yours, mine and Miss Price's! Not many barmaids get rooms like that, and private baths attached, in their places of employment, at the height of the season. Or have we got the wrong idea about barmaids?'

Henry grinned as he sat down on the edge of his bed.

'Laval did meet Nadine Price in the last war, sir,' he said firmly. 'You tricked that admission out of him all right. His face gave him away.'

The Super shook his head deprecatingly.

'That wasn't such a long shot, Henry. Don't forget Laval came to this country in the war.'

'It was beautifully timed, Mr. Greene.'

The Super eyed his young companion dubiously.

'I'm not sure you're not a bit too free with the bouquets, Henry,' he said. 'Let's be cautious and say it begins to look like Nadine Price came here and literally took the job. That doesn't get us much farther, but it's something. Also, the way I read him, our friend Laval wasn't so sorry to get rid of his guests and his staff as soon as possible after Nadine skedaddled. That's suggestive of something, if I only knew what.'

Henry grinned again delightedly.

'You darned well know what it's suggestive of,' he retorted. 'Laval even sweetened some of his departing staff to make them forget anything inconvenient to him they might remember.'

The Super frowned.

'You've got a suspicious mind, Henry; too suspicious by half for a kid your age. What did you make of our Gabriel on the Charlton-Radford angle?'

'He was either ready for you, sir,' Henry said promptly, 'or else he was stating an honest conviction — the same as Colonel Fielding's.'

The Super nodded gloomily.

'He disappointed me there,' he sighed. 'Well, don't let this business keep you awake, son. No good detective ever lets anything keep him awake when he hits the hay. We'll have more fun and games tomorrow. 'Night.'

In his own room across the passage the Super opened the window, and with the light burning and the curtains drawn back, he sat down and smoked a cigarette. Then he drew the curtains, switched off the light, set his door slightly ajar and lay down on his bed. He lay for an indefinite period listening to faint and distant sounds suggesting the closing-up of the establishment and the migration of various people to their rooms. Finally, after a longish spell of unbroken silence, he got up from his bed, armed himself with a small electric torch from his suitcase, and left the room.

The corridors and stairs he negotiated on his way to the third-floor landing were in darkness. But on his way from there back to the room lately occupied by Nadine Price, he passed two facing doors with lines of light showing under them; and he assumed that the receptionist and the barmaid were retiring behind them.

He found the door of Nadine Price's room unlocked, as he had left it. Inside, he laid a doubled-up mat against the bottom of the door, stuck a piece of paper in the keyhole of the lock, drew the window-curtains carefully and switched on the light. Then he began a more-than-cursory inspection of the room.

First, he visualized it as he imagined Nadine Price must have left it after her hurried packing and departure. Then he superimposed on that picture a picture of the room as the police should have left it after their search. Finally, he shook his head because the second picture he had visualized wasn't the one he was looking at now. There wasn't much difference between the two, but there was enough for his trained eye to distinguish as significant.

His experience was that policemen, searching such a room in the known circumstances, would have left it slightly tidier than they had found it, rather than the reverse. They wouldn't have left a part of the carpet crinkled in re-laying it; they wouldn't have left the bed as disturbed as it was; and they wouldn't have left the chest-of-drawers a couple of inches out of alignment with the wall behind it.

Someone else had searched this room, the Super decided, before and after the visit of the police. Hurriedly before, and very thoroughly afterwards. In the hope of finding something that even the police might have missed.

He found a silk slip under the bed that seemed to clinch the matter. There was a thick line of dust across one side of the garment; evidence, as he read it, that someone had searched in the space between the top of the picture-rail and the wall — and had been anxious not to leave their fingerprints behind them.

The Super examined every article that Nadine Price had left behind her; and he made his find in the bottom drawer of the chest-of-drawers, which contained nothing but a pile of used and discarded handkerchiefs — all of them the same size, texture and colour. One of these — it had obviously been used by someone with catarrh or a cold — was still stuck together very roughly and clumsily in the shape of a ball.

The Super pulled it open, cursing the policeman who had been guilty of what, in the circumstances, might seem a negligible lapse.

Across the centre of the small handkerchief someone had written '93 CHRISTINE' with a piece of tawny red lipstick.

He compared the shade of red with smears on other soiled handkerchiefs and found them all the same.

He got to his feet and was stowing his find away in his wallet when, from one of the rooms farther along the corridor, he heard voices raised in anger; then the unmistakable sound of the brutal assault of a hand on naked flesh; a woman's scream that was stifled almost as soon as it had begun . . . and silence.

He ran for the window and pulled back the curtains; he returned to the door, replaced the mat where he had found it, and turned out the light. Out in the passage, with the door shut behind him, he stood listening again.

He heard nothing more; but he could just make out the two lines of light still visible under the two facing doors he had passed on his way here. He was considering further investigation when

the line of light on the left side of
the passage went out. He reached for
the door of Nadine's room and stepped
back into the doorway a few seconds
before the door of the suddenly darkened
room opened and Gabriel Laval and his
French receptionist came out — both of
them wearing dressing-gowns.

They stood for a moment conversing
in whispers; then, watched by Laval,
the woman entered the lighted bedroom
opposite and locked the door behind her.
Laval re-entered the room they had left,
but re-appeared almost at once and went
off to the stairs and one of the floors
below.

The Super waited until the light went
out in the receptionist's room, and then
he made his silent way along to her door.
He heard her settling in bed. He stepped
across to the door opposite and could
hear a woman's half-stifled sobbing on
the other side of it.

'Janet, the barmaid,' he confirmed to
himself after a moment, and made his
way back to the first floor and his
own bed.

6

Five people were already at breakfast when the Super and Henry strolled into the dining-room that Thursday morning. Major Valentine waved to them from his corner table before burying himself again behind his newspaper; and the Super recognized a middle-aged couple whom he had seen at dinner the previous evening. The other two solitary guests had about them the bored, distracted air of commercial travellers.

The French receptionist-*cum*-waitress was more friendly when she came to express the hope that they had slept well, and to take their order.

'Bacon-and-eggs for me, miss,' the Super said hungrily. 'I slept with my window open and I could eat an ox.'

Henry ordered grapefruit and toast, and the Super shook his head at him as the woman went away.

'Summat wrong with people who can't

eat breakfast, son. Maybe you've got the artistic temperament. Well,' he went on cheerfully, 'this air and this weather is better'n doctor's medicine. We'll treat ourselves to a dose of 'em as soon as we're through here.'

He shook out a morning paper he had bought from the porter in the hall and proceeded to engross himself in it and his food. He was polishing off his seventh round of toast when Major Valentine came to their table on his way out.

'I don't usually breakfast here,' he told them, 'but I was up and about at an atrociously early hour, and I landed a couple of trout that I brought across to have cooked for my lunch. I'm going to try my luck again presently. Don't forget my standing invitation, Super.'

He nodded to Henry and left them. The Super gazed after him thoughtfully, and suddenly gulped down his coffee and pushed back his chair.

'Ready, son?'

Henry was ready and waiting. It was not the Super's intention to catch up with Valentine, however. Once outside the hotel he stood staring down at the river for several minutes, and then started wandering through the well-kept grounds. He stopped to admire a large, ornate summer house behind the hotel, and grunted with disappointment when he found it locked-up. He continued his wandering, pausing to view the hotel and its surroundings from various points of vantage; and only when he found himself back at his starting-point did he turn his footsteps in the direction of the promenade and the bridge.

They were half-way across the bridge when he stopped and leaned on the stone balustrade and stared once again down at the gently-flowing water. It was then that he told Henry of his return visit to Nadine Price's room, and showed him the handkerchief and the lipstick writing he had found there. Henry looked alarmed when he heard of the 'beating-up of Janet the barmaid', as the Super described it.

'Then you think the girl is in real danger from Laval and the Frenchwoman, sir?' he asked anxiously.

'I hope she is, and I hope she knows it,' the Super said grimly. 'People are more ready to talk when they're scared — whatever you may have heard to the contrary, son. Well, now we've docketed those bits and pieces, let's get on with the job as planned.'

He lit a cigarette as they moved on towards Colwin.

The main street of the village looked more unprepossessing than when they had seen it from a distance the previous evening. Most of the cottages were little better than hovels, and such shops as there were were shabby and poorly-stocked. The one redeeming feature of the scene was the fine old church standing with its vicarage, in well-kept grounds surrounded by tall trees. In contrast, the village school, just beyond the church, was as ugly and decrepit as the chapel by the bridge.

Where the main street ended, abruptly, at the war memorial, the road forked; and here, on the right, was also the mouth of a narrow lane that ran parallel with the river. The Super nodded at a small grey cottage just visible at the first slight bend in this lane, and said:

'That'll be Michael Amber's cottage, according to the directions I got from Colonel Fielding when I telephoned him from that café yesterday afternoon.'

They moved on, taking the right fork in the road, and stopped presently at the drive entrance to some extensive, well-timbered grounds. The name of the house partly visible among the trees was Sunnybrae.

'This house,' the Super announced, 'will be Miss Radford's house.'

He led the way into the grounds, and they followed the drive the short distance to a large, square, greystone building surrounded by lawns and gardens which, in spite of weeks of neglect, still made an impressive show.

The Super followed the drive round towards the back of the house and stopped when he came to two large windows of fairly recent erection, by the look of them, and a door between them. Farther on the drive terminated in a garage and some sheds. The Super stood with his back to the door at which he had stopped, and pointed ahead of him into the surrounding trees.

'Just a few yards in that direction, son, and you'd come to the lane and young Amber's cottage. Then, behind the cottage, the woods run down to the river; and somewhere in that piece of territory is that filled-in grave. Now, let's find them keys the local sergeant should have hidden here for us.'

He went to his knees and fumbled under and around the large flat stone that served as a step for the door between the windows. When he straightened he was holding two keys — both Yales. The first one he tried fitted the door, and this opened their way into a large airy kitchen.

It was a lofty, stone-floored room with cream-enamelled walls; and it was lavishly equipped with everything the modern housewife could desire. A huge patent stove dominated the scene; and in front of it stood a large square table with a single chair drawn up to it. Chair and table held the newcomer's attention for a long moment, for it must have been on that chair that Evelyn Radford had been sitting when she had taken her last fatal drink of poisoned cocoa.

The room was in perfect order and spotlessly clean. The Super spent some time examining the stove; he went outside and peered into the room through both windows; and then he came back to dismiss the scene with an almost impatient wave of his hand.

'Let's see what the rest of Miss Radford's house has to tell us, son.'

They passed through a doorway at the back of the kitchen and climbed three steps into the hall of the house that had been completely furnished as a lounge. On one side of the staircase was the dining-room, and here they found the first of Miss Radford's paintings adorning the cream walls and identified by her signature. They were a series of water-colours of country scenes typical of the locality; but the Super could only shake his head after inspecting them.

'I'm no judge of pictures,' he confessed, 'but these seem just plain ordinary to me.

Let's try the room across the hall.'

The sitting-room opposite presented a very different picture from the severely-furnished dining-room. It was a long room, low-ceilinged, with windows overlooking the lawn and gardens at the back of the house; and it was lavishly over-furnished. The walls were almost completely hidden by well-filled book-shelves. A persian carpet covered the floor. A large divan and several deep armchairs were arranged in front of a huge open fireplace where a log fire was stacked ready for lighting. Apart from a modern radiogram and a baby piano, the rest of the furniture was old or antique: the sort of stuff one collects over a long period of time — and some of which, the Super speculated, had been brought from Cumberland many years ago.

Here and there, on small easels, were other examples of Evelyn Radford's paintings, as unilluminating as those in the dining-room. But nowhere visible in the room was a single photograph. And a cursory inspection of the hundreds of books yielded no further clue to the character of the woman who had lived here.

The Super grunted his disappointment as they climbed the wide staircase to the landing above. He passed through an open doorway facing the stairs, and called over his shoulder:

'Well, this seems to be her bedroom, Henry. We ought to find something here.'

On the face of it the large room was the expensively-furnished bedroom of a well-to-do spinster without exotic tastes but with a definite liking for comfort. There was a great divan bed in the middle of the floor, but its silken covering was of the same pale grey as the plain carpet. There were mediocre paintings on the cream walls — and not a single photograph in sight.

The Super was intrigued by what he found in the huge bay window overlooking the grounds at the front of the house. A beautiful mahogany glass-topped dressing-table was bare except for a set of silver-backed brushes and hand-mirror; but a small mahogany table on the right of this, within easy reach, was literally crammed with the expensive make-up paraphernalia of the modern woman of means. The Super frowned at this odd arrangement; it baffled him and he couldn't imagine why. Then, to Henry Baxter's embarrassment, he turned his attention to the contents of the large wardrobe and many drawers.

This search proved excitingly revealing. The experience was, as he remarked bluntly, like inspecting the trousseau of a modern bride. All Evelyn Radford's clothes were expensive and new — and definitely *unspinsterish!* Some of the négligés made even the Super gasp.

It was in a small dressing-room that he found the collection of trunks in which were stored the discarded wardrobe of the solitary, unhopeful spinster Evelyn Radford had been before the advent of Robert Charlton . . .

He returned to the bedroom, frowning again, and wandered back to the landing. Then, with a hopeful exclamation, he stalked through another doorway into a large, bright room beyond.

'Here's her studio, Henry,' he called over his shoulder. 'Maybe it's here we'll find what I'm looking for . . . *My God!*'

Henry followed him into the room to find him standing in front of an unfinished portrait in oils. The canvas was fixed high on a tall easel, to the right of which was standing a large, oblong mirror.

The portrait was of a woman; and the woman — they recognized it from the one picture published in the newspapers — was Evelyn Radford.

Henry gasped, too, when he saw it; and stared at it wide-eyed and unbelieving, as the Super was staring.

'It's a self-portrait, Henry,' the latter said emotionally at length. 'It . . . it's a ruddy masterpiece! She must have been doing this for *him*.'

It was a bold, courageous piece of work, in startling contrast to the mediocre landscapes they had seen earlier; and, infinitely more, it was the work of an artist passionately inspired by her subject.

Yet it was the face itself that impressed

them most: the proud, passionate face of a woman in love; a woman who had shed years of loneliness and disillusionment, and re-discovered her youth and lost beauty.

' 'The female woman',' the Super said fervently, quoting from a source he could not have named. 'My God, Henry, no man could be worthy of a transformation like this.'

He passed his hand over his eyes and moved on to begin a thorough search of the studio. There were more countryside scenes, and studies of flowers, fruit, and *objets d'art;* but still the Super could not find the thing he was after, the thing he was confident must be somewhere in this house.

Suddenly he stopped and swung round to Henry.

'Damn it,' he cried, 'what are we doing here? It's in her bedroom. It's *got* to be in her bedroom — somewhere where she alone could find it!'

Back he went into the bedroom, searching behind pictures, pulling out drawers, disintegrating the divan bed.

Finally he returned to the scene that had baffled him before: the bare-topped dressing-table and the crowded little table nearby. Fretting, he rapped the glass top of the dressing-table with his knuckles.

'Can't be nothing hidden under this,' he growled. 'You can see the mahogany through the glass, unless — '

Swiftly he collected up the brushes and hand-mirror and laid them aside. Then, carefully, he lifted the glass top of the dressing-table and turned it over — and found his prize.

It was a beautifully-done head-and-shoulders portrait in oils of a handsome, clean-shaven man, apparently in early middle age. The canvas was stuck to the glass, and the back of the canvas had been painted the same colour as the mahogany of the dressing-table!

The Super propped up his discovery against a chair, and stood back to admire it.

'There it is, son,' he said triumphantly. 'There's the picture of Robert Charlton she had to paint from memory, and keep to herself to look at when she was alone — because she was a woman madly in love!'

Henry nodded dazedly.

'I see your point, sir,' he said humbly. 'She had to do this in secret, and keep it in secret, because he wouldn't have a picture of himself taken, one supposes. But what will you do with it now you've found it?'

The Super laughed as he picked up his prize.

'With a bit of luck, Henry, we'll find out a lot more about Robert Charlton, that's what we'll do with it. Come on down into the kitchen and we'll wrap it up ready to take away.'

A moment later, at the foot of the stairs, he stopped and crossed to the telephone standing on its small table against the wall.

'What's this, I wonder?' he said, beckoning his companion. 'More luck, or just more coincidence?'

He pointed with a stubby forefinger at the subscriber's number printed on the front of the instrument: COLWIN 93.

'Colwin ninety-three,' he muttered.

'Christine ninety-three. Hum . . . '

A sound from the kitchen made him turn abruptly and lead the way down the three steps and into that room.

They found the outside door wide open and, standing in the doorway, a woman.

7

She was a tall, finely-built creature, dark and handsome and dressed in a plain black frock that fitted her like a glove. Her arms and her legs were bare, and her hair was untidy as though she had just come from one menial task to another.

She stared at the Super and his companion in bewilderment but without panic; then, seeing the slab of glass the Super was carrying, she said:

'You'll be from Mr. Seascale. He didn't say anything about today, though.'

The Super laid the glass dressing-table top on the kitchen table and smiled at her.

'Who would Mr. Seascale be, missy?'

She looked mildly suspicious.

'Mr. Seascale is the solicitor dealing with Miss Radford's affairs. He wrote me he was coming down tomorrow to arrange for the sale, and — '

'You'll be Mrs. Ferndale who used to

work for Miss Radford?'

'That's right. Mavis Ferndale. But I don't — '

'Pleased to meet you, Mrs. Ferndale.' The Super smiled again. 'I am ex-Superintendent Greene of Scotland Yard. Now, there's nothing to be alarmed about, my dear. The police investigation into Miss Radford's death and so forth is officially closed. I'm down here in a private capacity, clearing up a point or two for the chief constable. Let's sit down, shall we?'

Mavis Ferndale hesitated a moment before she shut the door and perched on a nearby chair. The Super sat down on the chair at the table, ignoring the young woman's look of dismay that identified the chair beyond all doubt.

'Now then, Mrs. Ferndale,' he went on persuasively, 'I've taken you into my confidence because I'm sure I can trust you. This is a private, unofficial talk between us, you understand; and I want you to take me into *your* confidence.' He paused and let her have it. 'Do you believe that Miss Radford committed suicide?'

She started violently and turned pale at the blunt question. Henry Baxter barely succeeded in stifling a gasp of surprise and apprehension on his own account. But the Super's bold move was also a shrewd one, and it had the desired effect. It brought Mavis Ferndale face to face with what she had been thinking and feeling ever since the morning her mistress had been found dead in that room; and inevitably — if she was as transparently honest as she looked — it brought an honest answer.

'No, sir, I don't,' she cried; and then looked panic-stricken because of what she had said.

The Super nodded encouragingly.

'Please go on, Mrs. Ferndale.'

'Well,' she floundered after a moment, 'Miss Radford wasn't that sort of woman at all. I've been with her ever since she came here. That's sixteen years. I was fifteen when she came down from Cumberland. I was a bit frightened too, at first, because we all knew about her tragedy up there. But Miss Radford was kindness itself. 'You know who I am,

Mavis,' she said; I remember those words as if it was yesterday, and the smile that went with them. And that was all she ever said about herself the whole time I was with her. She was a fine, brave woman, and not the sort to take her own life. Why, I remember her reading me a bit out of the newspaper one day about a suicide, and saying how she despised people who did that sort of thing.'

The Super nodded again.

'Miss Radford lived very quietly here in Colwin, didn't she?'

'Very quietly indeed, sir.' She was more at ease now and seemed eager to talk. 'She never had any friends to stay, not the whole long time; and she never went anywhere much except for walks and her painting, and to church on Sunday evenings. She was deeply religious, Miss Radford was, without making a show of it, if you know what I mean. She preferred evening service because not so many go as in the morning. She had the vicar and such-like to tea now and again, but she was wonderful satisfied with her own company.' She made the latter statement as though naming another of her late mistress's virtues; and then she frowned. 'Until, of course — '

'Yes.' The Super turned over the slab of glass in front of him and showed her the portrait. 'Is this a good likeness of Mr. Charlton?'

Mavis Ferndale stared at the portrait in blank astonishment.

'It's a wonderful likeness,' she said dazedly. 'But isn't that the glass top of — '

'It is,' the Super agreed, 'but never mind that now. Tell me this: Was Miss Radford very much in love with Robert Charlton *right from the start?* Please think carefully before you answer.'

From her facial expression and long hesitation, it was clearly a question she had asked herself more than once.

'Yes,' she said emphatically at length, 'she was, right from their first meeting. I never saw a woman so much in love. And with a woman like Miss Radford you knew it was real.'

'Did she ever confide in you about the affair, Mrs. Ferndale?'

She shook her head.

'All them years she never said anything that mattered about herself. It don't seem possible, but there it is. But she did tell me she was going to marry Mr. Charlton.'

'Did it ever occur to you that she had met him before he came here to Colwin?'

She hesitated again.

'No, sir. At least, I couldn't hardly believe a lady like Miss Radford could have fallen for a man like that — right at their first meeting. But Miss Radford said that was how it was, and,' she added earnestly, 'she always told the truth. She hated lies.'

The Super waited a moment before putting his next, blunt question:

'Mrs. Ferndale, what was *your* honest opinion of Robert Charlton?'

'I didn't like him,' she said, promptly and almost eagerly. 'I didn't trust him.'

'Why not, Mrs. Ferndale?'

She blushed.

'Well, sir, I've got nothing *definite* against him. But I was very fond of

Miss Radford, and somehow . . . ' She tried again. 'He just wasn't worthy of her,' she exploded. 'He just wasn't her type. There was something mysterious about him too, though I couldn't place it exactly. He . . . I always felt he was up to something she didn't suspect. And once, while she was out, he tried some funny business with me. That washed him up completely so far as I was concerned. Oh, he was apologetic and all that, when I told him where to get off. He was scared, too; more scared than he need have been — that I'd let on to Miss Radford, of course. Anyway, he never took liberties again, so that was that.' She paused, frowning, as though there was a good deal else she would like to have said about Robert Charlton if she could have put her thoughts into words adequately; and then she shook her head and the Super nodded his understanding.

'Miss Radford never wore his engagement ring, did she?'

'No, sir. That,' she went on rather pityingly, 'was because she didn't want people to say they were actually engaged.

As though everyone couldn't see what was sticking out a mile.'

'Were there any definite plans for an early marriage, Mrs. Ferndale?'

Once again she hesitated, painfully uncertain.

'I couldn't say, sir. But what Miss Radford did say about getting rid of certain things, making changes . . . And once she asked me, if she moved from here when she was married, would I go with them. I was free to go,' she went on hurriedly, 'because my husband was killed in the war. But I couldn't make up my mind . . . because of *him*.'

'Thank you,' the Super said gratefully. 'Now, to come to the particular time of the tragedy, and Charlton's disappearance and the rest of it: Did you notice any sign of strain in the relationship between them? They hadn't quarrelled or anything like that?'

'Oh no, sir.' She was very emphatic. 'In fact, she was happier then than ever, if anything; and I was quite certain she would soon be telling me something definite in the way of plans.'

'When did you last see Miss Radford alive?'

She dropped her gaze again, finding herself in fresh difficulty.

'The evening it all happened, sir,' she said at length. 'I prepared a cold dinner, leaving the things for Miss Radford to take into the lounge. Mr. Charlton was with her. He'd been with her all afternoon. I left here about seven o'clock, having called out goodnight. And when I'd got as far as the gate I saw I'd forgotten my handbag, and . . . ' She stopped, floundering; and then, unconvincingly, she resumed: 'Well, that's all, sir. I came back for my bag, and then left again and went home.'

The Super shook his head reprovingly.

'That wasn't quite all about that, was it,' he protested. 'Come now, Mrs. Ferndale, you can talk quite frankly to me. Something else happened before you left here finally that night — something you didn't tell to the police, perhaps. What was it?'

Mavis Ferndale seemed on the verge of panic again, but the Super could be very reassuring and persuasive when he wanted to. After a long pause she braced herself to make the confession.

'It was the telephone, sir,' she said. 'Miss Radford *never* had any incoming calls unless they were wrong numbers. She disliked the telephone, in fact, and never even rang the tradesmen unless it was urgent. She even ticked off her solicitor at Hereford for ringing her, a short time back, over something she said he could have put in a letter . . .

'But all this,' she qualified, 'was apart from Mr. Charlton. He'd ring her several times a day, sometimes, from the cottage . . .

'The night we're speaking of, when I was at the gate and remembering my bag, I thought I heard the telephone. Quite startled me, it did. Then, when I got back into this room and was collecting my bag, I heard Miss Radford call out to Mr. Charlton from the hall. She called something like 'It's your sister, Bob.' And a second later she came into the kitchen — and looked quite startled to see me still there. I explained about my handbag, wondering why she seemed so flustered. And then, more for a joke than anything, I said I thought I'd heard the telephone ringing. But Miss Radford shook her head, and I laughed and said it must've been a ghost telephone . . . and off I went.'

The Super asked gently:

'Why didn't you tell this to the police, Mrs. Ferndale?'

The distressed woman flushed again, but her gaze was unflinching as she answered:

'Because I must have been mistaken. If Miss Radford said it hadn't rung — '

'Yes. But didn't you think it odd, Miss Radford calling out to Mr. Charlton like that, if there hadn't been a telephone call for him?'

'Yes,' she confessed, 'it did seem queer; but I supposed Miss Radford had just called that remark to Mr. Charlton as part of something she'd been saying when she left the lounge to come to the kitchen for the dinner things.'

The Super nodded sympathetically.

'That's natural enough. Now think

very carefully. What *exactly* did you hear Miss Radford call to Mr. Charlton? *Something like 'It's your sister, Bob'* won't quite do, you know. Was there another word in it, do you think?'

'Well,' she conceded, 'it did seem — '

'Was the word a name? The name Christine?'

Mavis Ferndale stared at him; then she nodded emphatically.

'It *was* Christine,' she cried. 'She called out, 'It's Christine, your sister, Bob.' I *knew* there was something . . . '

'Was that the first time you'd heard Miss Radford mention that name to Mr. Charlton?'

'It was the first time I knew Mr. Charlton had a sister, sir.'

'Right. We're almost through, Mrs. Ferndale. Did you do any work for Mr. Charlton in his cottage?'

'Yes, sir,' she said, her full lips tightening momentarily. 'Miss Radford asked me to, that's why. I went there three times a week to clean up. Miss Radford fussed over him like a hen with one chick.'

'When were you last at the cottage?'

'The day everything came out, sir. Sergeant Evans came for me. A fine muddle he'd left things in, too — Mr. Charlton, I mean.'

'Did Mr. Charlton have any callers at the cottage, besides Miss Radford?'

She shook her head, and then another memory caught her, as it were, almost in mid-stream. The Super said:

'You want to qualify that, don't you?'

She laughed impatiently.

'I don't, really. It was only something Willie Oaker said. He's the hunchback who works with Mike Amber, and he's always up to something. One moonlight night, months ago, he met me walking by the river, along by the woods behind the village, and he tried to frighten me with a story about a ghost he'd seen in the woods — a naked woman in a luminous black cape. Then, one night afterwards, when I'd been to Mr. Charlton's cottage with a parcel from Miss Radford, he tried to kid me he'd seen the same creature calling on Mr. Charlton the night before. A naked woman in a luminous black cape!' she scoffed. 'I oughtn't to have mentioned it, sir. Mr. Charlton never had no callers. He never spoke to anybody but Miss Radford if he could help it.'

The Super drummed on the table for a moment.

'Just one thing more, Mrs. Ferndale. Do you believe that Miss Radford and Mr. Charlton were lovers in the physical sense? This is strictly confidential, you know, and — '

'No, I don't, sir,' she cried, the warm colour flowing into her cheeks again. 'And you'd say the same if you'd known Miss Radford as I did. She was a good woman, and there aren't many of them about today. I . . . I know that,' she went on impulsively, 'for a positive fact. One day, not long before all this happened, I was passing the lounge, making no noise because of the thick carpet in the hall. The door was ajar, and Miss Radford and Mr. Charlton were on the divan. He was pleading for something, very passionately, and she told him to wait, and not to spoil everything. Oh, dear,' she rebuked herself again. 'I shouldn't have told you about that either, only — '

'I'm very grateful to you,' the Super said, getting up from his chair. 'Now, if you'll step outside a moment.'

He led the way out on to the drive.

'I want to know where the spade was kept, Mrs. Ferndale; the one that was borrowed to dig that grave in the woods.'

She pointed to the shed between them and the garage.

'It was taken from there, sir. That shed was never kept locked.' She gave him a half-frightened look. 'But Miss Radford never had nothing to do with *that* dreadful creature, sir,' she whispered. 'Nor Mr. Charlton either. He never went near the Riverside Hotel.'

The Super turned and pointed through the trees in the direction of the lane.

'Mr. Amber's cottage is over there, isn't it,' he said. 'Now tell me: If a light was burning in one of his front windows at night, could you see it plainly from here?'

'Oh yes, sir. I've often seen it. I'm . . . we all like Mike Amber.'

'You didn't see a light in his cottage on the night we've been talking about?'

'N-no, sir. But I didn't look particularly.'

The Super patted her shoulder reassuringly.

'You've done splendidly, Mrs. Ferndale. Have you much to do in the house, by the way?'

'No, sir. Nothing really. I just looked in as I've been doing every day since . . . '

'Then I wonder if you can spare us a little more of your time. How far is Mr. Charlton's cottage from here?'

'About a hundred yards,' she told him. 'You'll find a path in front of the house, unless you want to go by the road.'

'Right. Have you got a key with you? Then take this one,' he said, handing it over as she shook her head. 'Wait there for us, will you, and . . . Hello!' he exclaimed, as he consulted his watch. 'This won't do. It's nearly half-past twelve. How about you nipping home to your mother for a bite to eat and meetin' us at the cottage in an hour?'

'I live alone,' she smiled, 'so I haven't anyone to explain to. I'll be along to the cottage before half-past one, sir.'

A moment later the Super rejoined Henry in the kitchen. He nodded approvingly as he closed the door behind him.

'A smart girl that,' he said with warmth. 'Very convincing, too. She just can't see her late mistress as a suicide, can she?' He scratched his chin thoughtfully as he returned to his seat at the table. 'No more can I, Henry. No more can I.'

8

Henry Baxter thought this was one of the rare, exciting moments of his life. He photographed the scene mentally, to preserve every detail of it in his memory: the big, luxuriously-equipped kitchen with its gleaming chromium and cream and its spotless red-tiled floor; the two square windows full of sunlight; the big square table and the slab of glass with its exciting secret; and the Super lounging on the chair on which Evelyn Radford had met a violent death, and saying almost casually that he didn't believe it was suicide . . .

Henry returned to his own chair by the hall door. He knew the Super wanted to talk, to get things straightened out and neatly docketed in his mind before he passed on to the next scene of investigation. So he provoked him with his own incredulity.

'But surely, sir, Miss Radford could

have taken cyanide by accident?'

The Super went on as though he hadn't even heard the challenge:

'You know, Henry, it's a great pity that Colonel Fielding didn't call in the Yard at the start of all this. But he's not to be blamed too much for that. The same thing's always happening for one reason or another, and if anything's to be blamed it's the system rather than the man.

'Look at what must have happened here. Sergeant Evans would have been the first on the scene when this case began to break, as they say in America. And the worthy Evans brought a horribly prejudiced mind to the job! He couldn't help himself! He'd got his opinions about Gabriel Laval — who must have been working on him for a long time, because it's a publican's business to keep 'in' with the cops. He knew practically everyone in the locality, some of 'em intimately. Moreover, he was right in the thick of all this trouble that Nadine Price was responsible for. He was heartily fed up with Nadine, and doubtless relieved when

Laval sent for him and told him she'd packed up and vanished in the night. Evans didn't have to think twice about the situation. He'd expected it, hoped for it. One of Nadine's enemies had given her a real scare and she'd decided to clear out while the going was good! A glance at her bedroom was sufficient to ridicule the notion that there was more to it than that.

'Evans reported all this to Inspector Griffiths, who doubtless shared the sergeant's knowledge of the district and his convictions in relation to the whole set-up. So now there were two well-meaning, prejudiced minds on the job. They went out of their way to discourage the suggestion there'd been foul play, in their efforts to keep the public calm and avoid any sort of panic; and in doing so, of course, they deepened their own prejudices. So that when they found that open grave, and Nadine's hat in the bottom of it, they saw them as plain evidence of a plot to scare Nadine into flight. A thorough search of the locality merely served, as they saw it, to establish their case beyond all possible doubt. There had been no foul play!

'Now, Henry,' the Super went on sternly, 'you can see how those two worthy officers came to slip up over the handkerchief I found in Nadine's room. They must have tackled the search of that room as more or less a routine affair; because they never expected to find any evidence of foul play, or that Nadine would have been careless enough to leave behind anything incriminating as regards herself. A slip like that, son, would not have been possible in other circumstances. It would never have been made by a Yard man called in fresh to the case.

'So, when it came to dealing with the Colwin mystery, the minds of these two officers were doubly prejudiced. They knew — or thought they knew — Miss Radford and Robert Charlton as two of the last people who *could* be suspected of having been mixed up with Nadine Price and her escapades — or anything else that went on in the two villages for that matter! They knew also that the two had been keeping company, as well as keeping themselves to themselves. So once again the solution seemed obvious, didn't it! Charlton had walked out on his landlady-love; and that middle-aged spinster, in the throes of a belated love affair, had done herself in. It didn't matter whether Charlton had walked out because he'd tired of amusing himself with Miss Radford, or whether he'd been after her dough and had found out there was nothing doing in that direction. What did matter was that the disappearance of Nadine and the finding of the open grave were one story, and the Radford-Charlton affair was another story; and it was plain ridiculous to try and find any connection between 'em.

'That, Henry, was how matters stood when Colonel Fielding was called into the case. Inspector Griffiths and Sergeant Evans honestly believed they knew it all, barring the trimmings; and the results of subsequent inquiries tended to prove 'em right. There wasn't the vestige of a clue found to suggest there had been foul play — unless the grave was evidence of an abortive attempt in that direction. There was the remarkably detailed evidence of that seaman to indicate that Nadine had fled to France via Jersey. And, in relation to the Colwin tragedy, there seemed reason enough to believe Miss Radford had attempted to take her life once before, and might understandably have committed suicide in the throes of another emotional crisis over this mystery chap Charlton.

'A coroner's jury cautiously returned an open verdict over the death of Miss Radford. Colonel Fielding — loyal to his own officers and confident of their integrity and intelligence — ultimately felt it his duty to publish the police findings in both cases, and state that, pending something else turning up at any time, official investigations in the district were at an end.

'But,' the Super proclaimed, 'Colonel Fielding was far from satisfied. He was a darned sight more unhappy about the position, Henry, than he admitted to me yesterday. I dare say, moreover, he felt his hand might have been forced by the continued disquieting state of affairs in the locality and the threat of more trouble. I'd go even farther and say that his own officers were so confident, so emphatic, so contemptuous of the wild theories persisting among the local public, that he saw himself as being between two fires; and he feared that either of the fires might have singed his own judgments. Anyway, he went to Wynchester yesterday morning to talk things over with his son, Inspector Fielding, because he was getting pretty desperate in his own mind; and I'll bet he'd have gone to consult the Yard, even at that late stage, if Jim Dolly hadn't lured him along to me. That, Henry, was sheer inspiration on Jim's part. I'm the ideal chappie to tackle a situation like this. And apart from all my other virtues in relation to this business, I am absolutely impartial.

'So let's see where we are up to now. Let's start with Gabriel Laval. Inspector Griffiths and Sergeant Evans thought they knew all they needed to know about him when this case broke in the official sense. He was just a name to me;

except that what I had heard about him, mainly from the chief constable, didn't make sense. If, for one thing, he was the sort of fellow to take on a girl like Nadine purely on the strength of her physical testimonials, and exploit her as he appeared to have done, then he would surely have run his establishment on the same lines — and the police would have reported as much, if they hadn't closed him up? Frankly, Henry, the only other explanation of Laval I could see was that he was running a profitable, respectable establishment; but when Nadine turned up he just *had* to take her on as barmaid, and make the best of it. Well, we saw a good deal for ourselves at the Riverside Hotel last night; and I must admit we had a certain amount of luck. My present tentative views are that Nadine Price and Laval knew each other pretty intimately sometime during the war; that Nadine blackmailed him into giving her a job at the Riverside Hotel; that he was jolly glad to empty his hotel of guests *and* staff when she disappeared; and he'd give a year of his life right now to make sure the police don't find out more about any of this business than they have done up to now. Meanwhile, of course, the French receptionist and the Cockney barmaid are buddies helpin' to hold the fort; but, possibly in view of my advent and academic interest in things in general, Laval isn't so confident of the barmaid's discretion as he'd like to be.'

Once again, automatically, the Super produced a cigarette, stared at it and put it back into its packet with a regretful sigh. He got up from his chair, plunged his hands into his trouser pockets and prowled around the room.

'Now,' he said, 'we're over in Colwin along with Evelyn Radford, and I'm statin' my conviction that she never committed suicide in this room and never attempted suicide up in Cumberland all them years ago. That's where I've got myself, Henry, by approachin' Evelyn Radford with an open mind.

'Look at what that lady went through up in Cumberland. A drunken, lecherous, bullying brother; a life of misery and constant humiliation; the loss of the

134

one man she was fond of, apparently, because her brother couldn't bear to see her enjoying any sort of happiness; and then to be driven out of her home by vicious gossip brandin' 'er a murderess. Oh no, son, I haven't forgotten the story Colonel Fielding collected about her having attempted suicide in Cumberland. But I prefer, in the light of all else we've collected, to believe that Miss Radford was sincere in the remark she made to Mrs. Ferndale here about suicide. Why, for one thing, should she have made it if it wasn't sincere? And if she *did* attempt to take her life in Cumberland, then that remark to Mrs. Ferndale is pretty clear evidence of her determination never to try it on again.

'All that makes nonsense of the suggestion she kept a fatal dose of cyanide by her for years, just in case . . .

'No, Henry, Miss Radford, as I see her, had everything to live for here, with or without this chap Charlton or anyone else. Look at the brave, determined showing she made in Cumberland when her brother was dead, and she was free at last to live her own life, but gossip had branded her up there and was likely to follow her wherever she went. Most people, you might think, would have run away in the literal sense, and started a new life under a new name on the other side of the world — as they put it in the romance books. Miss Radford came to Colwin quite openly, bringing her past — and some of her furniture — with her. She settled among strangers as the notorious Evelyn Radford, and she made a new life for herself here — living down her past and winning the respect of people she didn't even mix with. She lived a full, satisfying life, too, the way she wanted it. She had her painting, her reading, her gardening, her housework, and the countryside; she was busy and happy; and she kept herself to herself, without overdoing it, because she was satisfied with her own company and just didn't want to talk or even think about the past.

'Then,' the Super almost snarled in his indignation, 'this chap Charlton came into the picture, and we're asked to believe a lot happened that never did because it never *could* have happened; not with a woman like Evelyn Radford. We're asked to believe that she fell head-over-heels on sight with a man who was a complete mystery to everybody; that she took him completely on trust and planned to marry him; that she guarded his secrets whatever they were, and was content to parade their relationship without giving it the respectability of an engagement ring.'

He swung round in his tracks and glared at Henry.

'Was it likely,' he demanded, 'that a woman of her strong character, after all she'd suffered at one man's hands already, and after spending years in building up a new life for herself, would have fallen like that for a total stranger like Charlton — and, presumably, have planned to place herself, her life and possibly her fortune in his keeping?'

'But surely,' Henry protested, 'that's exactly what she *did* do, sir! She told Mrs. Ferndale herself — '

The Super silenced him with a scornful wave of his arm.

'The operative word, as I see it, son, is 'stranger'. The only way I can explain Robert Charlton to my satisfaction, in relation to Evelyn Radford, is that he *wasn't* a stranger to her when he arrived here. He was a man she knew and trusted already. And it follows from that, in view of her solitary life in Colwin, that he was someone she had known intimately before she came to Colwin.'

Henry exclaimed:

'Do you mean that Charlton was her brother's estate manager in Cumberland years ago; the man her brother sent packing because she was in love with him?'

The Super laid his hand on the glass dressing-table top.

'This portrait of Charlton may help us find the answer to that question, son. If Robert Charlton and that estate manager are one and the same, then it makes sense of what happened here when he found her again — by chance or otherwise. It means that Evelyn Radford had never stopped loving him; which is something

138

I *can* certainly understand in a woman of her calibre.'

'Then why all the mystery about him, sir?'

'Because there was a good reason for it, son. And, more importantly, because he was able to convince Miss Radford that there *was* good reason for it. Suppose, for example, Charlton came here to wait for a divorce to put an end to a disastrous marriage, and if his identity became known, his relationship with Miss Radford might have ruined their prospects?

'But that's all surmise, at the moment,' he went on. 'We've got something more satisfactory than surmise in relation to what happened here on the night Nadine Price and Robert Charlton disappeared and Evelyn Radford died a violent death. We've got that lipstick writing — '93 CHRISTINE' — on Nadine's hand-kerchief. There's only one explanation of that that I can see, Henry; and it establishes beyond doubt a relationship between Charlton and the girl. Normally, if she wanted to get in touch with him, she could have telephoned his cottage. But Charlton was often here with Miss Radford; so it became necessary for her to reach him here in the event of an extreme emergency. Charlton gave her Miss Radford's telephone number, and told her to say, if Miss Radford took the call, that she was his sister Christine. Nadine wrote the name and number on her handkerchief to be on the safe side — and then forgot all about the handkerchief. At any rate, she didn't need to refer to it when the emergency cropped up — sometime before seven o'clock on the night of all these happenings. She tried the cottage and got no reply; so she rang this house, just as Mrs. Ferndale was leaving.

'So there we are, Henry,' he summed up. 'Nadine Price and Robert Charlton — and a third person who was responsible for that extreme emergency on the night in question.'

Henry frowned as he got up from his chair.

'She must have received a pretty serious threat from one of her victims in the district . . . ?' he suggested. The Super snorted.

'Rubbish! She'd been receivin' threats for long enough. She wouldn't have rated that sort of scare an extreme emergency that concerned Robert Charlton as well as herself.'

'Perhaps a letter . . . ?'

'You don't get postal deliveries at that time of the day in country villages, son. And she didn't get no telephone call either. She would have been on duty in the bar, remember, when she got the scare; and my gamble is it was delivered in person by someone who came into the bar of the hotel between six and seven. However, that's a line of inquiry we can follow up later,' he said brusquely, and glanced at his watch. 'In the meantime, we're keepin' a lady waitin'.'

He wrapped up the slab of glass in brown paper from a neatly-stocked cupboard and gave it to Henry to carry. Then they found the path that ran through the grounds, parallel with the street, to the cottage where Mavis Ferndale was waiting for them.

It was a small, double-fronted, two-storied house standing in its own small, well-tended garden. Mavis was waiting for them at the front door.

'I'm afraid you'll find everything in a terrible state, sir,' she said, 'but Sergeant Evans wouldn't let me touch nothing.'

'I'm glad he wouldn't, Mrs. Ferndale,' the Super replied as they trooped into the tiny hall, 'or the house might have had nothing to tell us. I suppose Miss Radford went to a good deal of trouble to make the place comfortable for her tenant?'

'That she did,' Mavis answered warmly. 'Had it done up inside and out, as you can see for yourselves; and the garden as well. She was always bringing along odd things she thought Mr. Charlton might like. Not that he brought much in the way of personal belongings himself. She even had to buy him shirts and socks to *my* knowledge.'

The downstairs rooms were a large sitting-room, a smaller dining-room and a well-equipped kitchen at the back. Upstairs there were two bedrooms, and a small but lavishly-equipped bathroom-lavatory. The furniture and fittings everywhere were of the best; indeed, Evelyn Radford had over-furnished the place in her concern for her tenant's comfort.

And the whole place was a shambles. Carpets had been turned up and carelessly replaced; drawers stood open in every room; and Robert Charlton's personal belongings — a pretty anonymous collection — were strewn all over the place.

'I can't think what he was doing,' an indignant Mavis remarked as their cursory inspection of the cottage ended up in the sitting-room, 'to leave things in such a mess. There's hardly a stick of furniture in its proper place. And just look at that table, sir!'

The Super was studying the table in the centre of the room with interest. Its top was bare, and books, papers, an ashtray and pipes had been pushed on the floor, apparently, to make it so. Meanwhile its well-polished surface had been defaced with an irregular pattern of deep, fresh scratches.

'Not much doubt as to how them

scratches got there,' the Super remarked. 'This was where Mr. Charlton did his packing.'

'Well,' Mavis informed them, 'that should have been simple enough, without turning the whole place upsi'down. He only had one large suitcase, and a battered old thing that was.'

'One suitcase,' the Super reflected, looking around again.

Ornaments on the mantelpiece had been disarranged, too; and an exclamation escaped Mavis as he picked up a sealed bottle of patent hair lotion that had been standing prominently in front of the clock.

'Well,' she cried, 'fancy his looking everywhere for his things and forgetting his hair oil! He wore his hair plastered with the stuff; he was terribly vain about it. He ran out of the stuff only the last morning he was here, and I had to go across to Larne to get that bottle specially. I left it there on the mantelpiece when I got back from shopping, and I told him about it when I went along to the house afterwards. I should have said that was the *last* thing he'd have overlooked.'

The Super glanced significantly at Henry.

'So should I,' he remarked, replacing the bottle. 'I noticed a similar bottle standing empty in the bathroom just now. We needn't keep you any longer. Don't forget now, not a word about our talk to a living soul. But if you do want to find me again, we shall be up at the Riverside Hotel for a few days.'

'Very well, sir.' The girl hesitated in the doorway. 'I don't know what else I can tell you. But I can't and never will believe Miss Radford took her own life.'

Henry saw her to the front door and closed it behind her. Then he watched the Super making a thorough, expert search of the cottage. It was a completely negative search as far as Henry could see. The Super wound up in the sitting-room again, with the bottle of hair lotion again in his hand.

'Well, Henry,' he said distractedly, 'what do you make of things here, I wonder.'

Henry laughed.

'It's pretty obvious, sir, isn't it. Robert Charlton spent a heck of a time going through the cottage to make sure he left behind no clues to his identity; and in his anxiety in that connection he overlooked his precious hair lotion.'

'When this bottle was starin' him in the face?'

'But the fact remains that he *did* overlook it, sir.'

The Super shook his head as he replaced the bottle in front of the clock once again.

'No, Henry,' he said, 'Charlton wouldn't have had to turn up the carpets to make sure he hadn't left anything incriminating behind him here. Charlton wouldn't have overlooked this bottle of hair lotion. So it looks as if someone else came along here to do his packing-up for him.'

Henry stared at him.

'You mean the mysterious individual who went to the Riverside Hotel and scared Nadine Price into ringing Charlton at Miss Radford's house? That makes an accomplice of him, doesn't it? Oh,

I see what the idea is!' he went on elatedly. 'This mysterious person *was* an accomplice. He went to the Riverside Hotel to *warn* Nadine and Charlton . . . ?'

The Super went on frowning at the bottle of hair lotion.

'You know, Henry,' he said after a moment, 'I've been wonderin' 'ow *I'd* carry cyanide about with me, small and handy and safe like, for use at short notice in an extreme emergency — if I had to, of course, in the way of business.'

Henry laughed again.

'You wouldn't carry it around in a bottle that size, I imagine.'

'No,' the Super answered. 'I was thinkin' of them capsules those chappies carried about in their waistcoat pockets, so to speak, in the war — in case they preferred sudden death to running the risk of talking under torture.'

'Oh, you mean our commando men, sir?' Henry suggested.

But again the Super shook his head.

'No, son, I was thinking of those

147

brave fellows who served in and with the French Resistance and that sort of thing. The kind of work Gabriel Laval did in the war — '

He broke off, consulting his watch once again, and mildly profaning.

'Twenty minutes to three!' he announced aggressively. 'Too late for lunch, but we may be in time for a pint and some bread-and-cheese at the Welsh Harp. What about it, son?'

He grabbed his hat and hurried into the hall as though the needs of his inner man had suddenly driven every other thought from his mind.

9

They found the main street deserted except for a small urchin playing in the gutter outside the village school. The Super insisted on their keeping to the middle of the broad, silent thoroughfare, without offering any reason for this, and Henry Baxter felt so self-conscious that he imagined a pair of eyes staring at them from behind every window in sight.

Then, as they came abreast of the urchin and the school, a piano struck up and a crowd of lusty infant voices united in the singing of 'Who Killed Cock Robin?' The Super stopped and listened, apparently enchanted; but he shook his head gravely when, the performance ended, they moved on slowly in the direction of the bridge.

'You know, Henry,' he confessed, 'whenever I find myself movin' too fast too soon on a new case, I always remember a particular nursery rhyme that brings me up with a jerk.'

He began to sing the verse in question, in a deep voice that was hardly more than a rumbling whisper of sound:

'Humpty Dumpty sat on a wall,
Humpty Dumpty had a great fall;
All the king's horses and all the
  king's men
Couldn't put the old So-and-so
  together again . . .

'You know, Henry,' he groaned in conclusion, 'I won't half look a fool if '93 CHRISTINE' turns out to be a new line in scent, and Landlord Laval was merely pasting that barmaid in her room last night because she'd drunk herself hysterical and he didn't want her wakin' the guests.'

A moment later they stopped in their tracks again as the unnatural stillness of the village scene was shattered a second time.

The door of the Welsh Harp — ten yards ahead of them — was crashed open, and two men staggered into the roadway.

One was a young hunchback with curly red hair; the other, dark and clean-shaven, was no more than a boy. The hunchback drove the terrified youngster in front of him, raining savage blows on his body and face, until, in the middle of the street, the youth fell headlong, lay stunned for two or three seconds, then picked himself up and scuttled away across the river. The hunchback, trembling with rage, shook his fists after his retreating victim and screamed: 'You come back and say that again and I'll kill you, I will! I'll kill you stone damned dead!'

Recovering himself, he returned to the inn, slamming the front door behind him and leaving Colwin's main street more ominously silent than ever.

The silence remained as though the shops and cottages were frozen in ice. Not a soul appeared in quest of an explanation of the rumpus; not a curtain moved that Henry Baxter could see. Nor did the Super make any comment as he took his arm and piloted him towards the inn.

The Super opened the door and led

the way inside. The hunchback, the only customer, was emptying his tankard at the bar while Hughie Grant, the landlord, remonstrated with him gently. At the sight of the newcomers the latter looked panic-stricken.

'Good afternoon,' the Super greeted him cheerfully. 'My friend and I have been wanderin' about and missed our lunch over the way, I reckon. How about some bread-and-cheese with a couple of pints of your excellent beer, landlord?'

Grant stared at them incredulously, because it was manifestly impossible for them to have missed the violent scene outside; then, looking relieved and grateful, he mustered a smile.

'Certainly, gentlemen,' he said. He served the beer and, turning to fetch the food from the kitchen, glanced apprehensively at the hunchback and forced a grin. 'Now, Willie,' he went on persuasively, 'these are the gentlemen Mike was talkin' about just now. Superintendent Greene, sir, this is Willie Oaker, the Man Friday of Mike Amber the woodman who introduced himself to you last night. I won't keep you a minute, gentlemen.'

He scuttled away and the Super turned to the hunchback. The latter was leaning heavily on the counter with his empty tankard in front of him. He had a round, red, boyish face without a hint of malice in it; but there was no friendliness in it, either, as he stared at the Super with blue, unnaturally bright eyes.

The latter held out his hand.

'Pleased to meet you, son.'

Willie Oaker ignored the hand, smiled unpleasantly and shook his head.

'You won't get anything out of me, sir,' he said in clipped not uncultured speech.

The Super grinned.

'What would I want out of you, son?'

The hunchback said nothing. He was still trying to stare the Super out, apparently, when Hughie Grant hurried back with two plates of bread-and-cheese.

'Sorry we're out of pickles, gentlemen,' he apologized, placing the plates on the counter. He looked anxiously at Willie Oaker as the Super spoke again.

'We'll have our grub here, standing,

eh, Henry? What about joining us in a pint, Mr Grant? You too, Oaker, your tankard looks as if it could do with some attention.'

The hunchback transferred his gaze from the Super to his tankard; but after a tussle with temptation he shook his head. Oddly, that gesture branded the Super as his enemy.

'A grand morning for a walk, sir,' Hughie Grant remarked, and he lifted his glass to his lips.

The hunchback's attention switched back to the Super as the latter handed Henry his plate and replied to the landlord with warmth:

'It's beautiful country around here in any sort of weather, I should imagine. Seems unbelievable there's been all these goings-on here, and folks are still at each other's throats after eight long weeks of — '

Willie Oaker banged his tankard on the counter and pushed out his chin aggressively.

'Ha!' he shrilled. 'So you saw me just now, did you? And you followed me in here to find out why. But you won't get anything out of me, *Superintendent,* and that's flat. You can ask and ask and ask and ask and I won't tell you a thing.' He flung round and glared at the landlord. 'What's more, you can tell that to Mike when you see him!'

He turned again and, stumbling in his haste, found his way to the front door and out of the inn.

The door banged. Hughie Grant seemed not to know where to look during the minute of silence that followed. The Super munched a mouthful of cheese, swallowed some beer and grunted.

'Well,' he said, 'he's a queer joker. What's it all about, Grant?' He fixed the landlord with a look that belied his cheerful friendliness. 'Including that demonstration in the street?'

There was something of fear in the landlord's embarrassment.

'I was afraid you was going to ask as much when you came in just now, sir,' he confessed. 'It was just a row between Willie Oaker and young Peter Pugh from over the river — '

155

'Pugh?' the Super interrupted sharply. 'A brother of Denis Pugh who was engaged to Nadine Price before she threw him over for Mike Amber?'

Grant stared at him in dismay.

'I thought, from what you said last night, sir,' he accused him, 'that you weren't interested in — '

'I didn't say I wasn't *informed* about the goings-on here,' the Super retorted, managing to imply at the same time that he was a great deal informed. 'That was Denis Pugh's brother, was it?'

'That's right, sir,' Grant replied unwillingly. 'His younger brother. Denis and Mike Amber have been at daggers drawn ever since that damned bitch switched over; and young Peter takes his brother's part whenever he sees a chance. He spoke out of turn with Willie Oaker just now; so Willie, being all out for Mike Amber, let him have it.'

The Super nodded.

'There wasn't much you could do about it, I suppose.'

The implication brought a flush of anger into the landlord's cheeks, but he struggled and got a grip on himself and answered earnestly:

'Look, sir, if you had more *personal* knowledge of what's been going on in these two villages you'd understand how a lot of us — me in particular — is placed. I'd have had the two of 'em on my hands if I'd butted in just now, and there *would* have been hell to pay. A lot of us only wish to God there *was* somebody who could do something about the troubles here, before there's more blood-letting or worse. But meantime we've got our living to get and our own skins to think about. I'll bet you didn't see anybody out in that street who was anxious to put in his spoke just now.'

'The street was empty,' the Super said. 'It stayed empty as far as I could see. Yes, Grant,' he went on more sympathetically, 'I understand what you were driving at. I suppose the police — '

'The police!' Grant cried bitterly. 'They're worse than useless the way things are — with half the locals calling 'em a lot of dunderheads, and determining on finding a murderer amongst themselves — '

He stopped in fresh dismay, realizing how far he had let his tongue run away with him. The Super pressed his advantage.

'You can talk freely with me, Grant,' he said persuasively. 'I dare say I know more about this business than you think, and I wish I could do something to help. But I'm not a copper any longer.' He grinned. 'I'm certainly not down here as a copper's nark.'

Henry Baxter was trying hard not to smile over that dubious proclamation of good faith when the landlord yielded to another impulse.

'I wish you *were* down here from the Yard, sir. I was only saying to the missus last night at supper that you seemed the right sort of gentleman for a situation like this — the way you handled the boys in the bar for one thing.'

'You were saying,' the Super reminded him, 'about the local police?'

'Well, sir, Sergeant Evans and Inspector Griffiths are two of the best, if you get my meaning; but they knew, or thought they knew, all about everything and everybody here when this trouble broke on us, so they thought they knew what had happened that night — almost before it had happened, if I make myself clear.'

While he floundered, the Super exchanged a meaning glance with Henry. Then the former nodded his sympathetic understanding of another point the landlord had been driving at none too successfully.

'That sort of thing is always happening, Grant,' he said blandly. 'The local police try to handle a case on their own, make a mess of it and send for the Yard when it's almost too late. But what was all this Willie Oaker screamed at me just now? What was behind it? What was I supposed to have been after getting out of him?'

Henry Baxter, noting the landlord's embarrassment at this abrupt return to a subject he had tried to evade, marvelled at the effective if completely unscrupulous tactics the Super was using to get Hughie Grant where he wanted him. He had begun by bullying and frightening him; he had disarmed him by assuring him of his good faith and official disinterest; now he was treating him almost as a fellow conspirator.

But Hughie Grant dodged the question of Willie Oaker yet again.

'That was just madness, sir,' he protested. 'Willie's madness. There's nothing to it. There's nothing to Willie, come to that, as far as knowing anything about all this business is concerned. Willie was drunk just now, though you mightn't have thought so.' He forced a laugh. 'He wouldn't have refused that drink if he'd been sober. The crazy things he says, the wild tales he tells when he's in the liquor — '

'Crazy tales,' the Super suggested, 'like the one about the naked woman in black?'

Hughie Grant paled suddenly under his florid complexion.

'My God, sir,' he cried hoarsely, 'where did you get *that* from? Not . . . not from the police, Mr. Greene?' he appealed quite desperately.

The Super eyed him owlishly.

'No,' he said, 'but I've been wondering

160

whether it might not be my duty to pass it on to them.'

'For God's sake don't, sir,' the landlord pleaded. 'There's nothing to it, I tell you. Nothing at all. We've got enough trouble with real things, without setting the place aflame with that crazy falseness!'

'Well,' the Super conceded, 'I'm open to conviction.'

Hughie Grant hesitated a long time before he capitulated. But once his mind was made up he told his story with complete frankness and unreserve. His speech was an odd mixture of Cockney and Scots, never definitely the one thing or the other.

Willie Oaker, he told them, came to Colwin between two and three years ago, to work with Mike Amber the woodman. Willie took lodgings with an old couple in Larne, because Mike Amber treasured his privacy too much to offer to put him up in his cottage, and no one else in Colwin could take him. Willie and Mike, the hunchback and the giant, became firm friends none the less. 'David and Jonathan', Hughie

Grant called them. They still worked together all day; came to the Welsh Harp for beer and sandwiches about mid-day; and met there again in the evenings, to play games and gossip with their friends. Most evenings, about eight o'clock or after, Mike would wander off on business of his own — which nearly always included a visit to the Riverside Hotel. Willie never left the Welsh Harp until closing-time. What he did then depended on whether he was sober or drunk.

If he was sober, Willie would wander to the other end of the village street to get a glimpse of Mike's cottage; then smoking a last cigarette, he would wander back into Larne and to his lodgings. There was more than sentiment in this nocturnal visit to his friend's cottage — to see whether there was a light showing or not. It was part of a game that had been the source of endless amusement in the bar; a game in which Willie would ask the good-natured Mike what he'd been up to and what time he'd got home the previous night, with the object of catching him out and proving him a liar. It was a rule of the game that the winner paid in pints . . .

But very frequently, when he left the inn at closing-time, Willie was drunk and he knew it. He dared not go straight home to his lodgings, for though the old people there didn't mind what time he came home they wouldn't have him the worse for drink. So, on such occasions, it was Willie's habit to 'walk it off'. And until recently, he had invariably gone for a walk past Mike Amber's cottage and into the woods behind the village — where, more often than not, he ended up by 'sleeping it off'. Time and again Mike Amber or other men from the village had found him asleep in the woods early next morning; and this had caused a great deal of fun in the bar. It was fun in which Willie had participated with gusto; he would tell the wildest tales of his nocturnal adventures in the woods the previous night — encounters with ghosts, strange tramps and other desperate characters, and even courting couples from the two villages whose amorous activities he would claim to have witnessed from behind a bush or the branch of a convenient tree.

One night, some considerable time — according to Hughie Grant — before the disappearance of Nadine Price and its accompanying sensations, Willie told of a particularly spectacular adventure in the woods the previous night. He stated he had seen a naked woman in a 'luminy' black cape come up out of the water and disappear in the woods along the path that led to the lane and Mike Amber's cottage. This statement caused an uproar of mirth, and pretended indignation from Mike. Hastily, however, Willie added that he had followed the apparition — if apparition it was — and had seen it hurrying past Miss Radford's house in the direction of Robert Charlton's cottage.

Nobody believed any of this for a moment. But Willie, even more drunk than usual, was strangely persistent in affirming the truth of it, and resentful of the jibes of his audience. That night, for the first and only time, Mike Amber took him home to his cottage to sleep.

At this point the story took a grim turn, with the disappearance of Nadine Price.

Mike Amber became a changed man overnight. In the words of Hughie Grant he 'simply closed up inside himself'. He seemed completely disinterested in the disappearance of his girl and the accompanying sensations, and contemptuous of the grave suspicions directed at him. On the two nights following these events he showed himself as usual at the Riverside Hotel and the Welsh Harp; but in neither did he join in the frenzied discussions or participate in the usual games.

Willie was visibly distressed by this change in his friend. On the second night after the disappearance of Nadine Price, he tried hard to draw Mike out of himself in the bar of the Welsh Harp. He joined spiritedly in the discussions and arguments, he even defended his friend against accusations he had overheard in the village that day. Mike merely ordered him to shut up. Willie got very, very drunk; and then he quarrelled with his friend for the first time, though it was a one-sided affair according to the landlord; and finally he went off, announcing it as his intention to sleep the night in the woods in which the police had completed their search that evening.

Nobody took Willie seriously in this promised act of bravado. But Willie was seen, later, going into the woods, stumbling about and muttering to himself.

Mike Amber went home to bed and to sleep. In the early hours of the following morning he was awakened by a banging on the front door of his cottage. He went down to admit a gibbering, hysterical and terrified Willie, whose face and head were smothered in blood.

Willie told a wildly fantastic story. He said he had been wandering in the woods when he had seen the naked woman in luminy black hanging by her neck from a rope attached to the branch of a tree. He had stumbled on this horror and touched it with his outstretched hand. Then, almost instantly, he had received a blow on the head that had knocked him unconscious. When he had come to and remembered everything, he had fled in terror to his friend's cottage.

Mike Amber got a torch and ordered his friend to take him back to the spot where he had encountered the horror. Willie took him there. But they found no body, and the branch from which Willie swore he had seen it hanging showed no marks of a rope. Nearby, however, they found a large jagged stone, with blood on it.

This was enough for Mike. He accused his friend of being drunk and the victim of a nightmare, told him to keep his mouth shut, cleaned up his face and head, and personally took him part of the way home to his lodgings.

Next day Willie stayed at his lodgings; Mike had ordered him to take a rest and get over his fright. In the evening, however, Willie turned up at the Welsh Harp. He looked sick and wasn't talkative to start with; but after a few drinks 'the devil seemed to possess him'. Possibly his friend's curt treatment and, even more importantly, the knowledge of Mike's disbelief, were more responsible than the drink for what happened. Suddenly hysterical, Willie threw his tankard on the floor and screamed out his story of his horrifying nocturnal experience. 'It did happen,' he shrilled at Mike. 'I'll *make* you believe me!'

Mike Amber got up from his seat, got hold of Willie by the scruff of the neck, and addressed the bar in turn. What had happened, he said soberly and convincingly, was obvious. Stumbling about in the woods, Willie had tripped and fallen, striking his head on the jagged stone and knocking himself out. Waking in terror, with his head and face covered in blood, he had rushed to Mike's cottage for sanctuary.

'We've got enough trouble in this place,' Mike summed up sternly, 'without adding this crazy tale to it.'

Quite soberly, he threatened Willie to thrash him within an inch of his life if he ever repeated his wild story. Then he appealed to the men in the bar to keep their mouths shut too. One and all, they promised.

Hughie Grant was leaning on his counter when he came to the end of his story. He, too, was soberly convincing when he said:

'I could name every man in this bar that night when the vow of silence was made. There weren't that many. We all respected Mike too much to break our word; and, on top of that, not one of us was likely to blab and get ourselves mixed up in what would happen if we did.' He stared appealingly at the Super. 'I'm only talking about it now, sir, because I'm telling you what you know already. Until you mentioned it just now I'd have sworn that not one of the chaps in this bar that night would have gone and — '

The Super pushed aside his empty plate.

'None of them did that I know of,' he said coolly. 'You misunderstood me, Grant. It was Willie's *first* alleged adventure with the naked woman in black that came to my ears: the time she was supposed to have paid a visit

169

to Robert Charlton's cottage.'

Hughie Grant's mouth dropped open. He looked stricken.

'My God!' he gasped at length. 'Then *I've* gone and given it away! Look here, sir,' he went on desperately, 'I wouldn't have told you a word of this if I hadn't thought you knew — '

'Don't worry,' the Super reassured him cheerfully. 'It's a crazy business altogether, as you say. It obviously happened the way Mike Amber said it did; and you fellows were wise, in the circumstances, to keep it under your hats. My friend and I will keep it under ours, Grant. Now let's have a couple more pints, and we'll be on our way.'

Hughie Grant looked so relieved, as he placed the replenished tankards on the counter, that he couldn't find words to express himself with. The Super came to his rescue.

'You did well to tell me what you did,' he said with a smile. 'Otherwise I might have felt it my duty to have taken Willie Oaker more seriously just now.'

He dismissed the whole business with a wave of his hand. 'What do *you* think happened in Colwin the night Nadine Price disappeared?'

Hughie Grant thought for a long moment before he shook his head. A cautious, almost furtive look had crept into his eyes.

'They should have sent for Scotland Yard,' he persisted evasively. 'It's too late now. But there'll be no peace, no safety either, for anyone, until *something* happens to kill all these wild suspicions that are keeping everyone at each other's throats as you said just now.'

'Why can't the local people accept the published conclusions of the police?'

Hughie Grant looked around the empty bar, and behind him at the kitchen doorway as well, before he answered.

'Because — between you and me, Mr. Greene — they believe Nadine Price was murdered; and one of them, or maybe more than one, did the deed. It's become almost like a . . . a spiritual conviction, if you know what I mean.'

171

'Then,' the Super said sternly, 'some of the local people must know, or suspect, more than they've owned up to the police. What do *you* think about that, Grant?'

Grant's lips seemed to have dried up; he moistened them with the tip of his tongue. He looked a badly frightened man.

'I've said too much, sir. You've had me once already. I've got myself and the missus to think of. Not that I know or suspect *anything*,' he went on rather wildly. 'And what I overhears behind this counter, not being able to help myself — '

He broke off as the wall clock behind him struck once.

'That's closing-time!' he cried. 'If you gentlemen don't mind — '

The Super finished his drink, set down the tankard and laughed.

'Your clock has just struck half-past three, Grant,' he said, 'and it's twenty minutes slow at that. Odd you should have become aware of time just then.'

Grant stared at the Super as the latter

buttoned up his jacket.

'Superintendent . . . Mr. Greene,' he appealed, 'you've no call to make a remark like that, me accommodating you as I have done. If you think I know anything I should have told the police, I can assure you — '

'My dear fellow,' the Super protested airily, 'I'm not supposed to do any thinking at all about this business. I'm an old pensioner from the Force down here on a sort of holiday. All the same, though, I wouldn't be too despondent about the local police. They'll re-open investigations the moment anything turns up to justify them doing so; and I've an odd feeling — an intuition, if you like — it will. So if *I* knew something the police ought to know and don't, I wouldn't like to keep *that* under my hat — for my own sake. See you later, Grant. Coming, Henry?'

A moment later Henry Baxter closed the inn door behind him and joined the Super in the sunshine outside.

'That shook him a bit, didn't it,' the latter grunted. 'Anyone'd think I'd *trapped* him into telling us all that about the naked woman in luminy black.'

Henry chuckled delightedly.

'It wasn't much use to you, was it, sir?' he said. 'I've never heard anything so completely crazy. I was quite disappointed.'

The Super gave him a mildly surprised look. One might almost have called it reproachful.

'Was you, Henry?' he said, *sotto voce*. 'Me, I'm beginning to wonder about the lady in question. She came out of the river and she went to Charlton's cottage. How else would Nadine Price get to Charlton, without coming openly by the bridge?'

Henry gasped.

'Nadine Price! But . . . surely you're joking, sir!'

'Look,' said the Super, pointing. 'I was just wondering what mischief we could be up to next. Here's somebody who might help us make up our minds.'

Major Valentine was striding towards them across the bridge, waving as he came.

'Maybe,' the Super suggested, 'he'll show us the grave.'

He began to hum the nursery rhyme they had heard the children singing, 'Who Killed Cock Robin . . . '

10

Valentine moved with an odd grace for so large a man; it was, the Super's practised eye detected, the grace of the trained athlete. He was smoking one of the big cigars he habitually affected, and belching clouds of silvery smoke.

'Hello there,' he greeted the pair as he joined them in front of the inn. 'This is an ungodly hour to be returning to one's hotel for lunch. What have you been up to?' he demanded, pointing accusingly at the large flat parcel Henry was carrying. 'Shopping?' He laughed. 'Surely not here in Colwin!'

'Let's say we've been collectin' a thing or two,' the Super twinkled. 'Incidentally, Major, ain't this an ungodly hour to be comin' home from lunch?'

Unwittingly, the Super had touched a raw spot. Valentine's face looked suddenly grey, and his eyes were haunted as he stared at him resentfully. Then, as suddenly, these revealing shadows were supplanted by an engaging grin.

'I fell asleep over an article I was reading,' he confessed. 'A damned bad habit for a man of my years.'

The Super was not deceived, however. Valentine had shown himself for a tragic moment as a sick man. Was that why he was here in Colwin — out of touch, perhaps, with his family and friends?

'As a matter of fact,' Valentine continued, 'I was also waiting for you, to begin with. I gave Laval a generous part of my catch this morning, for you two to enjoy at lunch. Afraid it's wasted now. But don't apologize,' he protested. 'Look, why not toddle along to my place and join me in a drink? Unless,' with another grin, 'you're hurrying back to your hotel to be in good time for tea.'

'Tea!' The Super shuddered. 'Not on top of them pints of beer, Major.' He nodded in the direction of the Welsh Harp. 'We'll be pleased to have a look at your place, though. Maybe you could show us the grave on the way through the woods.'

Valentine stared at him.

'Grave . . . ? Oh, you mean the grave they found that morning . . . But I thought,' he went on sharply, 'you were definitely not interested in — ?'

'Academic interest, I said,' the Super reminded him.

'Have a heart, Major. You don't go to London for a holiday and miss our Madame Tussaud's!'

Valentine laughed.

'All right then. It will mean going the long way round to my place, instead of taking the path by the river.'

'Plenty of time,' the Super retorted, as they turned back along the wide street. It seemed completely deserted now. An ominous silence oozed out of the village school.

'This street,' Valentine confided, 'gives me the creeps every time I walk the length of it. God knows when these people do their shopping.'

Just before they reached the fork they turned right into the lane that led them past Mike Amber's cottage. The Super did not even glance at the small greystone

178

building in its square overgrown garden. A few yards past the cottage they came to the path that plunged into the woods in the direction of the river. Valentine led the way along this for twenty yards or so. The trees and foliage had the smell of autumn about them, but the ground was still comparatively clear of fallen leaves. Valentine stopped where the path forked, one track seeming to run parallel with the lane they had left, while the other continued at a steeper angle towards the river. He followed the latter for a short distance, then stopped to get his bearings.

'It's somewhere over in this direction,' he called over his shoulder, and left the path to plunge into a dense part of the wood on the left of it. The scene was like a miniature jungle, in the Super's stated estimation. When they came to what looked like an impenetrable wall of foliage ahead of them Valentine announced, 'This is it.'

They plunged into the long grass and bushes, literally elbowing their way into an unexpected clearing shaded by the branches of a giant elm tree. In the middle of this space they found the grave, marked by an oblong of reddish soil — settling but still loose — bulging out of the ground.

'There's an easier approach,' Valentine apologized, pointing across the clearing, 'but I've only been here a couple of times and that wall of foliage we've just come through is the only landmark I know.'

The approach from the other side of the clearing was indeed much easier; and broken bushes still gave evidence of the invasion there must have been eight weeks ago after the discovery of the open grave.

The Super frowned at the grave for a long moment before he said:

'Do you happen to know who filled this in, Major, and when?'

'I certainly do,' Valentine answered promptly. 'I arrived here the day after the various sensations were discovered, and heard all about them from old Joe Early, who had been looking after The Retreat, my place, for the owner. He's a sort of caretaker gardener; incidentally, I believe he's one of Colwin's oldest inhabitants. Joe was full of the story, of course; and more to humour him than anything I let him bring me up here that evening. The police had completed their search of these woods by then. Sergeant Evans was here, with a constable and a number of locals; he wanted the grave filled in — the sooner the better, apparently. Joe Early volunteered to do the job for an agreed sum. He tackled it on his way to work at my place the following morning.'

The Super looked around the clearing once more.

'The chap who dug this grave, Major, knew where to find the ideal spot for the job, didn't he? Well, thanks for showin' us.'

They returned to the path leading down to the river, and thus reached the wider path on the river bank. The Super stopped at the junction of the two paths to look at the Riverside Hotel high up on the bank almost opposite.

'I reckon,' he mused, 'this piece of water's pretty dark some nights, after closing-time over there.'

Valentine nodded.

'It certainly is,' he agreed, 'if you try to find your way back to my place without a torch.'

'Fast flowing just here, is she?'

'Not particularly, but pretty deep. What's behind all this, Super?' he demanded with a smile.

'I was just wonderin' what might happen to me, son, if I fell in. But we're neglectin' them drinks.'

'It's not far,' Valentine said as he led the way again.

The Retreat, however, proved to be around a slight bend a good quarter-of-a-mile away. It stood well back among the trees, and they found an old man at work in the well-kept garden between them and the river. A tall, lean, bespectacled man who was carefully raking a circular flower-bed.

'This is Early,' Valentine informed the Super. 'Want a word with him?'

The Super paused to watch the old man straighten up and stare at them. He shook his head.

'One of my reasons for coming down

here was to get away from gardening, Major.'

They continued along the gravel path to the old stone house under the trees. Valentine climbed a short flight of stone steps, passed through the open front door and awaited his guests in a large, square, bare-furnished entrance hall.

'I'm afraid this is as badly appointed as most houses they let furnished nowadays at a reasonable price,' he apologized. 'But I'm not particular, and I've roughed it enough in the Army to know how to do for myself. The lounge is comfortable enough, though.'

They followed him into a large, long room with a row of tall windows overlooking the river — what was visible of it through the trees. The furniture was old and shabby, but certainly comfortable; and the Super sank gratefully on to the big, leather-covered couch on one side of an open fireplace in which a small log fire was burning. The place was so dark and cool that the fire was welcome.

'Early sees to the fire when I'm out,'

the major explained. 'He's a good chap, if a bit near-sighted and clumsy. Now, gentlemen, what will it be?'

The Super asked for whisky. Henry wanted a small bottle of beer. Major Valentine charged his own glass with neat brandy before he threw himself into an armchair facing the Super.

'This,' he said, and heaved a sigh, 'is how I like it, gentlemen. Peace and quiet, and not a soul to disturb me; plenty of books, a wireless, and fishing. Joe Early changes the linen and does what cleaning I want. I wasn't going to risk engaging some talkative female, with all these goings-on in the two villages. All the same, Super,' he smiled, 'I'd like to know what you and Baxter *were* collecting in the village during this morning and quite a part of the afternoon. If you could tell me in confidence, of course. I dabbled quite a bit in Intelligence in the war, quite apart from my other activities; and I'm as human as most men when it comes to mysteries.'

The Super took his time lighting a cigarette.

'Show the gentleman, Henry,' he requested at length. 'Frankly, Major,' he explained, 'I'm only doin' this because I think you may be able to help a bit.'

Henry opened the parcel he had dragged on to his lap, and the major frowned at the shaped and bevelled sheet of glass.

'Good heavens, what's that? The glass top of a piece of furniture?'

'Turn it over, Henry.'

Henry turned it over, slowly, and a sudden exclamation came from their host as he stared at the portrait in oils. He stared at it for the better part of a minute, an unreadable expression on his face. Then, slowly, his gaze moved back to the Super.

'Who *is* he?' he asked, dazedly.

The Super, watching him keenly, answered:

'I was hoping you'd be able to tell me, Major, from the way you reacted when you first saw the picture.'

Hugh Valentine studied the portrait again, and passed a hand over his eyes. He seemed to be searching his memory, but gave it up with a shake of his head.

'It's odd,' he confessed, 'that picture did seem to ring a bell somewhere . . . Wait. I've got it! I saw that chap on the river path here when I was looking round this place about a fortnight before I took over. He was staring up at the house, and I thought he might have been another potential tenant. I've got a pretty retentive memory for faces, you know, and — '

The Super groaned.

'Wrap it up, Henry.' He told the major: 'The subject of that portrait — painted on the back of a glass dressing-table top — is Robert Charlton, who disappeared from here the same night as Nadine Price. We found it in the house of Miss Radford, the woman he was friendly with.'

'Good heavens! But why was it painted on that — ?'

'Because she was in love with him, and had to have his picture, Major; and she had to have it without his knowing. And she was clever enough to keep it where even the police didn't find it.'

Valentine looked at him keenly.

'Then you've an idea why she committed

186

suicide that night?' he suggested.

'I've an idea she was murdered,' the Super replied bluntly. 'But that don't go any farther than this room.'

Valentine got to his feet abruptly. He refilled his glass and the Super's and returned to his chair.

'You seem to know a lot more about this business than the police,' he remarked grimly then. 'Just when the good people here are hoping and praying this affair might begin to blow over — '

'The police weren't looking for a murderer,' said the Super. 'I was. I'm quite liable to be barkin' up the wrong trees, but I'm going on barking, if you get my meaning.' He gave the other a straight look. 'Still want to be mixed up in it, Major?'

Valentine did not reply at once. His face was a grey mask as he returned the Super's gaze, and the haunted, almost despairing look returned to his eyes. Finally, he made a gesture as if he had reached a decision and nodded.

'I'd better explain myself, Super,' he

said. 'I'm a sick man; never mind how sick. I came here to get away from everything and find peace. Peace of mind as well as of body. Instead, I found myself trapped in a cauldron. My first impulse was to clear out, but I left it just too late. Call it an incurable curiosity if you like; before I realized what was happening it had become much more than that. This horror and mystery grows on one; and I found myself trapped. I've got to know many of the people here; there's something appealing and pathetic about some of them in their turmoil of suspicion and uncertainty and strife; one feels that even in a few weeks one has become part of the pattern, the horror. One can run away from most things in the physical sense; the mind, emotional attachments, are a different matter. Even more inescapable, perhaps, are the impressions one forms, the convictions . . .

'No, Super,' he wound up decisively, 'this place and its troubles have become part of my sickness. I want to stay, and if there's anything I can do, I want to

188

help. I'm still a comparative stranger, of course, but — '

'Very often,' the Super reminded him warmly, 'the comparative stranger sees most of the truth. That's what I'm after, Major — the truth, whatever it is.'

'Then I'm your man,' Valentine said emphatically. 'What do you want me to do?'

'First of all, son, I want you to protect me from any suspicious-minded people here who may find it difficult to accept me at my face value. I'm just a retired police detective on holiday; a good-natured old so-and-so who's not averse to pottering around in a strictly private capacity if it'd help the cause of justice generally, and the good people in Larne and Colwin in particular. And, naturally, I'm interested in Madame Tussaud's.'

'In other words, Super, you want an accomplice and a cover for your nefarious activities.'

'Yes. And a few odd bits of information right now. What d'you think of Gabriel Laval?'

Valentine frowned.

'As a hotel proprietor? Superlative. As a host and drinking companion? Charming. As a man? I want to trust him and I can't. You know when you've been through the thick of a war you can always tell about somebody else who lays claim to the same sort of experience. Laval won't talk about his war experiences; but it's not just the reticence of your modest hero; and I'm damned sure it's not that his lips are sealed officially. My impression, for what it's worth, is that Laval won't talk about his wartime experiences because there are some he *daren't* talk about. I've no proof, mind you — '

'No. Now, you were a customer when the new receptionist, Lucille Something-or-other, turned up?'

'Yes. She's very efficient. Laval says he engaged her through an agency. But I'm pretty sure they were far from strangers when she came here. In fact, I spotted them together on her first evening here, and — '

'We'll take that as read. Now the barmaid, Janet.'

'Look here,' Valentine protested, 'once

again I can only give my personal conviction — if that isn't too strong a word. Janet's a common little thing, as hard as nails in some ways; but I'm convinced she wasn't a stranger to Laval or the receptionist either, when she arrived here the day after Lucille Everard, to give that lady her full name. I've an idea — I can't say exactly why — she's rather scared of'em.'

'Which of them two ladies wears the pearls?'

Valentine stared at him in bewilderment.

'Why, Janet. Until last evening. She was very proud of her pearls. Last night she wasn't wearing them and I asked, jokingly, if she had lost them. Why she should have blushed when she said she had forgotten to put them on — '

'It ain't important.' The Super emptied his glass, got up from his chair and held out his hand. 'Gone half-past five, Major, so we'll be toddling back. You'll be up to dinner, at the Riverside Hotel at the usual time, won't you?'

'Certainly. You'll see me in the bar about seven. Look here, why not move to

191

my table? Laval knows already that you were a friend of my father's, so — '

'The friend business is a good line,' the Super agreed as they shook hands, 'but the table idea may present complications. You leave the initiative to me, son, and we'll get along fine. By the way,' he branched off at a tangent again, 'you know that ornate summer house in the grounds of the hotel? We found it locked this morning. I suppose Laval keeps the key in the office?'

'No, it's hidden on a ledge over the summer house door. Guests are welcome to the use of the place; it's kept locked because of casual callers who are notoriously light-fingered and inquisitive. I've sat out there myself once or twice in the evenings. But what's the gist of — ?'

The Super grinned reassuringly.

'No more puzzlers, Major. Henry Baxter and I've got to be getting along.'

Valentine came to the door to see them off. The greyness had gone from his face. He looked flushed and mildly excited, a

192

man with a new purpose. Henry Baxter remarked as much as he and the Super walked along the river path towards the bridge.

'It's nerves, I should say,' he diagnosed. 'You've done him a bit of good already, sir.'

'It's more than nerves,' the Super said gravely. 'Neurotics *tell* you how sick they are.' There was a harsh note of sympathy in his voice that kept Henry from pursuing the subject.

When they came to the path that led up through the woods to the lane the Super stopped abruptly.

'Let's take the long way round, Henry,' he said, and shot off into the wood.

'It's not the grave again, surely!' Henry protested, feeling the weight of his considerable burden in brown paper.

The Super did not reply. He found his way, almost without hesitation, to the clearing and the grave. Here, while a mystified Henry waited patiently, he scouted around. He was out of sight for several minutes, and all Henry could hear were the vague sounds of his movements in the vicinity. Then, suddenly, he reappeared looking annoyed with himself.

'We'd better come back and try again tomorrow,' he announced. 'The morning light's always better in this sort of jungle. I been wasting my time, Henry. Getting too impatient in my old age.'

He started off to find the path again; then, suddenly, he stopped in his tracks and motioned Henry to do the same. Henry had just caught the sound of footsteps in the near distance when the Super, moving with the caution of a cat, pulled him back into the shelter of some tall bushes.

From this point of vantage they watched. They saw the figure of Willie Oaker, the hunchback, coming along the path that was just visible ten yards nearer the river. He was moving with the stealth of a burglar. Henry thought he was still the worse for drink.

Willie stopped where a stout branch of a tree overhung the path a couple of feet above his head. He stared up at it as though to identify it; and then he turned, retraced his steps a few yards, and searched the ground on either side of the path. He was out of sight of Henry Baxter, but not of the Super. Presently, Henry heard an exclamation of satisfaction, and Willie came hastening along the path to the river at a run. He was carrying something bulky under his jacket.

The Super remained motionless. A long two minutes passed, and then there came the sound of a splash.

Willie did not reappear. After another minute the Super moved down to the path and stood glaring aggrievedly up at the overhanging branch in which Willie had been interested.

'Damn this light,' he exploded at length. Nevertheless, with surprising agility he began to climb the tree; and a moment later he was perched on the trunk end of the branch, leaning over it precariously and feeling along the bark with podgy but sensitive fingers which crept along inch by inch.

This performance looked absurd and yielded nothing. With a groan of resignation, then, the Super produced from a pocket of his waistcoat the magnifying glass he was never without.

Leaning still more dangerously out on the branch, he searched along the top of it again with his glass. Each of four successive grunts announced a find which, when all four were collected between thumb and forefinger of his left hand, he contrived to transfer to his wallet.

His both hands free again, he started to climb down — and fell. Badly shaken, he rested on his bottom for a long and painful minute before he levered himself to his feet.

His face, when he took Henry's arm and piloted him along the path down to the river, was fiercely elated.

'I'll have to sleep on my side tonight, Henry,' he confessed. 'But it was worth it. A bit of luck, Willie Oaker coming here like that and showing me what I was looking for. Now why do you suppose he did come here, after eight weeks, to find that blood-stained stone and dump it in the river?'

'I think,' Henry answered with unusual spirit, 'he must be drunk or unbalanced. Probably both. He certainly struck me that way at the Welsh Harp. I can't imagine how he *can* have found that particular stone, either, after such a length of time. Bloodstains — '

The Super shook his arm impatiently. 'Never mind the bloodstains,' he rebuked him. 'Willie knew within a yard or two where the stone was lying. When he found it he must have recognized it on sight.'

'But why,' Henry protested, 'should he want to find it and dump it in the river, sir? I mean, the whole thing's too crazy — '

'Not so crazy as you think,' the Super went on patiently, stopping just before they reached the riverside path and pulling Henry into the shelter of a clump of bushes. 'Willie Oaker knows who I am. The way he turned on me this afternoon, and his activities here just now, are pretty plain indication he thinks I was interested in that bloodstained stone. Because of the blood on it, Henry. *His* blood. And if you'll think a moment you'll realize that bloodstains might very easily have been identifiable, if not plainly visible, on that stone. Willie bled a lot, and probably left some clotted hair behind as well. There's been no rain for more'n eight weeks; and that stone was shaded and sheltered all that time by undergrowth and overhanging trees. Willie was taking no chances, anyway. He came here to put that stone beyond my reach.'

'I realize all that, sir,' Henry agreed, 'but *why* did he want to go to all that trouble to . . . well, it's tantamount to destroying that story of his that nobody would believe!'

'Exactly, son. You're a bit slower than Willie right now, but you're coming to it. Willie Oaker wanted to destroy his story — *because that story is true. He did find a body swinging from that branch back there that night.*'

He produced his wallet and, from an envelope inside it, four inch-long shreds of light brown fibre.

'Sacking, Henry,' he explained confidently. 'What was used to prevent the rope bearing the weight of the body marking the bark of that overhanging branch. And when the rope and the sacking were taken down, these four bits of telltale fibre were left behind. So you see, son, there *was* a body.'

Henry Baxter looked stupefied.

'So someone planted a body there for Willie Oaker to see that night, and then took it away before Mike Amber came on the scene — to prove Willie a liar! It's the craziest thing I ever heard, sir. If you weren't looking so dashed serious about it — '

The Super returned his wallet to its pocket and turned back to the river.

'We can carry on along the bank to the bridge now,' he said. 'We've given Willie Oaker plenty of time to make himself scarce. Yes, Henry,' he went on, 'I'm serious all right. And before long we're going to find a sane and serious reason to explain what you call the craziest story you ever heard. Willie may be mentally abnormal, and he may have been very drunk that night; but the person who staged that performance under and around that tree was neither.'

Henry Baxter suddenly saw the light — or so he thought.

'There wasn't a real corpse!' he proclaimed. 'It was just a practical joke played on Willie Oaker because of his alleged experience with that fantastic 'naked woman in luminy black'.'

The Super gave him a withering look.

'In a minute, Henry,' he said, 'I shall be sorry I brought you here. You'll eat them words.'

He quickened his pace perceptibly. Henry, abashed but still stubbornly loyal to his theory, accompanied him in silence across the bridge, along the promenade and up the drive to the Riverside Hotel. At the entrance the Super stopped and turned to him.

'Take that parcel up to my room and lock the door when you leave,' he ordered under his breath. 'You'll find me in the vicinity of the summer house.'

When Henry entered the hotel he found Gabriel Laval at the reception counter. The proprietor hastened towards him.

'Mr. Baxter . . . ' he began, and stopped short when he saw Henry was alone. 'Mr. Greene is not with you?' he questioned. He frowned but waved the question aside when Henry vouchsafed no information. 'It is nothing really,' he beamed. 'Except a special lunch we had ready for you. Some trout Major Valentine caught. You wouldn't like it cold with a salad for dinner? No,' when Henry hesitated on the problem, 'I'm sure you wouldn't. Not as palatable as hot roast chicken and all the trimmings, no? Then we'll throw the trout away.' He pointed at the parcel under Henry's arms. 'You've been shopping, eh? A picture you've found in one of our antique shops, perhaps?'

Henry smiled angelically.

'Mr. Greene,' he said, 'will be in presently. Excuse me.'

He left Laval defeated, and climbed the stairs to the floor above. He hid the precious package under the mattress of the Super's bed, and, leaving the room, locked the door with the key the Super had given him. Then he went into his own room to wash and brush his hair. When he returned downstairs he stood in the hotel entrance for a minute or two as though awaiting the Super, before he wandered out in search of him.

He found the door of the summer house unlocked. He pushed it open and went inside. It was almost dark there. All Henry could see were chairs and tables lining two walls, and several tiers of lockers half-covering the wall at the far end of the place. The Super was standing there, his tiny torch in his hand, examining something he had taken apparently from one of the lockers.

'All right, Henry,' the Super called to him. 'We're in luck again, son, though this was the logical place to look for the stuff. Come on over.'

He turned from an open locker as Henry joined him.

'Exhibit A,' he announced, and displayed a pair of black rubber bathing shoes. 'Exhibit B,' he said, and held up, in his other hand, a black one-piece bathing costume. He laid these objects down on a nearby chair, searched in the locker again and turned with 'Exhibit C,' held up by both his hands. It was a black rubber cape and hood. 'There's a black rubber bathing cap still in the locker,' he added, 'but these ought to satisfy you, eh?'

Watched by a dazedly admiring Henry, he returned his finds to the locker, picked up some sacking from the floor and stowed it away in the locker in front of the other things.

'I guessed she would use this place,' he explained, turning to confront Henry again. 'She wouldn't dare change in her room. She'd slip out here in her ordinary clothes, change into this black kit, and swim across the river to Charlton when the coast was clear. She'd come back the same way, and leave her swimming kit here when she returned to the hotel. *Now* do you believe in the 'naked woman in luminy black', son?'

Henry nodded gravely.

'Nadine Price and the woman in black were one and the same,' he stated emphatically, and gasped in dismay a second later. 'But Willie Oaker saw the woman in black hanging from that tree two nights after Nadine's disappearance. How — ?'

'I found this locker unlocked,' the Super went on. 'There are scratches on the lock that attracted me to it. The lock has been clumsily forced with a knife. So you see, son, Nadine Price wasn't the last person to take these things from this locker.'

'Good God!' Henry cried. 'Then *another* woman borrowed them and swam across the river to her death that night?'

'Well,' the Super remarked dryly, 'it was obviously someone more lively than a corpse who *returned* the black things to this locker. A murderer most likely. Very neat sort of chap. Very thorough. Always puts things back when he's finished with them.

'Never mind, son,' he wound up, dropping a reassuring hand on Henry's shoulder, 'there's no sense of thinkin' ourselves into knots when there's more useful work to be done. Let's get back to where we belong before they come lookin' for us . . . '

11

The Super said, as they climbed the front steps of the hotel: 'Wait for me in the bar, Henry. I got a little job to do upstairs.'

Henry noticed it was seven-fifteen precisely when he strolled into the bar. There were only two or three customers in the place, and Janet was reading a newspaper. She put it down quickly to welcome Henry to her counter, and he was quite stunned by her gushing friendliness.

Had he and Mr. Greene had a pleasant day? They'd been over to Colwin, hadn't they? Had they walked far? Did Major Valentine encounter them on his way home? A *real* gentleman, Major Valentine. And so on and so on.

It was all very flattering until Henry noticed how she kept watching the door from the entrance hall, as though her performance was for her employer's benefit and she was hoping he was within earshot. He also noticed there was a small cut on her left cheek which just showed through her make-up; and he remembered that someone had done violence to her late last night, and that Gabriel Laval wore a diamond ring on his right hand.

Henry was sipping his modest half-pint and dodging neatly the barmaid's unsubtle questions when the Super and Major Valentine came in together. The latter had just arrived; the two men had met in the hall.

'I'm late,' Valentine apologized, glancing up at the clock that stood at half-past seven. 'I was delayed by rather a lengthy telephone call from Scotland. I'm expecting another from the same source later on; they're ringing me here. Affairs of estate are a damned nuisance, Super, when a man wants to be left alone. Margetson, my agent, is quite a youngster, and hasn't been with me long. He's a good chap, but over-conscientious and rather frightened of making decisions on his own.'

The Super chuckled as he picked up the tankard Janet had just served with a beaming smile.

'I was like that myself years ago in the Force, Major,' he reminisced. 'Then I got wise to the fact that I knew better than my superiors, and from then on I didn't give a damn for the whole bloomin' Force. As you may have occasion,' he confided out of a corner of his mouth, 'to see for yourself.'

The dinner-gong sounded. Valentine reached for his glass.

'We'd better not keep them waiting,' he said. 'I don't think there are many diners to serve this evening. At least, Laval told me at lunchtime he wasn't expecting any new guests — or wanting 'em, as things are.'

They found Lucille Everard tying on her apron in the dining-room. She looked flushed, and had apparently been busy in the kitchen. She informed them they were the only three to be served that evening, and that the Super and Henry were, so far, the only guests staying at the hotel. The few they had seen that morning had all departed.

'Come and share my table for once, Super,' Valentine appealed. 'It will be more cosy, and make things easier for Mam'selle.'

They settled at the major's corner table while Lucille — who was also noticeably more pleasant than hitherto — fetched them drinks from the bar. She hovered around impatiently while they drank their soup. When she had served the main course and left them, the Super looked across at Hugh Valentine and said:

'They're pretty extensive woods around you over in Colwin, Major. Ever heard of 'em being haunted?'

Valentine gave his questioner such a long, searching look that the Super laughed.

'You ain't contemplating withholding information, I hope.'

Valentine glanced at the service door before he answered:

'As a matter of fact, I was, because the information is totally irrelevant to what we were discussing this afternoon. I'm rather sorry for the chap concerned.'

'You mean Willie Oaker?'

'So you know about — ?'

' 'The naked lady in luminy black'?'

Valentine sighed resignedly.

'Joe Early frequents the Welsh Harp. Willie Oaker was one of the locals around that open grave when Joe took me to see it. Willie was there with a pal of his . . . Amber's the name, I believe. The hunchback and the giant. I remarked on the strangely contrasted pair to Joe on our way back to The Retreat. The old chap told me of Willie's habit of sleeping in the woods when tight; and yes, about his supposed encounter with the woman in black.'

'So Willie and Mike Amber were up there that evening,' the Super remarked. 'Did Joe Early ever tell you that Willie was up there much later the same night?'

'No.' Valentine put down his knife and fork. 'What happened?'

'It's a long story,' the Super replied. 'I'll tell it you some other time, Major. Right now I'm supposed to be pumpin' you. I suppose *you* never encountered Willie in them woods?'

Valentine laughed, but uneasily.

'Good heavens, no. I've never been in those woods after dark.'

'Ever encounter anyone or anything unusual on your way home along that river path o' nights?'

Lucille came in to take their plates. She seemed in a hurry. When she had served the dessert and departed, Valentine said sternly:

'I promised to help, Super, so I'd better come clean about something I've honestly only just remembered. Local people avoid that path after dark, for obvious reasons. During all the weeks I've used it I've only met one person there after dark, and he was a stranger. A tramp, I imagined. A most unpleasantly colourful character, the little I saw of him. A big fellow about my own build; unshaven, dirty, with long black hair and yellow teeth. He wore a blue or black jersey, and corduroy trousers. And he spoke English with a French accent you could have cut with a knife. He carried his belongings in an Army pack slung over one shoulder. I don't know why, but I gathered the impression he'd been a French sailor at some time or another.

'Anyway, he was coming towards me as I made my way homewards, just about ten o'clock. It was strong moonlight at the time. He stopped and asked me for a light. I saw he was wearing a massive, curiously-shaped ring on the little finger of his left hand. He asked me if I was a stranger to the district. When I said that I was, comparatively, he pointed across the water at this place and asked what it was. I told him. Then,' Valentine went on, dropping his voice, 'he asked me if the proprietor was one Gabriel Laval. I was so taken aback that I replied in the affirmative without giving myself time to consider the situation. The tramp merely nodded, however, bade me goodnight in French, and moved on. And I don't mind admitting I got back to my place as quickly as possible — in case he'd been paying the house a visit in my absence. I found everything intact, however.'

The Super nodded.

'Did you mention the encounter to Laval, Major?'

'No. For one thing it was early days and I hardly knew him. For another, it was no business of mine, anyway.'

'Did you ever see this tramp again, Major?'

'Nope, but I overheard from a conversation in the bar one evening that he was still about. A casual caller at the Welsh Harp, I understood.'

Lucille returned to serve biscuits-and-cheese.

'I bring your coffee now, gentlemen,' she said, 'if you don't mind. Then I am off for the rest of the evening.'

'But of course,' Valentine said. 'As soon as you like, Mam'selle.'

She came at once with the coffees.

'I have to prepare part of the dinner myself,' she explained, 'and I am famish for a leetle fresh air. Mr. Laval will answer the bell if there is anything else.'

The Super was relating one of his adventures as a young constable in the Force ten minutes later when the telephone rang in the reception office. Almost immediately Gabriel Laval appeared in the hall doorway. He was wearing his chef's white uniform minus the hat.

'It is a trunk call for you, Major Valentine,' he announced. 'Will you take it in my private office?'

'Very kind of you, Laval.' Valentine got up from his chair. 'It will be more comfortable in your office. Super, I'll see you presently in the bar, eh?'

He left them, and the Super produced the inevitable crumpled packet of cigarettes and lit up. For the next ten minutes he sat huddled in his chair with his eyes closed, smoke drifting from his hairy nostrils.

Then, suddenly, he jumped to his feet, emptied his cup and said, 'We'll get across to the bar, son, and wait for the major there.'

They were crossing the hall when Laval — who had changed out of his chef's uniform — called to them from the reception office.

'The major is still at it, gentlemen.'

'I'm just finished, Laval!' Valentine called from the private office. 'O.K., Jim. Thanks a lot for ringing. Goodnight.' A second later a bell tinkled as he replaced the receiver. He came out into the hall looking oddly preoccupied, and accompanied the Super and Henry into the bar.

The huge room was half full now, and rather noisy. The Super looked in vain for Mike Amber and his ex-rival for the favours of Nadine Price, however, as he found a place for himself and his companions at one end of the bar.

Valentine lit one of his big cigars and smoked in silence for several minutes; then, with an impatient exclamation he came out of himself and apologized for his unsociability.

'It's just some farm business that's a bit worrying,' he explained. He gave the Super a straight look and said, 'Look, Super, I wonder if I might glance at that portrait again.' He went on with some embarrassment: 'I'm not so sure I haven't seen that chap somewhere else than where and when I told you this afternoon. Since you left me I've been haunted by a queer feeling there's more to it than that. Possibly something to do with the war. I don't want to raise any false hopes, but, as I told you, I've a pretty retentive memory for faces, and if I could look at that picture again . . . ?'

'But of course, Major,' the Super replied warmly. 'Let's go up to my room at once.'

He finished his drink, nodded to Henry to accompany them. Laval was still busy with his books in the reception office when they crossed the hall to the stairs and climbed to the first floor.

'You know, Major,' the Super called over his shoulder as he led the way down the corridor to his room, 'this ain't a new thing in my experience by a long chalk. What you want to do is to cut this place and its associations right out of your mind when you look at — '

He stopped abruptly outside the door of his room with an exclamation that might have meant anything.

'This is queer, Major,' he said as they joined him. 'I left this door locked when I went down to dinner.' The door was ajar. He examined it more closely and swore. 'It's been forced open!'

He pushed the door open and switched

215

on the light as he strode into the room, which smelt strongly of turpentine though the window was wide open.

Lying on the bed was the glass-backed 'portrait' of Robert Charlton. It had been attacked with turpentine; and what had been a vivid and colourful picture was now a meaningless smear of shining oil-paint.

Valentine was horrified, as he stared at the Super's flushed and angry countenance.

'Look here, Super,' he cried indignantly, 'the sooner we get Laval on to this the better, don't you think? Shall I fetch him?'

The Super nodded.

'Fetch him quick, Major,' he rasped. 'Henry, you shut the door and stay with me.'

When Valentine had gone the Super looked into the bathroom, shut the window and made a swift inspection of the bedroom. Then he planted himself in front of Henry, and the ferocious glare on his face became, incredibly, a grin.

'So someone in this place has declared himself, Henry,' he said. 'That picture has brought results sooner'n I expected.'

'But there isn't any picture, sir!' the stupefied Henry protested.

'Oh, yes, there is.' The Super tapped a bulge in the righthand pocket of his jacket. 'There's six of 'em in this little camera of mine. That's the job I came up here to do before dinner, son. But,' and the glare returned, 'if you let on about this by so much as a look — '

He broke off at the sound of running footsteps in the corridor outside, five seconds before the door was pushed open and Valentine appeared in the doorway. His face was drained of colour, his eyes were wide with horror.

'You'd better come with me, Super,' he said. 'There's been a murder.'

He turned and hurried away. The Super, curtly telling Henry to stay where he was, ran after him. Valentine waited for him at the end of the corridor. He pointed at the mouth of a narrow passage on the other side of the stairs.

'I went that way,' he explained breathlessly, 'to avoid risking a scene in the hall downstairs. There are stairs at the end of that passage leading down to the kitchen and a back way into the reception office.'

He strode past the head of the staircase, dived into the passage beyond, and stopped when he came to a lighted doorway half-way down.

The door was wide open. The room beyond was a wash-room.

Sprawled on his back in the middle of the stone-tiled floor, his arms outflung, his sightless eyes shining glassily in the light from the powerful electric bulb overhead, was Gabriel Laval.

'He's dead all right,' Valentine said as he followed the Super into the room. 'The weapon is over there.'

He pointed to a silver-handled dagger lying near the line of washbasins, its point darkly shining with uncongealed blood.

12

The Super glanced at the dagger as he sank to his knees by the body. Valentine, who seemed oddly excited for a man of his calibre and experience, went on explaining:

'The door of this room was open and the lights were on, just as you see them, when I got here just now. That was how I came to spot the poor devil. He was lying on his face when I found him, by the way. If you'll turn him over you'll see where the knife went in at the base of the spine. I killed a German sentry with the same trick on a commando raid in the war. A sharp dig in the vital spot and they drop like a stone. Incidentally,' he added, 'that knife over there is a commando knife. It may be the one Laval kept on his desk for use as a paper-knife; I noticed it wasn't there when I used his telephone this evening.'

The Super sniffed and grunted.

'Turpentine on his clothes,' he said as he got to his feet. 'Got your torch on you, Major?'

Valentine nodded.

'Wait a minute,' he exclaimed. 'Constable Taft, in plain clothes, was playing darts when we left the bar just now — '

'Your observation does you credit, Major,' the Super said warmly. 'You and Constable Taft will 'ave to pretend you're a police force for the next half-hour. Take him outside the building and tell him what's happened. Tell him no one is to leave the premises until further notice. I shall also want to know who entered or left the bar during the past fifteen minutes. And as from this minute, I want the grounds covered as best you can, in case anyone tries to sneak away. In your spare time,' he added with a twinkle, 'you might look around outside underneath my bedroom window.'

Valentine hurried away. The Super followed him into the corridor, locked the door of the washroom behind him and pocketed the key. He continued along the corridor, descended narrow stairs at the end, and found himself in a short, stone-floored passage with three doors opening into it. The one at the end on the left of the stairs was obviously the back way into the reception office. He tried the door at the opposite end; it was unlocked and opened on to a lawn overlooking the river. The Super retraced his steps to the door facing the stairs, threw it open and walked into a large kitchen.

John the porter, not in uniform, was reading a newspaper at the far end of the kitchen table. He explained he had been having his afternoon off, and had returned to the hotel merely for his supper before going home to sleep. If the gentleman wanted anything urgent, however, he would be happy to oblige.

'I want to know whether you've seen or heard anyone in this part of the building since you came in for your supper, John,' the Super told him.

The puzzled porter shook his head. 'Only Mr. Laval, sir. He came in with them things a few minutes ago, and then went up them stairs behind you.' He pointed to Laval's chef's clothes lying on the table, and asked anxiously if anything was amiss.

'Mr. Laval,' the Super told him bluntly, 'has been murdered, and I need your help. Fetch me a master key to begin with.'

The porter's promptness did him credit in the circumstances. Without a word of exclamation he went off to the reception office and returned with the master key.

'Now hurry around,' the Super ordered him, 'and lock all the outside doors excepting the bar and the front entrance. Bring me the keys in the hall.'

The Super himself made a swift tour of inspection of the cellars and all the rooms on the ground floor, missing only the bar. He then found the porter awaiting him in the hall with three keys in his hand.

'Hang on to them, John,' he told him, 'and stay right here.'

He crossed to the main staircase, climbed to the first-floor landing and bawled, 'Henry!'

Henry Baxter came at a run, his eyes full of questions.

'Laval was stabbed in a washroom along there, son,' the Super informed him. 'I want you to take this master key and look into every room from this floor upwards. If you run into trouble, or find anything suspicious, yell for me.'

He went downstairs again and into Gabriel Laval's private office, where he sat down behind the desk, searched for a number in the local telephone directory, and dialled it on the instrument in front of him. A deep, drowsy voice answered after almost a minute:

'Sergeant Evans speaking. What is it?'

'This,' the Super barked, 'is ex-Superintendent Greene speaking from the Riverside Hotel.'

'The Superintendent!' the very Welsh voice exclaimed, suddenly awake. 'I've heard about you, sir, from the chief constable. He told me to give you a very wide berth, Mr. Greene, until — '

'Well, Sergeant, this is it. Gabriel Laval has just been murdered in one of the washrooms here. Get down here in a hurry, will you.'

He rang off without more ado, dialled

'O' and gave the operator a number he had obtained from Colonel Fielding the previous morning and kept in his head. Two minutes later the chief constable was speaking to him from his private residence in Levenstone.

'Hello, Greene,' he began anxiously. 'I hardly expected you to call me as soon as this — '

'Gabriel Laval has just been murdered,' the Super repeated himself, 'here at the Riverside Hotel.'

'Laval? Good God!' There was a long pause before Colonel Fielding went on: 'I'll be with you as soon as I can make it, Super. In the meantime my men are to take their orders from you.'

'Very good, sir.'

The Super rang off. He was frowning at the expensive array of articles on the desk, and noting the absence of the commando knife to which Valentine had referred, when the major himself came in. He was carrying something wrapped in a handkerchief.

'I thought I'd better report, Super,' he said. 'No one entered the bar during the material fifteen minutes. Taft was watching out for a pal of his who might have come through either door, so he was able to vouch for that. We found no one outside we could question as to anyone having left the building recently; but we did find this stuff strewn on the grass verge under your bedroom window.'

He opened the handkerchief on the desk, revealing a medicine bottle about one-third full of turpentine, a small hand towel that had obviously been used in the defacement of the oil-painting in the Super's bedroom, and a pair of red rubber gloves.

The Super opened the middle drawer of the desk, deposited the collection of articles inside, and handed Valentine his handkerchief.

'Has anyone tried to leave the hotel so far, Major?'

'No. Nothing has leaked out in the bar up to now, either, but — '

'Good work. Do you mind going back to the bar and keeping your eyes skinned until I can hand over that part of the business to Sergeant Evans? I want you to keep a special eye on Janet, the barmaid, when she learns what's happened to her boss.'

A moment after the major had departed, Henry Baxter came into the office very much out of breath.

'I didn't meet a soul up there, sir,' he reported. 'Nothing unusual either, so far as I could see.'

The Super pushed himself out of his chair with difficulty, for he was a tight fit.

'I didn't expect you would find anything, Henry,' he said. 'The murderer was probably on his way out when Major Valentine found the body — '

He broke off as a burly figure in the uniform of a police sergeant appeared in the doorway, and, recognizing the famous ex-superintendent on sight, saluted smartly and introduced himself as Sergeant Evans. He was a florid-faced man of late middle age.

'I had a word with Constable Taft on my way in, sir,' he began. 'This is indeed a dreadful business to be happening at this time. I take it you have had a word already with the chief constable?'

'That's right, Sergeant,' the Super replied. 'He's on his way. Meanwhile I'm acting as his mouthpiece.' He pointed to the telephone on the desk. 'Will you get on to Inspector Griffiths, and do the necessary about the surgeon and the ambulance? Then collect Constable Taft, seal off the bar and take names and particulars.'

'Very good, Superintendent.'

He left the sergeant squeezing himself into the chair behind the desk, nodded to Henry Baxter to follow him, and went upstairs to the washroom where he showed Henry the corpse.

He went to his knees again by the body, and ran his hand over the front of the jacket and waistcoat.

'Not only smells of turpentine, Henry,' he grunted. 'There's a damp patch of it on his waistcoat.' He looked up over his shoulder. 'Go and get John, the porter, to take you to the kitchen. You'll find Laval's chef's clothes on the table there. Give 'em a good sniffing over, and look for traces of oil-paint.'

Left alone, he went through the dead man's pockets. He turned out a gold pencil and pen, a gold lighter and a large, heavy gold cigarette-case containing a dozen cigarettes of an expensive brand. In a hip pocket he found a smaller and slimmer case containing a half-dozen cigarettes, unmarked and brownish in colour. 'Dope,' he muttered disgustedly. 'I suspected as much last night.'

He found and pocketed Laval's ring of keys, and searched through his wallet. The latter contained a substantial sum in paper money, and nothing else excepting several printed hotel cards. On the back of one of the cards, however, someone had scribbled in pencil: *Kenton* 6148. *F. after* 10.

The Super slipped the card into his own wallet; and finding nothing else of interest in the dead man's pockets, he was about to get to his feet when his attention was caught by the watch gleaming on Laval's left wrist. He removed it to examine it still more closely.

It was a gold watch fitted with the additional hands of a stop-watch. The expanding gold bracelet was unusually wide and substantial. It consisted of a series of small gold cylinders held together by a spring attachment at the back. A tiny, barely-visible line near the top of one of the cylinders caught the Super's eye. He flicked at it with a fingernail, and a cap composing the top of the cylinder sprang open, revealing the hollow cylinder — a cavity large enough to contain an object about twice as thick as an ordinary match and half as long.

When Henry Baxter returned to the washroom the Super had completed his preliminary examination of the scene of the crime. He was standing with his hands in his trouser pockets and scowling down at the mortal remains of Gabriel Laval.

'No, Mr. Greene,' Henry said, 'there's not a whiff of turpentine on those chef's clothes, and nothing that looks like a smudge of oil-paint.'

The Super sighed regretfully.

'Then all I can say, son, is that Gabriel Laval must 'ave been a very careless chap with a very poor sense of smell. Come in!' he called in response to a knock on the door.

It was Major Valentine.

'I thought I'd find you here, Super,' he said. 'The sergeant and Taft have got things under control in the bar. Janet looks scared out of her wits, but there's no risk of her bolting.' He paused. 'There's something queer I think you ought to know. When I went down into the bar to take Taft outside and tell him about the murder, I took a quick look around to note the faces of all the people I know — as a matter of routine observation. I even looked into the men's lavatory. That hunchback and that big fellow Amber weren't there then. But when I left you in Laval's office and returned to the bar just now they were drinking together there. Taft or I would have spotted them if they'd come up the drive after the murder; so the implication is pretty obvious, isn't it? They must have been together out in the grounds at the time of the murder, and have slipped into the bar after I'd taken Taft outside.'

The Super stared at him for a long

moment, then threw open the door of the washroom, waved his companions out into the passage, followed them and locked the door behind him.

'Major Valentine, I want you to get back to the bar. Tell Sergeant Evans I want to see Mike Amber in Laval's private office. Henry, you stick with me.'

The trio separated in the hall. The Super grinned at Henry as he pushed himself again into the chair behind Laval's desk.

'Henry,' he said, 'you're watchin' the investigation of a truly bafflin' mystery. It's unique even in my long and varied experience. So don't look surprised whatever happens.'

His smile vanished when Michael Amber came into the room. The latter looked more of a giant than ever in a well-fitting blue lounge suit complete with collar-and-tie. His fair hair was creamed and brushed straight back from his forehead, and his face was newly-shaven and shining. But he looked grim and prepared for anything as he glanced at Henry and faced the Super.

'Shut the door, Henry,' the Super ordered sternly. 'Now, Amber, things are rather different from what they were when we met yesterday. I'm going to ask you a question that'll probably startle you: a question about the girl you were engaged to. Did Nadine Price wear any special piece of jewellery? Did she have a special piece, for example, that she wore all the time?'

Mike Amber stared at him with smouldering eyes. He seemed to suspect a trap.

'She had a lot of jewellery,' he replied. 'I don't know what you mean by — '

'I spoke plain enough, son. A special piece of jewellery she was particularly attached to?'

Mike Amber jesitated for a long time before he answered:

'I don't know what all this is about, Superintendent, but she had a gold watch with a wide, expanding bracelet that she wore all the time. It was the dead spit of Laval's watch. She used to say that was coincidence, but I could never bring myself to believe her. I was always haunted by the suspicion she'd coveted Laval's watch, and he'd given her one like it for favours received. The last night we were together I forbade her to wear the watch again. She laughed at me and said I could go throw myself in the river. And she wouldn't deny that Laval had given it to her for a price. We quarrelled; and that was why we had no definite date the night she disappeared.'

The Super's eyes gleamed as he nodded.

'Did she ever say anything else about her watch to you, son; anything you thought was queer?'

Amber frowned.

'No, sir, nothing I can remember anyhow — except she said she would be wearing the watch on her dying day, and then she laughed as though she'd made a joke.'

'Thanks, Amber.' The Super gestured to Henry to open the door. 'Let's see, you've got that hunchback friend of yours with you in the bar, haven't you. Well, tell Sergeant Evans from me that you two are free to go as soon as he's asked you the routine questions.'

Amber thanked him and looked very relieved as he strode out of the room. Henry Baxter closed the door again and gaped at the Super.

'Excuse me, sir,' he stammered, 'but w-what's all that about jewellery got to do with Amber and his friend being out of the bar when the murder was committed?'

The Super laughed.

'Oh, that,' he said. 'It's much too soon to ask 'em about *that*, Henry. But the jewellery was urgent.'

'So I gather, sir,' Henry said dazedly. 'Was Laval wearing a wrist watch when he was murdered? I didn't see one — '

'He was, Henry, but he ain't any more.' He tapped the left-hand pocket of his jacket. 'You'll hear more about them watches,' he promised, and suddenly began to drum with his fingers on the desk. 'Now where the dickens *is* the chief constable?' he demanded complainingly. 'He could have walked it from Levenstone by now . . . '

The clock in the hall was just striking ten.

Henry Baxter thought, 'You're enjoying yourself thoroughly, you delightful old hypocrite!'

13

It was half-past eleven when the Super and Colonel Fielding sat down together, facing each other across the hearth in that over-heated office. The Super certainly wasn't enjoying himself, and the chief constable looked haggard, haunted and exhausted.

'Well, that's that,' the latter sighed, producing a pipe and sticking it empty between his teeth. 'We've drawn a blank with the crowd from the bar and got rid of them. The ambulance has taken Gabriel Laval to the mortuary. The police surgeon has confirmed the obvious time and cause of death. My photographer and fingerprint men have finished their work and cleared off. At your request, we have drafted in six additional officers to patrol the streets and the environs of this hotel. Inspector Griffiths and Sergeant Evans are kicking their heels in the bar and heaven knows when I'll have time to talk to them. You let that porter go, didn't you, and Major Valentine?'

The Super nodded, fingering a cigarette he had apparently no intention of smoking at the moment.

'The porter sleeps out, Colonel,' he explained. 'Major Valentine has been very helpful, and he'll be back for breakfast — eager to lend a hand again.'

Fielding frowned.

'Was there any particular point in sending the barmaid and the receptionist off to their beds without questioning them?'

'Yes,' the Super replied. 'I've an idea they'll be much more useful to us in the morning.'

'I see.' The colonel smiled faintly. 'I suppose you packed Henry Baxter off to bed for the same reason?'

'Henry's not in his bed,' the Super corrected him. 'He's stretched out on a mattress on the landing of the top floor, to make sure the barmaid and the receptionist stay put.'

The chief constable puzzled over that for a moment and frowned again.

'Then it only remains for you to explain, Greene, why you insisted on my excluding Inspector Griffiths and Sergeant Evans from this conference. I seem to know less about this murder than when I arrived here,' he added with a touch of bitterness, 'and I imagine they're not much better off.'

'Bluntly, sir,' the Super replied, 'I feel it'll be better for us all if I talk to you like this, and then you talk to them. They're probably having a comfortable snooze right now in any case.'

'You mean we've made a mess of things, don't you? You've turned the tables on us, and produced a murder into the bargain, in the space of thirty hours or so?'

The Super lighted a cigarette for which he had no appetite, to give him time to choose his words.

'Your men,' he said at length, 'started off on the wrong foot. The more familiar you are with people, in my experience, the less you can trust your judgment of 'em in certain circumstances.'

Fielding smiled bitterly.

238

'Very discreetly put, Super. You might have added that the responsibility was mine and I should have called in Scotland Yard at the start of things.'

'I'm not going to say that, Colonel. I will say, though, that I started here from scratch — with results that are going to shake you pretty badly.'

'Fire away then, and for God's sake don't try to be too tactful with the object of letting me down lightly.'

'Very well, Colonel. I appreciate that. First of all let me make the emphatic assertion that everything that's happened here in Larne and Colwin in the past eight weeks or so comes under one heading. It's all part and parcel of the same drama, the same case. And the only element of coincidence about it is that Gabriel Laval happened to be the proprietor of this hotel at the same time that Miss Evelyn Radford was living in Colwin.

'Nadine Price and Robert Charlton were very much hand-in-glove when they came here,' he went on confidently. 'And my present theory is that they came here because they wanted a hide-out; and they chose this place because Laval was here and Miss Radford was over at Colwin.'

Fielding was too stunned to grasp the whole of it.

'A hide-out!' he exclaimed. 'Good heavens, man, how can you say Nadine Price came here to *hide herself*? That immoral creature couldn't have advertised herself more — '

'There are different ways of hiding, Colonel. One way I can think of is advertisin' yourself as somebody you're not — if you get my meaning. In this connection there is the significant fact that Nadine Price would never let any of her numerous admirers take her picture; and there is the fact that Robert Charlton was equally reticent on the same subject — so reticent that the only way Evelyn Radford could get herself a picture of him was to paint it in secret and hide it in her bedroom. I found that picture today, on the back of the glass top of her dressing-table . . . '

'So that's the mess you showed me in your room here, Super. That's why Laval was murdered tonight!'

The Super shook his head reprovingly.

'We'll come to that later, Colonel, if you don't mind. Let's stick to the story as I see it, and get the picture clear before you start to tear it to pieces.'

He began again:

'Robert Charlton came here first to spy out the land. Nadine came shortly afterwards and blackmailed Gabriel Laval into giving her a job as barmaid. Then Charlton came and made himself known to Evelyn Radford, because he was dam' confident that if she would let that cottage of hers to anyone in this world it would be himself.'

Fielding warded him off with a gesture.

'This is much too fast for my digestion, Super. It's common knowledge here that Charlton and Evelyn Radford were strangers when he came here; she fell in love with him more or less at first sight, as I understand — '

The Super laughed ironically.

'Stuff and nonsense, Colonel! Evelyn Radford wasn't that sort of spinster, as I'll try and convince you presently. I'm going to hazard a guess, on the strength of what I know of her life and character, that Evelyn Radford had been in love with Charlton for years; that he was the only man she had ever loved. But the answer to that is to be found in Cumberland, I imagine.'

'Great heavens! Are you trying to tell me that Charlton was the young estate manager in Cumberland when she and her brother — ?'

'We shall see, Colonel,' the Super persisted. 'In the meantime I am perfectly satisfied that she not only accepted him as her future husband, but she lied — possibly for the first time in her thoroughly respectable life — to preserve here the secret of his true identity for what she considered good enough reasons.'

He smoked the rest of his cigarette in silence, and threw it into the fireplace.

'So there we have it,' he continued at length, 'the original set-up. Nadine and Charlton were nicely settled in their hide-out; and while Nadine was amusing herself quite profitably with her various admirers, Charlton was amusing himself with Evelyn Radford — and, in spite of what you said on the subject yesterday, I shall be very surprised if it wasn't his intention to make a very profitable marriage with Evelyn Radford before he ultimately walked out on her.'

'I suppose,' the chief constable suggested cynically, 'you haven't any idea as to whom Charlton and Nadine Price were hiding here *from?*'

'I've a sort of an idea,' the Super replied calmly. 'It might simplify things a bit if we hazard a guess it was a man, and call him 'X' for the purpose of this imaginative story of mine.

'Charlton and Nadine were absolute strangers to each other on the surface, of course. That was part of their policy. But there's pretty strong evidence that she visited him frequently at his cottage late at night. They'd certainly arranged how she could get him on the 'phone in an extreme emergency.

'That extreme emergency arose, as I believe it, between six and seven o'clock on the evening of the night they both disappeared. As a result, she telephoned him at Miss Radford's house, telling that lady she was Charlton's sister. Later that night, she packed her things and risked crossing the river by the bridge, and met Charlton as arranged on the 'phone. I believe she was in a panic because she had seen 'X', or she knew he had discovered her whereabouts and was on her track. So . . . well,' he ended, 'she and Charlton disappeared.'

Fielding looked savagely incredulous.

'So I suppose Miss Radford, hitherto completely unsuspecting, discovered the horrible truth about them both at that late hour that night, and went straight back to her house to commit suicide?'

'I think,' the Super said quietly, 'that Evelyn Radford followed Charlton when he left her house that night. I think she found him with Nadine and overheard enough for them to decide it was too dangerous to let her go on living.'

'Murder!' Fielding gasped. 'So Evelyn Radford was murdered, was she?'

'I'm dam' sure she was murdered, Colonel,' the Super proclaimed aggressively. 'And her murderer had the cyanide handy in a contraption which has been described as the dead spit of this one.'

He produced Laval's wrist watch and showed the stupefied Fielding the secret cavity in the bracelet.

But he hadn't finished with Fielding yet.

'But was that the only murder committed that night?' he demanded, after a dramatic pause. 'Nadine and Charlton certainly disappeared; but did they go under their own steam? One reason I've got for posing them questions, Colonel, is this: Charlton didn't do his own packing. It was done by someone who had to turn the cottage upside down to make sure that nothing was left behind in the nature of a clue to Charlton's identity.

'I'm not *asserting* anything,' he went on blandly, 'I'm merely *wondering aloud*, whether 'X' caught up with Charlton and Nadine that night, and did Charlton's packing for him because Charlton was in no condition to do it for himself?'

'My God, Greene!' Fielding sounded almost hysterical. 'So you want to make it three murders now, do you? What do you think this mysterious, problematical person 'X' did with the bodies, then? I can assure you that the police search of the entire district — '

'We'll come back to that again,' the Super promised.

Fielding pulled out a handkerchief to wipe his perspiring face.

'Turn out that damned fire, will you?' he pleaded. 'This room is like an oven, and my brain's on fire. Well,' when the Super had obliged, 'is that the end of your story, Greene? Or is there more of the same kind? By heavens,' he cried, 'you've hardly brought Laval into the picture yet, except as a corpse. And there's still that open grave in Colwin to be explained.'

The Super got to his feet.

'Before we go on, Colonel, don't you think we could both do with a drink?'

'I do!' Fielding almost shouted the words. 'Bring me a whisky neat, Super, and make it a big one. And make it snappy,' he begged, as the Super turned to the door.

14

The Super returned within ten minutes with two very large whiskies. Colonel Fielding's hand trembled as he took his glass. He looked completely crushed, but was still concerned for the comfort of his two officers waiting in the bar.

'They're doin' themselves nicely,' the Super reassured him cheerfully, sampling his own drink and setting it aside. 'Now, Colonel, let's look at this thing rationally. Your men started their investigations from the wrong angle, and it brought 'em to a dead end. That's why your published conclusions satisfied no one — not even yourself. But lor' bless you, sir — and I speak from a very long experience — that's just what happens in six investigations out of ten, isn't it? It was always happenin' to me, I assure you. I started from the wrong angle and got to a dead end; then I began again from a different angle . . . and so on until I found the right road that led me to the criminal.

'I've had all the luck in this business,' he went on generously. 'I saw possible snags in the story you told me yesterday in Drawbridge — yesterday being now the day before yesterday,' he corrected himself, glancing at the electric clock on the wall behind his companion. 'And I happened to strike the right road straight away. I don't claim much credit for bein' able to put two and two together in them circumstances.

'Well now, sir, let's have a go at putting some flesh on the skeleton I've been rattlin' so alarmingly . . . '

Cautiously, cunningly, devastatingly, he began to build up his case. He began with Laval, and his conversation with the Frenchman had tentatively convinced him that he had known Nadine Price during the war. He went on to deal with his inspection of Nadine's luxury room-with-a-bath, and his conviction that someone other than the police had searched the place thoroughly since the barmaid's disappearance. Then, shatteringly, he

248

mentioned the handkerchief he had found there, with the lipstick writing on it; and he exploited to the full the importance and implications of '93 *Christine*'. 'In my opinion, Colonel, that discovery establishes beyond all doubt the relationship between Price and Charlton.'

He described what he had heard and seen when he had left Nadine's room. 'That's something up my sleeve,' he chuckled, 'for when I tackle them two ladies in the morning.'

Then, with an authority that held his listener fascinated, he went on to describe his visit that morning to Evelyn Radford's house, and his interview with Mavis Ferndale, the daily woman. 'What I found in that house, what I heard from Mrs. Ferndale, on top of what I knew already about Miss Radford's earlier life, made nonsense of nearly everything you'd told me about her, Colonel. She wasn't, she couldn't have been that sort of woman at all.' He repeated most of his earlier oration to Henry Baxter on the character of Evelyn Radford, and ended:

'She was incapable of suicide, Colonel.

'So, as far as I can see, there's only one possible explanation of what happened to her on the night she died. She caught Charlton and Nadine together and learned, from their conversation, the truth about them. Then, like the sensible woman she was, she went back to her house and made herself a cup of cocoa to soothe her nerves. My guess is that Nadine Price, knowing what Miss Radford had overheard, followed her to the house, saw her making that cocoa, and saw her chance. She had the cyanide virtually in her hand. She was carryin' it in the wristlet of her watch which was identical to Laval's watch; I reckon he'd given it her during the war, and she had worn it ever since, to have that poison handy for use — possibly on herself — in extreme emergency. Anyway, all this is in keepin' with her character as I read her.

'Well now, she had the means of silencing Miss Radford, and it was easy enough to use it. She had only to nip round and ring the front-door bell, nip back and into that kitchen while Miss Radford was answering the door, break the capsule of cyanide into the cup of cocoa . . . and there you were!'

'You're certain about that watch, Super?'

'Mike Amber is, Colonel. He told me about it. She made a joke to him about carrying it to her dying day . . . '

The Super carried the story of his investigations on to the cottage Charlton had occupied. He emphasized the implications of the chaotic state of the rooms, and the bottle of hair lotion on the mantelpiece.

'That's about the first real thing we know about 'X',' he added half-seriously. 'He didn't know about Charlton and his hair lotion.'

Then, having refreshed himself with another mouthful of whisky from his glass, he plunged into his and Henry Baxter's experience at the Welsh Harp, during their lunch on bread-and-cheese. He gave a very dramatic account of Willie Oaker's outburst, and Hughie Grant's story of the hunchback's nocturnal

251

adventures in the wood behind Colwin. But he stopped at the point where the landlord had told them of Oaker's alleged adventures in those woods two nights after the disappearance of Nadine Price.

Fielding had listened with an expression of scepticism and distaste on his grey face. He laughed impatiently when the Super stopped his narration abruptly.

'Willie Oaker, from what I've heard of him,' he said, 'is a habitual drunkard who is definitely not normal when he's sober. 'A naked woman in luminy black'! Rubbish, Greene! I'd believe him if it was pink elephants.'

'Well,' the Super supplied, 'he told the same story — of seeing the black woman visiting Charlton at his cottage — to Mavis Ferndale.'

'I don't suppose that sensible woman believed him either, did she? Anyway,' the chief constable protested in exasperation, 'what's the point of this unpleasant story?'

'Just this, Colonel. Nadine Price was the woman in luminy black. She reached Charlton's cottage, on her nocturnal visits to him, by swimming the river from this hotel when she was certain the coast was clear, and making her way through the woods.'

'Can you prove that, Greene?'

'Well, if you look in one of the lockers in the summer house in these grounds, you'll find the black rubber outfit she used, Colonel.'

Fielding stared at him for a long moment, and then he shrugged.

'All right. That's how Nadine Price made her clandestine visits to Charlton. Is there anything more to it than that?'

'Very much so,' the Super said sternly, and proceeded to relate Willie Oaker's alleged encounter with the body of the woman in black two nights after Nadine's disappearance, his subsequent return to the spot with Mike Amber, and his hysterical outburst in the bar of the Welsh Harp the following day.

Fielding listened with incredulity and horror in his eyes. But his subsequent reaction was an outburst of angry scepticism.

'You're not going to tell me you believe

this crazy hunchback saw and touched the dead body of Nadine Price, are you,' he demanded, 'near that open grave in those woods two nights after her disappearance? It's perfectly obvious the fellow hit his head on that stone and had a nightmare — or delirium tremens, more likely. A disappearing corpse into the bargain! Great heavens, Greene, I've had enough of this craziness. Unless you come to a sane point to it pretty quickly — '

'I will,' the Super retorted sternly. 'I am convinced Willie Oaker saw and touched the body of Nadine Price hanging from that tree that night, though I don't suggest even now he knows the woman in luminy black *was* Nadine Price. I am convinced, moreover, that when Mike Amber took him back to the spot, the corpse was no longer there.'

'Go on,' the chief constable invited, harshly.

The Super went on. He told how he and Henry Baxter had seen Willie Oaker collect the bloodstained stone and drop it into the river early that evening.

Fielding was not impressed.

'Of course,' he sneered. 'The hunch-back thought you and the police were after him on account of his crazy story. So he drowned that stone; and if you tackle him now he'll deny the whole thing. What you've just told me simply proves the abnormal working of the poor devil's mind.'

'No,' the Super persisted, 'there's more to it than that. Take a look at these, Colonel.'

He produced from his wallet the pieces of fibre he had taken from the branch of the tree in the woods.

'Sacking was used, when the corpse was hung from that tree, Colonel, to prevent the rope marking the bark. I found these bits of it still caught in the bark of that branch when I examined it this evening — eight weeks after the event. And I'm going to get 'em identified for what they are.'

Fielding reached for his glass and drained it.

'God in Heaven, Super,' he said hoarsely, 'what are you coming to now?'

'Simply, sir, that what Willie Oaker said happened that night *did* happen. He encountered that hanging corpse just before he was knocked on the head with that stone. And immediately afterwards the corpse was removed.'

Colonel Fielding drew a shaking hand across his eyes as though he was finding difficulty in seeing his companion.

'Why, man?' he demanded faintly. '*Why —* ?'

'Well, there is one very sane explanation,' the Super replied. 'Willie Oaker habitually frequented those woods at night, didn't he? And someone — a murderer — had to scare him out of them that night, and make certain he wouldn't return. As it happened, Mike Amber made the scare doubly effective.'

'All right.' Fielding was too dazed to argue any more. 'But why did this murderer go to such fantastic lengths to achieve that end?'

'Because the murderer had to be absolutely sure he would be alone in those woods until daylight. He had a job to do there; at all costs he had to make sure of doing it unseen.'

'A job? What job?'

'A job that had to be completed before morning, *when that grave was going to be filled in*.'

Before the chief constable could say anything in reply to that, the Super added sternly:

'I think, Colonel, we should re-open that grave.'

15

Half an hour later Colonel Fielding, holding a replenished glass in his hand, said:

'No wonder they talk at the Yard of your uncanny mind, Greene. It was a staggering achievement to have made sense, horrible sense, out of that Oaker story.'

'There is a reason for everything,' the Super replied. 'Even the actions of a lunatic. The only other explanation possible of what you called the disappearing corpse is that a practical joke was played on Willie Oaker. Circumstances ridicule that notion.'

'I agree,' Fielding nodded. 'Was the re-opening of the grave in your mind when you asked for those six men to be drafted into Larne, Super?'

'Well, sir, we don't want a crowd invading those woods while the job's being done.'

Fielding sighed heavily.

'I hope to God your theories are wrong,' he said fervently, 'but we'll start re-opening that grave as soon as it's daylight. Excuse me a moment.'

He left the room, returning with the news that he had ordered Sergeant Evans to make the necessary arrangements.

'The pair of them think I must have gone off my rocker,' he said, as he resumed his seat and picked up his glass. 'Well now, Super, perhaps we can now come to the incidental matter of Laval's murder.'

The Super smiled grimly.

'Make quite a pleasant diversion, won't it, Colonel?'

'I'd like to know how it fits into the general pattern you've been devastating me with.'

'So should I, sir. We don't even know it had any connection with the mucking up of that oil-painting in my bedroom.'

'But hang it all, Super, that turpentine on Laval's waistcoat — ?'

'Let's put the oil-painting back on Miss Radford's dressing-table for a moment.

The police didn't find it there, and it's fairly certain the murderer was unaware of its existence when Henry and I went to the house yesterday morning. We brought it away wrapped in brown paper. The only person I showed it to was Major Valentine. Laval was inquisitive about it when Henry got back here with it in the early evening. He shoved it under the mattress in my room and locked the door when he came away. Anyone with a key could have got in and had a look at it, of course, between then and when I went up there just before dinner. It was undamaged when I came down to dinner. At approximately eight-forty-five, when Valentine and Henry and I were in the bar, the major asked to see the picture again. He had an idea that face ought to mean more to him than it had. I took him up at once, and, excepting the smell, we found my room as you saw it when you arrived, Colonel.'

'I see. So Major Valentine is the only person who saw the portrait to your personal knowledge.'

'Yes. But the major is absolutely in

the clear. He was entering the hall when I came down to dinner. He was with Henry and me until Laval called 'im to take a call from Scotland in this office. He was still on the 'phone, with Laval in the reception office, when Henry and I left the dining-room to make for the bar. We waited for Valentine, who was just finishing his call, and the three of us trooped into the bar together. When we found that mess in my room I sent Valentine to fetch Laval. He made for those back stairs to avoid making a scene in the hall. That's how he came to find Laval in the washroom; the lights were on there and the door was open. He came straight back to fetch me. He wasn't gone more'n a couple of shakes.

'Laval must have followed us upstairs,' he summed up, 'and walked straight into it in that washroom. It looks like the murderer got away down them back stairs and out of a door I found unlocked in the passage below. John, the porter, isn't too good at hearing; and at the time he had his nose in the evening paper on the other side of the kitchen door. A good way on the other side of the kitchen door,' he added.

'You were certainly smart in covering the premises as you did,' Fielding praised. But the Super shook his head.

'I was lucky, Major Valentine remembering that constable in the bar.'

'Yes. Well . . . who *could* have defaced that oil painting?'

'Anyone — excepting Valentine, Henry and me — who could have got into my room after I went down to dinner. Obviously, though, we've got to consider the household staff first. Constable Taft is able to vouch for Janet, the barmaid, during the material time; she never left the bar, not even to powder her nose. That Taft, by the way, is a pretty smart chap . . . Well, then there's Lucille Everard, the waitress. She was in and out of the dining-room and the kitchen. I suppose she could have nipped upstairs and done the dirty deed — at Laval's bidding, or with his knowledge. But it'd have been taking a big risk, handlin' turpentine while she was fussin' around our table.

'That brings us to Laval,' he went on more seriously. 'Laval could have done it during dinner. But if he did he must have changed out of his chef's clothes when he left the kitchen, and back into them when he got back there. Otherwise we'd have found turps on 'em, and not on his waistcoat. That's the snag in the ointment, Colonel — or whatever the sayin' is. Why did he waste time changing out of his chef's clothes when he knew darned well he wouldn't meet a soul — Henry and me bein' the sole survivin' guests — on his way to and from my room? I know he had to cross the head of the main staircase, but he'd have peeked down to make sure the hall was empty, in any case, before nipping across that bit of no man's land.'

Fielding smiled faintly.

'Staying up late, and telling horrific tales, seems good for your temper, Super. I believe you're enjoying this.'

'I'm beginnin' to,' the Super replied naively. 'But about Laval. The odds are he did the defacin' during dinner, or his murderer did it during dinner or just afterwards. It's possible the murderer did it, had to hide in that washroom to avoid me and my companions when we went upstairs, and was surprised by Laval there a minute afterwards. Or it's possible he was in the washroom for another reason when Laval found him there. His motive, then, would seem to be that he had to silence Laval because he had seen him on the premises.' He shook his head. 'Too many snags in that for my liking, Colonel.'

'I'm with you there,' Fielding agreed.

'One argument washes it out almost completely as sense,' the Super proceeded. 'How could the murderer — who couldn't afford to be seen by Laval in that hotel — have known about that portrait in my room?

'No, sir. On the present evidence, I vote for Laval. He had a date with his murderer in that washroom. He followed us upstairs and walked straight into it.'

'Yes, I'm with you there, too,' Fielding stated emphatically. 'But why did the murderer leave the door open and the lights on?'

'The obvious answer to that, sir, is that he heard Valentine coming along the corridor from my room and bolted.' He frowned as though a little cloud was crossing his mind. 'Yes, I suppose he could have heard the major, in spite of the carpet in that corridor. A lot of floor boards creak there; Major Valentine takes big strides and he was in a hurry. But the murderer might have heard something from somewhere quite different.'

Fielding nodded.

'Motive?'

The Super shook his head.

'I'd like to think the murderer was my mystery man, 'X', but doin' that would be practically a criminal offence at this juncture.'

'Would it? Remembering that 'X' was desperately anxious to conceal the identity of Robert Charlton; and if he knew Laval had seen that portrait?'

The Super grinned.

'Late hours ain't good for you, sir,' he admonished him. 'Laval had already seen the original of Robert Charlton twice at least.'

'Yes, damn it, I'm getting wool in my brain box.' He passed his hand over his eyes again. 'Well, let me see, you spoke of finding a card in Laval's wallet.'

The Super produced it from his own, and read the writing on the back: *Kenton* 6148. *J. after* 10. He went on: 'That telephone number used to belong to a club in Soho I've particular reasons for rememberin'. The Peacock Club. It's one of those borderline clubs the police find it profitable to have in existence. It's the haunt of all sorts of people, includin' crooks and coppers' narks. This memo is in Laval's handwriting; I've checked up on that. It's clearly a reminder that a chap whose name begins with 'J' can be reached at the club — if the number still holds good, of course — after ten o'clock at night.'

He held out the card to the chief constable.

'I'd like you to put the Yard on to this, sir. Have a man at the club tonight in time to see who comes in about ten o'clock. I want to interview this chap 'J'.'

The chief constable nodded as he took the card.

'We might be able to induce him to come to you,' he said. 'You're needed here badly right now, Super.' He went on when he had stowed the card away in his wallet: 'A pity about that oil portrait. I suppose it's completely worthless now?'

The Super chuckled.

'I anticipated somethin' might 'appen to it, Colonel; so I went up to my room before dinner to take six photographs of it. I gave the spool to your photographer, so we should have some nice enlargements here by breakfast time.'

Fielding laughed warmly.

'Do you *ever* make mistakes, Greene?'

'I've probably made half a dozen talking to you in this room, sir. The trouble with us chaps is when we try to justify our mistakes. I'm always *looking* for mine. I look on mistakes as opportunities. The more of 'em you spot the more you're gettin' ahead.'

'A fine philosophy, Super, if rather involved. I shall have to pass it on to

Inspector Griffiths and the good Evans. If they'd been less sure of themselves in their estimations of certain people here ... However ... ' He seemed to be clearing up loose ends in his mind. 'Look here, haven't you any notion who and what this chap 'X' is, in relation to Charlton and the Price woman? I mean, *why* were they hiding from him? Why was Nadine Price, anyway, in mortal terror of him as you seem to suggest she was?'

The Super shrugged.

'Your guess is as good as mine at this stage of our journey, Colonel. As I said before, there are different ways of hidin' out; and the one clue we've got to the relationship between 'X' and Charlton and Nadine P. is the *way* they hid themselves out, so to speak, in these two adjoining villages. Charlton never went near Nadine in public; and she swam the river late at night whenever she wanted to visit him. Also, she worked hard, as you say, to advertise herself as a gold-digger and worse, maybe, while making sure nobody got a picture of 'er. What all that adds up to is beyond me at the moment.'

268

'Then it's no use *me* puzzling my brains about it,' Fielding retorted. 'Is there anything else you want done?'

The Super produced Laval's wrist watch and handed it over. 'I'd like to know where Laval got this from, and the one he gave to Nadine Price. It's a long time ago, but MI5 could probably put you in touch with someone who knew Laval in the Free French organization over here in the war; in Laval's particular branch of it. Laval; wrist watches; cyanide. Do you get me, Colonel?'

'Yes.' Fielding pocketed the watch, and consulted his own. 'Well, it's getting on for two o'clock. I'll stretch out here and take a nap after telephoning my missus. You'd better find yourself a bed, Super. It ought to be light enough for my men to start work on that grave at six o'clock. Time enough to send for an ambulance and a surgeon when we find out if there's anything for them to deal with. If there is, on top of the murder of Gabriel Laval,' he ended gravely, 'we're going to need all those six additional officers, Greene.'

'Have your nap and forget it for a

269

bit, sir,' the Super advised, rising to his feet. 'I'm just going to take a look at Henry, and then I won't be here either. Goodnight, sir.'

''*Night*!' Fielding laughed. He picked up the telephone as the door closed.

16

In the bleak, unfriendly half-light in Colwin Woods at six o'clock that morning, two stalwart constables, stripped to their shirts and equipped with spades borrowed from the Riverside Hotel, began the work of emptying the grave of its still unsettled earth.

Four men watched them: Inspector Griffiths — a tall, dark-complexioned, clean-shaven man in his late thirties; Colonel Fielding, looking more haggard and apprehensive then ever in the half-light that was more cruelly revealing than any sunshine; Sergeant Evans who, through lack of sleep, looked like a toper with a hangover; and ex-Superintendent Greene who, despite his grim expression, looked as fresh as a daisy.

At four points of vantage on the edge of the woods, police sentries had been posted to keep inquisitive villagers away; while Constable Taft, in charge of this defensive force, roamed the woods with a roving commission.

The work on the grave proceeded in a silence broken only by the laboured breathing of the diggers, the impact of steel spades on earth and an occasional stone, and the melodious, mocking, persistent singing of a bird high up on a nearby tree.

Colonel Fielding's breathing became audible, too, and contributed to this uncanny cacophony of sound when the constables were clearly nearing the end of their task.

'You know, Super,' the chief constable confided, 'I could never understand why the digger dug so deep a grave.'

'Can't you, sir?' the Super replied in a voice hardly louder than a whisper — for he, too, was sensitive to the atmosphere around the deepening grave, and the victim of a tensing excitement, despite a long and hardening experience. 'I can think of two good reasons. Which is the right one depends on who dug the grave and why.'

Fielding shot him a startled, searching look.

'*Who* dug the grave? But I thought — '

An exclamation from one of the constables silenced him, and brought himself, Tubby Greene, and the two police officers closer to the edge of the grave.

It took the two constables ten minutes of careful work to uncover a piece of sacking and whatever was beneath it. Then the Super ordered them out of the grave, and climbed down into it to gently remove the sacking.

A shuddering sigh accompanied the horrible revelation of two bodies stretched out together in the bottom of the grave, a coil of rope between them.

One of the bodies was wearing the clothes of a woman; the other was in male attire. The bloated, rotting faces meant little to the Super.

A question burning in his mind made him brace himself and bend over the hideous display of death, and pull gently back the left arm of the woman's jacket. There was nothing there but decay.

He tried the right arm — and found it. A gold watch with a wide, expanding bracelet made up of little golden cylinders. The dead spit of Laval's watch . . .

He did not examine it more closely, but climbed out of the grave and looked across at Colonel Fielding.

Five minutes after that the Super, Colonel Fielding and Inspector Griffiths were walking along the riverside path towards the bridge, on their way back to the hotel. They could see silent, apparently motionless little groups of staring people on the bridge, the promenade across the river, and the zig-zagging street leading up to the village beyond the church.

Inspector Griffiths was a desperately agitated man. He saw himself as directly responsible for a colossal blunder; and the fact itself seemed to worry him more than possible consequences to himself.

'It's like a nightmare, sir,' he said to ex-Superintendent Greene, in a voice shrill with emotional appeal. 'Old Joe Early, the gardener at The Retreat, filled in that grave. He reported to Sergeant Evans by telephone immediately afterwards. It

274

seems impossible that the murderer can have returned after that, and emptied and re-filled a grave as deep as that, without . . . Dash it, sir, it was taking fantastic risks.'

The Super and Fielding exchanged a look as the worried inspector went on:

'Besides, where could the bodies have been hidden in the interim? I'm willing to stake my reputation on the fact that every inch of ground, every building for miles around was thoroughly searched, and — '

'The bodies were put in the bottom of that grave, Inspector,' the Super enlightened him, 'during the night before the morning on which Joe Early filled it in. All the murderer had to do was to make a false bottom to the grave, to deceive Joe Early. It was a diabolically clever move on the murderer's part, too. Don't you see, son, that that grave was the one safe spot in the country to hide them bodies in?'

'By God, yes!' the stunned Griffiths exclaimed. 'But where did he hide the bodies during the time we were searching for them? We left absolutely nothing to chance. We even went over The Retreat, which Joe Early was getting ready for Major Valentine. I'm ready to swear — '

The Super laughed ironically.

'Son, you need your breakfast,' he said. 'Did your search extend as far as Glasgow or Land's End?'

The inspector exclaimed again:

'You mean — ?'

'I mean I want my breakfast, too,' the Super answered testily. His own nerves were on edge at the moment, and a sympathetic glance from the chief constable warned the inspector to silence.

'Joe Early is short-sighted into the bargain, too,' the Super growled, half to himself, as the trio began to cross the bridge.

They ran the gauntlet of the staring groups of people between the bridge and the hotel grounds. But they were no longer silent people; they were chattering like magpies — for uncannily, like a swift, invisible messenger, the news of the finding of the bodies had escaped the woods and sped from group to group.

'Breakfast, and a big 'un,' the Super grunted, as they climbed the steps at the front of the hotel. 'What about you, Colonel?'

'I'll eat with you, of course,' Fielding replied.

Henry Baxter, looking very old because he was very tired, was awaiting them in the hall. The Super stopped to speak to him.

'The women,' Henry reported, 'didn't budge from their rooms until they went on duty a few minutes ago. I don't think they're even on speaking terms.'

The Super nodded approvingly.

'All to the good, son. Come and have breakfast and then find your bed. Sleepin' on the floor with one eye open is worse'n not sleepin' at all.'

'I'm all right, sir,' Henry replied determinedly. He knew where the Super had been and why. 'Did you find — ?'

'We did, son. The pair of them. Plus evidence provin' that Willie Oaker didn't have no nightmare that night.'

Fielding, Henry and the Super were

settling themselves at a table in the dining-room when Major Valentine came in. He had just arrived, and was looking far from his best.

'Good morning, gentlemen.' He stopped at their table and searched their faces anxiously. 'I saw what was happening in those woods from the river path, and learned from a constable what you found in that grave.' He looked suddenly sick, and the Super remembered sympathetically that he *was* a sick man. 'What's the meaning of it all, Super?' he appealed. 'How did you — ?'

'It's a long story, Major. Better get your breakfast too, as soon as you can. I'll be needin' your help again before long.'

John, the porter, came in to hand the major a morning newspaper. Valentine took it, distractedly, and went off to his corner table.

Lucille Everard came in and went to Valentine's table. She looked pale, defiant, and coarsely ugly under a hurried and indifferent make-up.

'It will have to be eggs and bacon,

Major Valentine,' she told him in a loud voice. 'In the circumstances you are fortunate to 'ave that.'

She glanced at the other occupied table as she spoke, and went back to the kitchen.

'I suppose,' Major Valentine remarked bitterly over his paper, 'we shall be invaded by the reporters again in a few hours. I'm damned sorry for the people of these two villages, Super.'

'So,' Fielding said warmly, as though grateful for the opportunity, 'am I. But not half as sorry as I am for my men. By the way, Super, I sent Inspector Griffiths home for his breakfast. Got to consider our wives as far as we can. He'll be right back. Evans will have to have something when he gets here with the ambulance.'

John, the porter, looked in through the doorway.

'A messenger for Mr. Greene,' he announced. 'Says his orders is to speak to him privately.'

The Super glanced significantly at the chief constable as he got up from his chair. He found a constable motor-cyclist awaiting him in the hall. The man saluted smartly and held out a bulky, sealed envelope which the Super grabbed with avidity.

He dismissed the man, beckoned Colonel Fielding from the dining-room, and went into Laval's private office where Fielding joined him. The latter found the Super opening his package.

'Shut the door, Colonel,' the Super said urgently. 'This is top secret.'

He pulled six photographs out of the envelope. They were all excellent reproductions of the oil portrait of Robert Charlton, three inches square.

'Your man's an expert, Colonel,' the Super said warmly, and handed two of them across the desk. 'One of those 'as got to fly to Cumberland faster than the speed of sound. One must get to Scotland Yard even quicker.' He thrust the remaining four into his wallet. 'It will be something if they find somebody in Cumberland who can identify Charlton as Stanley Weaver, the Radford estate manager who was sacked in 1938 or '39 because Evelyn Radford was sweet on him — allegedly. It will be better still if someone can tell us a bit more about Weaver's personality and background, and his relations with Evelyn Radford and his employer up there. But it ain't no good hopin' too much from that end. What matters is what happened to the feller between the time he left Cumberland and turned up here as Robert Charlton.'

The chief constable frowned bewilderment.

'Then why all this top secret? Surely the quickest way of finding out that is to publish this picture in every national newspaper, and — '

The Super shook his head aggressively.

'I'm ashamed of you for suggestin' such a thing, Colonel,' he rebuked him. 'It'd be like sending your enemy a gratuitous warning of an impending attack. We'd better get back to our breakfast,' he went on, rising. 'We got a lot to do.'

Lucille Everard was serving their table when they returned to the dining-room. She gave the Super a furtive glance as he resumed his chair; he glared at her in return.

'Soon after breakfast,' he barked at her, 'I shall want to see you and the barmaid in the private office.'

The Frenchwoman was so taken aback by his tone and manner that she almost dropped the tray in her hands. Then, pulling herself together, she tossed her head and walked away.

The Super caught Valentine's questioning gaze as the service door closed behind the waitress. He grinned at him.

'I'd like you to sit in with me at the inquisition, Major,' he said, 'to see fair play. Then,' he went on darkly, 'we're going to see if we can find out anything more about that French sailor tramp you mentioned yesterday.'

Thoroughly enjoying the confusion of thought around him, he picked up his knife and fork and tackled his food with relish.

17

The Super was the first to finish his breakfast. He nodded to Henry Baxter as he pushed back his chair.

'Take your time, son. Come to the office in ten minutes.'

When Henry joined him there he found him in the throes of a telephone conversation. The Super broke off to speak to him. 'Tell the major I'm ready for him, son. Then find the ladies and bring 'em as soon as they're ready.'

Major Valentine found the Super finishing off the same telephone conversation. 'No, there's no necessity for a written confirmation.' He waved the major to an armchair in a corner. 'It was just routine. Thanks very much.' He replaced the telephone and looked sternly across at his companion. 'I have just been checking up on your Scottish call last night,' he said, severely.

Valentine looked startled, then mildly

incredulous as the Super burst out laughing.

'Don't worry, Major,' he reassured him. 'You're in the clear. We can't afford to overlook anything in an investigation like this.'

Valentine heaved a sigh of relief and laughed in turn.

'You have a habit of startling people, Super,' he protested half-resentfully. 'As a matter of fact, I've been uncomfortably aware of the fact that I'm one of the few people you must have shown that oil painting to, if not the only one.'

'You're absolutely in the clear,' the Super repeated emphatically. 'You're about the only one in this place who is, worse luck. Tell me, did Laval seem like his normal self when he took you to this telephone last night? Did he give any reason for waiting in the reception office while you were in here?'

'As a matter of fact,' Valentine said after a moment, 'he did seem a bit on edge. He told me he was waiting for a call himself, and I imagined that was why he hung on. He divested himself of his chef's uniform while he waited, I remember — '

'I noticed that,' the Super nodded. 'Come in, Henry. The ladies are ready and waiting, are they. All right, show them in.'

Lucille Everard and Janet, the barmaid, came slowly into the room. The Super pointed to the lounge on the left of the fire. The Frenchwoman moved to it and sat down, stiffly. The barmaid followed her, unwillingly, and sat down with a yard of space between them.

'Shut the door, Henry. Stay this side of it, will you.'

In a strained silence the three men appraised the two women. The latter made a startlingly contrasting pair. Lucille Everard was no longer defiant; she was as cold as steel, ready for anything, and, apparently, completely unafraid. Janet, on the other hand, was petrified. She looked a wild thing, newly-trapped, paralysed with terror. It was equally obvious too, that the two women were separated by a gap much greater than the visible space between them.

The Super opened the drawer in front of him, took out the bottle of turpentine, the red rubber gloves, and the stained hand towel, and laid them on the desk. 'These things mean anything to either of you?' he demanded, abruptly.

Janet merely stared at the articles. Lucille Everard pointed, after a brief hesitation that might have meant anything, at the rubber gloves.

'I use a pair like those in the washplace in the kitchen some time before dinner las' night,' she stated. 'They are not there this morning when I want them before breakfast. John, the porter, said he did not see them either when he wash up there first thing today.'

The Super looked hard at Janet, who found it painfully difficult to speak at all.

'I never touch anything in the kitchen,' she said in a small voice. 'I have a pair like that in the bar . . . still there.'

Janet was obviously terrified of the woman at her side, apart from anything else. Aware of this, the Super returned the three articles to the drawer, and said:

'Very well. Perhaps you'll wait outside, Janet, or get on with your work in the bar.'

The girl's relief was pathetic. She almost ran from the room. As the door closed the Super turned to the Frenchwoman.

'Now, mam'selle. The sooner you can satisfy us as to yourself and your movements last night, the sooner you can get away from this hotel and back where you came from.'

The Frenchwoman laughed shortly.

'That,' she said, 'is what I want to do. I'm nothing to do with that girl. I first meet Gabriel Laval when he come to England early in the war, and I work as a waitress in a West End café. He take a flat in Soho, a little place, and I keep house for him there. He had many friends, many activities, none of them my business — '

'Were you also his mistress?' the Super asked bluntly.

She did not turn a hair.

'Laval,' she said, 'had many women. He paid me well to keep house and

mind my own business. I do just that
. . . and sleep with him once or twice if
he want.'

'How long did this go on?'

She shrugged.

'Laval marry just after the war and
have another place. But I still keep the
little flat for when he wants it. He gave
it up when he came to this 'otel. Then
he set me up, with my sister, in a small
café, and I do not see him much again.
Until,' and her eyes narrowed perceptibly
as she hesitated, 'the trouble here about
eight weeks ago. The staff leave. Laval
want someone he can trust, so he send
for me . . . and here I am.'

'I see. You came here when Nadine
Price disappeared. What did Laval tell
you about her?'

'Nothing at all.' She was lying; the
Super knew it and she knew that he
knew it; but the unflinching look in her
eyes was plain indication that she was
not going to give away a thing more
than was necessary to her own interests.
'It was not my business. I did not want
to know anything. I was well paid to work

here to help him over his difficulty, and that was all.'

'Nadine Price, nevertheless,' the Super persisted, 'was intimately connected with Laval during the war. You must have seen her in his company then?'

She shrugged again.

'I do not know the name. How can I tell, either, when I never saw the girl who worked for him here?'

'What about Janet? She came here to see Laval through his troubles, too.'

'You must ask Janet,' she replied coolly. 'I told you Laval had many women.'

The Super leaned forward on his elbow and fixed her with a truculent glare.

'So you know nothing about Janet either, eh?'

'Nothing, monsieur, except that she came from London and I think Laval send for her.'

'The night before last,' he went on, 'you accompanied Laval to Janet's bedroom. Violence was done to her there. I heard her scream. How, mam'selle, do you account for your participation in that incident?'

She was taken aback, but not shaken. There was even a smile of amusement around her sensual mouth as she answered:

'Your coming here, monsieur, upset Laval. He was afraid that Janet might make things more difficult for him. He ask me to come with him to her room while he talk to her. He slapped her, that's all.'

'And you still don't know what Laval was talking to her about?'

'No, except he threaten her what might happen if she run away or lose her 'ead. Why do you not ask the girl yourself?'

'I will,' the Super promised. 'Presently. You told us you did most of the preparing for dinner last night — remember? What was Laval doing during that time?'

'Other things elsewhere. I don' know what. I do not ask.'

'Laval came into the kitchen in time to take over the dishing up, as chef?'

'Yes.'

'Was he in the kitchen during the whole time Major Valentine and I were at dinner?'

She hesitated again; then she shook her head slowly and with an odd deliberation.

'No. He was not there when I went back after serving the main course. I saw him once again, when I had put on my coat and hat and was leaving the hotel by the front entrance. He was in the reception office.'

'So Laval was absent from the kitchen when you returned there after serving the main course. Had he left his chef's clothes behind him?'

She gave him a long, searching stare, obviously wondering what was behind the question. She decided, as obviously, to dodge it.

'I am busy,' she said. 'I do not notice small things like that.'

'Busy?' he barked at her. 'Doing what?'

She smiled at him with her lips.

'There are always many things to do in a kitchen during dinner, particularly when there are only two of you.'

'But you must have wondered why Laval had gone off like that when there was still part of the dinner to be served?'

'No, m'sieur. One did not wonder

what Gabriel Laval was doing, if one was wise.'

'Well, you must have left the building — you were careful to tell us you went by the front entrance — when Major Valentine was using the telephone in this office?'

She glanced at Valentine and hesitated.

'I heard the telephone ring, I did not know who — '

'You didn't go to your room before leaving the hotel? Not even to powder your nose?'

'No. I make myself ready in the kitchen. I had no man to meet. It was fresh air I wanted.'

'John, the porter, was having his supper there when you left, was he?'

Her eyes mocked him as she shook her head.

'John, the porter, had not come in for his supper when I left, m'sieur.'

'Where did you go while you were out of the hotel?'

'A long walk, m'sieur,' she answered stonily, 'along the path beyond the bridge, this side of the river. I have a torch and am quite content with myself. I sit on a stile, and then I return.'

'You met no one you recognized during the walk, mam'selle?'

She shook her head.

'Did Laval say anything to you about expecting a caller or a telephone call that evening?'

'No, m'sieur. In fac' Laval has no personal callers to my knowledge all the time I am here.'

'You saw no stranger in the establishment that afternoon or evening?'

'No, m'sieur. I don' know about the bar, but — '

'Thank you. I suppose you have work to do in the dining-room and the kitchen, mam'selle. We shall know where to find you when we want you again.'

She got up and walked to the door and opened it. The Super sent Henry to fetch the barmaid and turned to Valentine.

'A nice mess I made of that bit of questionin',' he growled. 'What did you make of her, Major?'

Valentine looked puzzled and vaguely worried.

293

'Frankly,' he said, 'I believed her to a large extent. She was well paid to serve Laval and mind her own business. She'll say nothing more than she has to for her own safety. She always struck me as indifferent to Laval as a man, though on one occasion — he'd been drinking — I did see her in his arms. What baffles me and disturbs me, Super, is the girl Janet. She seemed slavishly in love with Laval, and rather scared of him, but otherwise as hard as nails. Until . . . yes, until you arrived on the scene. But that, as I recall it now, was nothing more than the jitters. Now, when Laval is dead, and you'd think she had nothing to be scared of in that direction, she's *petrified*.'

The Super nodded.

'Maybe she knows too much for Laval's murderer's comfort, Major.'

'Good God, I hadn't thought of that. But why should Laval have brought her down here, at the time he did, if he couldn't trust her in the way he could trust Lucille Everard?'

'Well,' the Super hazarded, 'he may have wanted her under his eye because she knew too much about himself and Nadine Price.' He went on after a moment, 'What did you make of the relationship between those two women?'

'There wasn't any relationship, to my knowledge, except that I imagined Janet was jealous. Lucille seemed completely indifferent to her.'

The Super shifted impatiently in his chair and glanced at the door. He was wondering why Henry was taking so long in bringing the barmaid. Valentine changed the subject:

'You mentioned making further inquiries about this French tramp I spoke to you about at dinner last night, Super. Have you turned up anything fresh in that direction?'

The Super cogitated for a moment and answered cautiously:

'No, but you said you'd heard he'd been hanging around the district. And I'm looking for a murderer who was most likely doing just that.'

Valentine jerked in his chair and stared at him.

'Then you believe an outsider was

responsible for what happened to Nadine Price and Robert Charlton? And to Laval last night?'

'An outsider,' the Super qualified, 'who did a lot of clandestine reconnaissance work in the district before he struck, Major.'

Valentine looked stunned.

'Then all this suspicion among the local people — ?'

'It's just possible,' the Super replied darkly, 'that some of the locals dug that grave.'

'Then how in the name of reason — ?'

The Super pushed himself out of his chair. He was worried.

'Where the devil is that barmaid?' he demanded. 'Henry's had time enough to — '

The door of the office was burst open as he spoke, and Henry came in. He was painfully out of breath, and there was a look of horror on his pale, twisted face.

'I found her in her room, Super,' he got out with difficulty. 'I . . . I think she's dead.'

18

The Super swore savagely, pushed Henry out of the way and dashed for the main staircase. He cursed himself bitterly, as he took the stairs two at a time, for having allowed himself to be deceived by the barmaid's hard-boiled Cockney facade, and insufficiently impressed by her almost speechless terror half an hour ago. Then, his portly frame literally heaving with breathlessness, he found himself standing by a narrow bed in a small, plainly-furnished room, staring down defeatedly at the tragic figure of the girl.

She was lying on her back. Her eyes and her mouth were open, as though she had been struggling for air when death had transfixed her. There was an expression of dumb, pathetic appeal in her hazel eyes that the Super told himself he would remember to his dying day — probably *on* his dying day.

Henry Baxter and Major Valentine found him bending over the body, peering into the small mouth he had prised further open with his fingers. His face was dark with rage and frustration when he straightened up and glared at them.

'Cyanide,' he rasped. 'She must have got it from that watch bracelet of Laval's. Bits of the capsule are still in her mouth. Major Valentine, will you find the police surgeon and tell 'im 'e's wanted 'ere? This won't take him long. Henry,' he went on harshly, 'send that Everard woman to me, and don't tell 'er what's happened to this poor girl.'

Left alone, he looked around him again, contrasting his present surroundings with the room Nadine Price had occupied when she had worked here as barmaid . . . and what else besides.

It was a painfully tidy room. There was a cheap wicker chair between the dressing-table and the chest-of-drawers. On top of the latter was a neat row of novelettes and magazines, and a box of cigarettes. The top of the dressing-table was crowded with cheap toilet articles, and cheap cosmetics in their gaudy containers.

The Super returned his gaze to the body, to the outflung right arm and the small hand overhanging the side of the bed; and then he reached down and picked up an oval of pasteboard lying on the floor, directly under the hand and half-hidden by the covering of the bed.

It was a snapshot, small enough to go in a locket; the picture of a baby's face. A chubby, serious face; and there was something about the wee mouth and the big, dark eyes that reminded him of Gabriel Laval. He was still fascinated by the picture cupped in his podgy left hand when a voice as calm and cool as a mountain lake addressed him from the doorway:

'You sent for me, m'sieur.'

The Super started more in angry dismay than surprise. He glared at the bleak-eyed Frenchwoman, cursing himself because he had allowed her to steal a march on him. She had caught him unprepared, when he had intended it to be the other way round. She had already seen the still figure on the bed; she was ready for him again.

Nevertheless, he tried — perhaps because she was a woman. He beckoned her to the bed, and nodded at the pathetic, pallid face on the pillow.

'She must have come straight here,' he said harshly, 'when I let her out of that office, and lay down on this bed and done herself in. A capsule of cyanide it was.' He watched her bent head with fiercely observing eyes. 'She must have got it from Laval.' He saw her painted mouth quiver for a second, as she stared down at the lifeless face; it was a barely-perceptible movement, but he took a chance on it and appealed to her: 'Don't this move you to want to say anything? Who's going to look after *this* now, I wonder?'

He thrust in front of her his left hand, cupping the baby picture.

Her mouth trembled slightly — he was sure of it this time — as she gazed at the tiny photograph. He waited, hating the ludicrous appeal he had made, hating himself and her. But he saw, though he could never have said exactly why, that he had reached her, moved her. It was as though he could feel her mind searching for something she could safely give him in return — because of that dead girl, because of that baby, because she herself was a woman after all . . .

She turned herself slowly until she was facing him, her body between him and the dead. Her dark eyes seemed almost human as they looked into his own.

'You are a clever man, Superintendent,' she said softly. 'You find Nadine Price. Then perhaps you find all you want to know about this poor child an' 'er baby. Other things too. I don't know.'

The Super's jaw tightened; that was his only betrayal of surprise. Then he realized how unlikely it was that this morning's grim news *could* have reached her yet.

'We found Nadine Price soon after dawn,' he told her abruptly. 'In that grave in the woods. Eight weeks dead.'

Lucille Everard was more than surprised; she was staggered.

'Dead!' she cried. 'But that is impossible.

Laval was looking for her everywhere. He was frantically worried because — '

She checked herself. He let her have it again.

'We found them both. Nadine and Robert Charlton. There was a false bottom to that grave when it was filled in. It was a damned clever bit of work, mam'selle.'

He saw through her eyes the agony of rage, bewilderment and threatened panic in her brain. He hoped it would break out somewhere before she regained complete control of herself; and it did.

'Then Laval murdered them!' she hissed, her eyes blazing black. 'He must have sent for this Janet to murder 'er too! But . . . las' night . . . I do not understand . . . Who . . . ?'

She froze into herself again. The dark eyes died. She shook her head slowly.

'I do *not* understand . . . anything,' she said convincingly. 'I have spoken too much already.'

It was the moment for playing a card the Super had withheld deliberately.

'Mam'selle,' he said, 'you told me you

encountered no one on your walk by the river last night. Did anyone see you leave this hotel by the front entrance?'

'No,' she said, 'I don't remember — '

'That's a pity,' he retorted, 'because it means you still need an alibi for the time when Laval was murdered.'

She laughed unsteadily, in sudden alarm.

'That is ridiculous,' she cried impulsively. 'I remember now Janet saw me leave. I waved to her from — '

She broke off, catching her breath as she remembered the girl on the bed. The Super grunted, disgustedly.

'So you see,' he went on, 'you could have gone from the kitchen to that washroom by those back stairs knowing Laval would join you there; you could even have beckoned to him from the landing to join you; it would have taken you but a moment to have used that dagger, slipped out of the building through the door I found unlocked at the foot of them back stairs, and then have gone for your walk — '

'*Imbécile!*' she spat at him. 'Why

should I murder Laval?'

They heard voices from the direction of the stairs. He waved her away.

'Think over the advice I gave you in the office just now, mam'selle,' was his parting shot.

Henry Baxter was standing in the corridor. 'It's Major Valentine with the police surgeon, sir,' he warned the Super.

A moment later a dapper little man with a black beard presented himself in the doorway. He was the surgeon who had collected the body of Laval.

'Well, Mr. Greene,' he began with the breezy air of the hardened forensic specialist, 'you seem to be establishing a record.' He made a move towards the bed but the Super stopped him with a gesture.

'Before you tackle this, Dr. Powell, have you anything definite from across the water?'

The doctor shrugged.

'I have emptied the grave, and sent the ambulance to the mortuary. Tentatively, I should say the deaths occurred about the time the victims disappeared. It may be impossible to do better than that. Tentatively, too, I would say it was strangulation in both cases.'

'There's no doubt, I suppose, of their identity?'

'Sergeant Evans says not. But there is one curious thing. The man's pockets are empty; even a signet ring, I think, had been taken from his left hand. Nor is there anything to the woman but her clothes and a rather substantial gold bracelet watch for a woman to be wearing — '

The Super stepped aside.

'Thanks, Doctor.' He nodded at the bed. 'I think you'll find this poor girl swallowed a capsule of cyanide. Only she knew what she was doin'. Miss Radford didn't.'

He ignored the doctor's exclamation of astonishment as he passed into the corridor. He ordered Henry Baxter to lock the door and bring him the key when the surgeon was through with the body; then, beckoning Major Valentine to follow him, he strode away towards the stairs.

He reached the hall as Inspector Griffiths came in through the front door. The latter explained he had just returned from his breakfast and asked for his chief.

'Colonel Fielding should be back at his office by now,' the Super told him. 'The surgeon is taking a look at another corpse on the top floor. Janet, the barmaid. Perhaps you'll telephone for another ambulance, and pass on the news to the colonel.'

He left the startled inspector and walked out on to the front steps where Valentine joined him. Together they stared in the direction of the drive gates, where a constable was vainly trying to disperse a crowd of excited people. The promenade was like a fairground, too; and the bridge was lined with people staring across at the hotel like spectators at a football match.

The Super swore softly under his breath.

'Prisoners, Major, that's what we are,' he growled. He saw Constable Taft striding towards them up the drive, and waited for him. 'Constable,' he ordered, 'I want you to get Hughie Grant, the landlord of the Welsh Harp, up here as soon as you can. Don't bring him; send him. Then find Mike Amber and Willie Oaker, and do the same with them. Hello, here's Sergeant Evans, too. Off you go, Taft.'

Sergeant Evans was carrying a large brown paper parcel under an arm. He saluted the Super and offered him his parcel.

'The sacking, Superintendent, and the coil of rope,' he reported. 'I've seen the ambulance away and left a man on duty at the grave.'

The Super nodded approvingly. He opened his wallet, produced the envelope containing the pieces of fibre he had taken from the tree in Colwin Woods, and thrust it into the officer's hand.

'This is a bit more of that sacking, I hope,' he explained. 'Get it off to the chief constable's office as quick as you can. I'll have a word with him as to what I want done.'

He re-entered the hotel and met Dr.

Powell coming down the stairs with Henry in his wake.

'You were right, Superintendent,' the doctor said brusquely. 'Bits of the container still in the mouth. No signs of violence. The sooner you send her along to the mortuary the better. I've got my work cut out there.' He laid an urgent hand hand on the Super's arm. 'Where *is* this damned cyanide coming from?'

The Super shook his head, beckoned Henry and started to climb the stairs, jingling in his trouser pocket Laval's ring of keys.

19

On the first-floor landing the Super turned into the corridor opposite his own. He stopped at the door of Room 34. John, the porter, had given him the number of his late employer's room the previous night.

'You know, Henry,' he said extravagantly as he searched for a key on Laval's ring, 'you can often learn more about a man from his bedroom than from reading 'is autobiography. That is, of course, if 'e doesn't share it with a woman.'

He opened the door and led the way into the large, airy room. 'Yes,' he said, as Henry followed and closed the door behind him, 'this is exactly what I expected.'

Laval's bed-sitting-room was the last word in luxury and comfort and bad taste. It was a gaudy room, in which gilt clashed with chromium, oak with mahogany, modern furniture with antiques. Laval had bought the best of everything he had wanted, regardless; and the result was literally a showroom.

The silver-coloured divan bed in the middle of the room was, the Super muttered disgustedly, the biggest he'd ever seen or ever would. He said the same of the wardrobe and the massive desk standing in front of the middle of the three windows overlooking the summer house and the bend in the river that hid The Retreat from view.

Laval had even indulged himself to the extent of a cocktail bar in the corner of the room.

The Super discovered a wall safe hidden behind an oil painting heavily framed in gilt. It was not a combination affair, and he found the key to it on the ring. It was a small safe. Henry emptied the contents — wads of notes, packets of silver, batches of documents tied together with red tape, some loose letters and a brown leather-covered album — on to a nearby table, while the Super went through them. The batches of documents were exclusively concerned with the Riverside Hotel, its clientele and its fishing rights. The loose letters were an equally uninteresting collection — with one exception. This letter brought an exclamation of satisfaction from the Super as he opened it. It was written to Laval from Nadine Price, on the notepaper of a popular London hotel, and dated just over ten months earlier. The handwriting was an elegant scrawl, but there was something impressively fierce about it:

Gabriel darling!

How exciting it was to see your advertisement for a 'superior barmaid' in this morning's paper — just when little me was looking for a congenial situation in the country for a while — for reasons which are exclusively my own! Indeed, I could hardly believe my luck; though I knew, of course, you had a flourishing hotel somewhere in that part of England.

Darling, I've decided to take the job. (How exciting this news must be for you!) So you won't have to bother

311

*with other applicants; and we can
settle the salary, etc., when I arrive
on Thursday.*

*Needless to say, darling, I shouldn't
dream of causing you any embarrassment,
in relation to our wartime partnership
of which I retain certain interesting
souvenirs — always providing, of
course, that you make this impending
association as pleasant.*

Until Thursday, then,

Nadine Price.

P.S. — A room with a private bath,
of course . . . !

The Super grunted as he handed the
letter to Henry to read.

'Clever of Laval to have kept that
letter,' he remarked. 'He might have
found it useful in certain circumstances.
Wonder what he kept in this gilt-edged
album.' He picked it up, opened it and
turned the pages. 'Crikey, Henry, this
does look like a bit of luck for us.
It's a blinkin' picture gallery of Laval's
women. One per page, and forty pages if
there's one! No names to any of 'em, but

there's somethin' even more interesting than names. The blinkin' mormon has labelled each of 'em with a date; the date, apparently, when he took 'em on. The first one is 1930. The last one's dated last year — a darn' pretty brunette, but her face don't mean anything to me.' He turned the pages backwards slowly, muttering: 'I wonder which of these dames is Nadine Price. I wonder where . . . By golly, Henry, here's a couple of 'em together, and one is Janet!'

Henry moved eagerly closer to join the Super in studying an enlarged snapshot of two women in a well-kept garden. One was a strikingly beautiful blonde, lounging on a deck-chair; the other, a young girl in a maid's uniform, was undeniably Janet — as she must have been in her 'teens.

The Super said disgustedly: 'It wasn't so clever of Laval to have kept a thing like this to testify to his lurid past. But there's no accounting for vanity. 'Vanity, like murder, will out,' ' he quoted. 'That's Shakespeare.'

Henry dragged his fascinated gaze from

the snapshot to grin at his companion.

'Excuse me, sir,' he said, 'those words were written by a lady named Hannah Cowley, over a century ago.'

The Super glared at him.

'Hannah Cowley!' he exploded. 'You mean to tell me them inspirin' words came out of a dame with a name like *that*! You disappoint me, Henry.'

Then, triumphantly, he stabbed at the photograph with a forefinger.

'That woman in the chair,' he cried. 'I'll bet you a fiver that's Nadine Price! I got something out of that Everard woman just now, when I showed her the body of that girl — '

Henry remembered too, and cut in:

'You mean, when she told you to find Nadine Price if you wanted to find out more about Janet, sir?'

'Well,' the Super reflected, studying the picture again, 'that blonde looks glamorous enough for Nadine, don't she?'

Carefully, he detached the photograph from its page, folded it and put it away in his wallet. He continued to search backwards through the album, and presently came to another picture they both recognized on sight. It was a full-length photograph of Lucille Everard posed in the nude; a younger and slimmer Lucille, but as hard-faced as she was today. The date beneath it was '1940'.

'Leave the album where it is, son,' the Super ordered, 'and shove the rest of the stuff back in that safe. I'm going back to Janet's room now. Meantime, you can amuse yourself searching the rest of this room . . . '

A minute later, he unlocked the door of the barmaid's room and went inside. The still form on the bed was covered with a sheet. The Super shook his head as he began a methodical search of the place. He did not expect to find anything of interest; Laval would have seen to it that this girl from his past did not leave anything incriminating lying around in her room. He wondered, as he worked his way through the untidy drawers, how the girl had contrived to retain possession of that baby photograph without the Frenchman's knowledge.

Her handbag was on the dressing-table. He left it until last. And it was in the bag that he found the unopened letter, addressed in an illiterate scrawl to 'Mrs. Janet Chesterfield' at the Riverside Hotel, and carrying a London postmark and the previous day's date.

Obviously, the Super reflected as he produced his penknife to slit open the envelope, Janet had collected it from the reception office that morning, and had been too distracted, or too afraid, to open it at once.

The envelope contained a single sheet of cheap white notepaper on which had been written:

Thursday a.m.
When you comin back honey. The babys all right but the girl has give notis and you no i cant manedge on my own, besides the men doant like it. Youd better tell him the rents due anyway, and let me no quick about the baby,

Lots of love,
Alayne.

The Super scowled at the pathetic communication that told him much more than it put into words. He could visualize the small flat in a mean street in the West End of London which Janet and her baby had shared with 'Alayne'. He could imagine the anxiety of the good-natured 'Alayne' with a baby on her hands, when her living depended on the men she picked up on the streets and entertained at the flat. Men of that calibre didn't like to hear a baby crying when they were being entertained.

He moved to the bed and reverently uncovered the head and shoulders of the dead girl. He remembered the date he had seen under the snapshot of Janet and that glamorous blonde: 1941.

So, he reflected, she must have been no more than a child when Laval had seduced her. Laval had 'kept' her for fourteen years; and for fourteen years she had loved and feared him. Obviously, one of the Frenchman's reasons for concerning himself with her for so long had been the necessity for keeping her mouth shut. But for how long, the

Super wondered, had he been running her — for his profit or convenience — as a prostitute?

'Scared to death, girlie, that's what you were,' the Super muttered. 'But who of, I wonder: Laval's murderer or me?' He sighed as he replaced the sheet. 'Well, you don't have to worry about your baby, Janet. The Super'll see to that.'

He stowed the letter away in his wallet and stood with his hands pushed deep into his trouser pockets, scowling at the floor. He admitted bluntly to himself that he didn't like the way his case was developing; and that admission had nothing to do with sentiment or sensation, it merely related to an instinctive feeling — he had experienced the same thing many times before in his career — that he was losing his grasp of things, that the pattern he had made embracing all the known facts was in danger of falling apart.

He knew precisely where the trouble was. He was bothering himself continually and ineffectually with two questions: Who had murdered Laval and why. The more he considered them and worried over them, the more he felt that murder ought not to have happened, and did not belong to his case. It was an absurd theory on the face of it, yet it was fast becoming an obsession; and the next thing, if he didn't deal with it he would be making mistakes.

He dealt with it by refusing to deal with it. He stared at it, and picked it up like a baffling piece of a puzzle, and set it firmly aside. He told himself convincingly he would have nothing more to do with it until it forced its own way back into the puzzle and dropped into the only possible place for it.

Then, feeling his old, confident self again, he left the room with the intention of finding Inspector Griffiths downstairs. At the head of the main staircase, however, he stopped short in dismay. There was pandemonium in the hall below. Half a dozen men and two women were crowding the space in front of the reception counter, and, from behind it, a furious Lucille Everard was screaming at them that she didn't care a hang who or what they were; the hotel was closed; they couldn't have a room, or a meal, or even a drink; and if they didn't go away quickly she would fetch a gun and shoot them all dead.

Inspector Griffiths appeared on the scene as the Super watched, and firmly took charge of the situation.

'The lady is quite correct, gentlemen,' he told them, sternly. 'I shall have something to say about this to the constable who let you through the gate. The entire hotel is closed to the public, and that includes the Press.'

Suddenly a big man in a shabby raincoat thrust his way towards the inspector and demanded, truculently: 'Tubby Greene's staying here, isn't he? So my informant said, anyhow, when he 'phoned through the murder of this chap Laval. Well, you send for ex-Superintendent Greene and let me talk to him. He's a pal of mine, and — '

'That,' the Super roared indignantly from the landing, 'is a ruddy lie, Ted Graham. You may be a big noise on *The Trumpet*, but you're a pain in the neck to me — as I've told you more'n a dozen times already.' A burst of laughter from some of the other reporters did nothing to soothe him as he went on: 'If a fat-headed constable had no more sense than to let you on to the premises, your sense of decency ought to 'ave stopped you short of the sort of demonstration I saw just now. I'm speakin' with the authority of the chief constable of Levenshire when I tell you people you're on the scene of a crime, and order you out of it at the double.'

Ted Graham, undaunted, walked to the foot of the stairs and demanded: 'Tell us, anyway, Superintendent, what you're doing here right now. Damn it all, man, you can't expect us to believe it's sheer coincidence that you — '

'I'm writin' my memoirs,' the Super bawled down at him, 'and I'm not open to offers for the serial rights.'

Ted Graham laughed.

'That's a darned original lie, Super! All right, we'll clear out if you give us a statement first. We all came rushing down here to cover the murder of the proprietor of this hotel. What else has been happening here since then?'

The Super hesitated a moment and then he let them have it in no uncertain manner:

'For one thing, the barmaid here has committed suicide. For another, the police have just dug out of that grave in Colwin Woods the bodies of Nadine Price and Robert Charlton. Now go away and make what you can of that. Inspector Griffiths, I suggest you clear these people out and put an officer on duty at the drive gates who can't be bribed, bullied or otherwise bedevilled by the Press.'

He turned abruptly and made his way back to Laval's room, where he found Henry working his way through the Frenchman's wardrobe.

'I've never seen so many suits outside a shop, sir,' Henry told him. 'But Laval was a very orderly person; almost too much so for a man.' He closed the doors of the massive, antique piece of furniture, and turned away. 'I'm afraid I haven't found anything for you, Mr. Greene.'

'That wardrobe's a fine piece of

furniture,' the Super remarked. 'Looks like there's a hollow space at the top behind that strip of carving. Have you taken a peek, Henry?'

'No, sir. I noticed it, but surely it's the last place Laval would have put anything, when he had so much cupboard space — '

'Take a look, Henry. Never take chances.'

Henry pulled an occasional chair in front of the wardrobe, climbed on to it and took a look.

'No, sir,' he began, 'there doesn't seem . . . Holy smoke!' A moment later he climbed off the chair with two objects in his hands. One was a small square, flat brown-paper parcel; the other was a little pearl-handled revolver.

'Bring 'em over here.' The Super moved to the table on which lay Laval's album of women. 'Better put down that revolver while there's still a chance of findin' somebody else's fingerprint on it.' He took the brown-paper parcel and opened it. It contained a red leather-covered memorandum book which he opened in turn. He gasped and held his breath when he saw and read the handwriting on the first page:

A diary of
activities at Threeways,
Boxsted, Dorset,
By
Nadine 'Laval'
from September 1940
to . . . .

The Super motioned Henry away as the latter craned his neck to study their find more closely.

'Give me ten minutes with this,' he said harshly, feeling his way to a chair while he went on reading. 'Carry on with your search.'

Henry carried on, patiently and fruitlessly, glancing anxiously at the Super from time to time and wondering what was provoking the expression of angry disgust on his florid face. The Super only skimmed through the many pages filled with writing. He came to an end of this inspection abruptly, and called Henry back to his side.

'Recognize this handwriting, son? It's Nadine Price's,' he rasped, 'only she called herself Laval in them days. Well, here's the story behind this diary — for that's what it is. Laval was a frequent visitor to this country before the war; he was mixed up in the dope traffic. Soon after he escaped from France in 1940 he took this house Threeways, in the Dorset country, and installed Nadine there as his 'wife'. Laval spent part of his time in London, contacting men and women with money to burn — at a time when a lot of wealthy people of all ages were apt to go off the rails — and organizing week-end parties for Threeways. Those parties were orgies,' he went on bitterly. 'The sinister main purpose behind them was to induce new guests to try the excitement of drug-taking, and so make new dope victims, new customers for their vile trade. Laval was conducting these foul activities while, apparently, playing the hero in the Free French organization; and, according to Nadine, he was mixing his dope smuggling with his trips to and from France to contact the Resistance there.

'All this went on without a hitch, until July 1942; and believe me, even in them war days that wanted a bit of doing. The last entry in this diary concerns one of the usual week-end parties; and the next page in this book has been torn out. That means, of course, that a later entry has been removed.'

He shut the book and thrust it aside.

'There's not a shadow of doubt why Nadine kept the diary,' he summed up. 'It was partly for self-protection in case Laval tried to shop her; and partly in case she decided to try a spot of blackmail on him some time — as she did, of course, when she came here as barmaid.'

'So this diary,' Henry said, 'is one of the souvenirs she mentioned in her letter to Laval.' He frowned as he looked across at the wardrobe. 'That was a pretty casual place for him to leave such a damning document, Mr. Greene, after getting his hands on it.'

The Super snorted impatiently as he

took out a handkerchief and reached for the pearl-handled revolver.

'Use your loaf, Henry! The only person who could have put these two things up there was Nadine herself. She bought the diary with her in case she found it necessary to show it to Laval; and she bought the toy gun to protect herself and the diary. She hid 'em up there where they were handy, because it was the last place Laval was likely to find 'em.'

'But why, sir, did she leave the diary behind her when she cleared out? Why, for that matter, did she leave the revolver?'

The Super shrugged as he put down the revolver, and walked to one of the three long windows.

'She may have overlooked 'em in her panic to get to Charlton and away from 'X',' he hazarded. 'More likely, in my opinion, she thought it better to leave the diary behind her there, than to risk being caught by 'X' in possession of it.

'Well, Henry,' he said, turning from the window, 'we've had it so far as free movement is concerned. Half the population of these two villages seems to be out in the streets, and half the London Press have been trying to book rooms 'ere. So there's nothing else for it, son: I'm going to be a real-life armchair detective and conduct the investigations from this room from now on, with you and Major Valentine and that telephone over there to assist me. Maybe the atmosphere of this room will be a help too,' he added with a grimace. 'Anyway, anything is better than playin' 'ide-and-seek with that bunch of reporters in an isolated spot like this. I wouldn't even 'ave time to think straight.'

Henry stared at him incredulously.

'You really mean you're going to *live* in this room, sir, until you — ?'

'I'm going to live and work and sleep here,' the Super shouted recklessly, 'until I'm through with this case. And that means when the case is solved and the murderer — unless there should be more than one — is on 'is way to the dock.'

There was a knock on the door. The Super bawled, 'Come in!' and Major Valentine entered the room.

'So this is where you are,' he smiled. 'Inspector Griffiths asked me to find you and tell you that the three people you wanted to interview are downstairs in the hall.'

'Good.' The Super grunted. 'That's Hughie Grant, Mike Amber and Willie Oaker. I'll see Amber first. Bring him up and stay with us, will you, Major.'

He pulled out a packet of Players and planted himself in the leather-upholstered chair behind Laval's massive desk.

20

Mike Amber was in his working clothes when he strode into the room, looking grim but impressively self-confident. Major Valentine followed him, closed the door quietly and moved to an armchair in the corner beyond the wardrobe.

The Super was virtually a shadow against the window as he pointed the young woodman towards a chair Henry had placed in the middle of the room, facing him.

'Smoke if you want to, Amber,' he began cheerfully. 'I got some questions to ask you — '

Amber did not sit down, nor did he want to smoke.

'I'll answer all your questions, Superintendent,' he said, firmly, 'but only in the presence of Willie Oaker — since they concern us both. Willie's a loyal friend of mine, and a grand worker; but he's not up to facing a thing like this on his own. You'll get the truth if you do what I say,' he added.

The Super hesitated only for a moment. He was always ready to change his mind.

'All right, Amber. Sit down. Henry, you fetch up Willie.' He offered his packet of cigarettes to the woodman, but Amber shook his head. 'Not in the daytime when I'm working, sir.'

Two minutes later Willie Oaker shuffled into the room, with Henry in his wake. He was flushed, frightened and defiant as he fingered his cap and looked the length of the room at the Super's dark silhouette against the light; but when he saw his friend he heaved a sigh of relief, and moved without protest to an armchair near him.

'Now, Amber,' the Super began again, rather less cheerfully, 'you and Oaker were absent from the bar downstairs last night, during the time a murder was bein' committed on this floor. Where were you and why? You were absent, I understand, for a quarter of an hour at least.'

Willie Oaker started forwards in his

chair, whimpering what might have been a denial or an appeal to his friend. Amber turned to give him a straight look and said:

'You leave this to me, boy.' He moved his level gaze back to the Super. 'Willie had something to tell me, and I had something to tell him, so we went out into the grounds for a private talk. We sat on the steps of the summer house all the time.'

'I see. What did you talk about?'

Willie whimpered again.

'Shut up, Willie,' Amber snapped at him without turning his head. 'I'm afraid it's going to take some time to answer that,' he told the Super. 'It goes back to — '

'P'raps I can 'elp you,' the Super intervened. 'Are you goin' to tell me about Willie sleepin' in them woods, and about his encounter with the luminy woman in black — swingin' at the end of a rope?'

Willie screamed a protest at this, and then was silent. Amber went on looking at the Super with unflinching gaze.

'Yes,' he said, 'that's about it. Some of it, anyway. Though I don't know how you got hold of it. I believed Willie had just been seeing things when he told me of his first encounter with that apparition in black, sir, but I humoured him. It was rather different that night he came screaming to my cottage with a story of having found the woman hanging from a tree. I took him straight back there to prove he'd been seeing things. There was a lot of blood on a stone, where he'd fallen and knocked himself out — '

'Yes,' the Super rasped, 'you went to a lot of trouble to hush up that business, Amber. Why?'

Willie Oaker shrilled, 'Don't tell 'em, Mike!'

Mike Amber glared over his shoulder. 'Shut up, can't you.' He addressed the Super again: 'We were in trouble enough, sir, without that. You see,' and he drew a breath, 'we dug that grave. Or rather, I dug it while Willie kept doggo.'

Willie subsided in his chair with a groan. Then, after a dramatic silence, Amber went on:

'I'd determined to finish with Nadine, sir. I'd made up my mind about her: she was a bitch of the first water, playing me for a sucker as she'd played Denis Pugh and other poor devils like us. I'd decided to get rid of her, so far as this community was concerned, for the benefit of us all. There was only one way of doing that, and that was to scare her out of the place; and believe me, Superintendent, she needed some scaring.

'Anyway, that grave and her hat were my idea and my doing. I was fairly certain that even Nadine would take a hint like that, when it was discovered, and get out while the going was good. Needless to say, Willie and I never reckoned on what else happened on the night she did disappear. We had nothing to do with any of that, on my word of honour; but you can understand the trouble we found ourselves in, on account of the grave.'

'When exactly did you dig that grave, Amber?'

'Three nights before Nadine disappeared,' Amber replied promptly. 'We chose that particular spot hoping a week or so might go by before anyone discovered it — giving us plenty of time to cover our tracks.'

'So that was why you were anxious to keep quiet the story of Willie's alleged adventures in those woods two nights after the two disappearances and the supposed suicide of Miss Radford?'

'Yes, sir. Willie's loyal enough; but if the police had started questioning him about that crazy business . . . well, I wanted to make sure he'd not give me away about the grave. Shut up, Willie!' He silenced another protest from the hunchback. 'Nobody's questioning your loyalty.'

'Well,' the Super said, 'was that what Willie wanted to talk to you about in the grounds last night?'

'Not exactly, sir. You see, you saw Willie make a bit of a fool of himself outside the Welsh Harp yesterday afternoon; and he made a bit of a fool of himself inside, afterwards, because he'd made up his mind you'd heard about the woman in black and the rest of it, and were after him about it. Willie's not quite normal in the way he reasons some things,' he went on in a gentler voice. 'He was all set to deny everything, regardless, for my sake. He went into the woods yesterday afternoon to find that bloodstained stone and drop it in the river, to remove a piece of evidence. That was what he wanted to talk to me about in private yesterday. What I told him,' he added with a grim smile, 'is nobody's business.'

'What *did* you tell 'im, exactly?'

'Well, I told him to shut up and leave everything to me. I told him that if things got to a certain stage, with you here on the job, I should own up about the grave.'

'I see.' The Super drummed on the desk. 'So you didn't believe in the woman in luminy black?'

Amber smiled again and shook his head. The Super leaned forward over the desk.

'You told us you'd rumbled Nadine for what she was, Amber. Did you suspect she was carrying on, among others of course, with Robert Charlton?'

The atmosphere in the room changed suddenly. Willie Oaker uttered a half-stifled cry and sat petrified in his chair. Mike Amber's handsome face hardened into a grey-brown mask.

'That news about them this morning,' he said at last, 'stunned us all, Superintendent. I don't understand any of it. Charlton never came to this pub; he never talked to anyone but Miss Radford. All I can say is that . . . bitch must have been deeper and darker than even I imagined. I don't mind telling you,' he added, 'that after the horror broke this morning I was determined to come and see you whether you sent for me or not.'

'Did Willie ever suggest he'd been close enough to the woman in black to recognize her — as Nadine Price?'

'I never did!' Willie screamed, jumping to his feet. 'I never saw her face. I swear — '

Mike Amber waited for Willie to shut up this time, before he answered:

'No, sir.' His voice was hoarse with

strain. 'What are you getting at, Superintendent?'

The Super hesitated a long moment before he replied:

'The luminy woman in black existed all right, Amber. She was Nadine Price. She had a special black rubber outfit in which she used to swim the river at night, to get to Charlton's cottage without going round by the bridge.'

Amber looked stunned. The Super gave him a little time to adjust himself before he went on:

'So you and Willie were sitting on the summer house steps last night when Laval was murdered. Then you must have been there when the murderer escaped from the hotel by one of them three back doors.'

'We never saw a soul!' Willie shrilled.

Amber thought for a moment before he shook his head.

'Listen, Superintendent,' he said quietly, 'from those summer house steps you can see all those three back doors to the hotel; you can even see if anyone enters or leaves the bar. What's more, the hotel was framed in the outside lights, last night as every night; and I was watching all round, not wanting to be spotted there with Willie; so I can tell you that no one left the hotel by either of those four doors while we were out there last night. Damn it,' he exploded, 'I should have seen anyone who'd even got out through a window!'

The Super straightened up in his chair. 'Thanks,' he said, tersely. 'That's definite enough. There's just one thing more on which you might be able to help us. Major Valentine has told me about a tramp he encountered on the river path to his house one night fairly recently. I understand the fellow has been seen hanging around since then. I wonder if you or Willie — '

'Just a minute, Super.' Major Valentine got up from his chair and walked to the middle of the room, where he turned to face Amber. 'I only saw the chap once, very briefly; so perhaps it would be better if I repeated my description of him and you corrected me if I'm wrong. That is, of course, if you have seen him?'

Amber looked puzzled, but he nodded emphatically.

'I've seen *a* tramp, Major; and there's only been one around here during the past three months so far as I know. A big chap in a blue jersey and corduroys. About my build I made him. Yellow teeth. He only spoke once in my hearing, to order a drink. A deep, guttural voice, sort of French he sounded. He's been several times on and off to the Welsh Harp. Never talks to a soul. I tried to draw him out once, but it didn't work. Still, tramps are like that.'

Major Valentine shrugged and smiled as he returned to his chair.

'It's the same man all right, of course. You've got him pat,' he said. 'I needn't have interrupted, Super.'

The Super turned to Amber again.

'Can you remember when you saw him first?'

Amber shook his head. It was Willie who chimed in, almost eagerly:

'The first time was the night we dug that grave, Mike.'

Amber shook his head.

'He was there before then,' he corrected him. 'I remember someone saying that night, when he came in, that he'd been in before.'

'When did you last see him, Amber?' the Super persisted.

'Two, three weeks ago. Hughie Grant will be able to tell you better, Superintendent. He's good at remembering things like that.'

'I'll ask him,' the Super promised with a smile. 'All right, you two can go.'

Amber got slowly to his feet, looked around him as though momentarily uncertain of himself; then, with a nod to his friend, he led the way from the room.

The door closed. There was a long silence, broken only by the drumming of the Super's fingers on the desk. Finally, he looked a question at Major Valentine.

Valentine spoke at length, apparently unwillingly, but with harsh conviction:

'I went to have a close look at Amber just now, Super, because I couldn't for the life of me make up my mind about him. It was either the truth, or he's

341

the most brazen, ingenious liar I've encountered in a pretty comprehensive experience of liars. It was a superlative performance whatever it was. Personally . . . well, damn it all, Super, he *could* have found Charlton and Nadine together and have done 'em both in. He *could* have dug that grave for his victims and have been prevented from using it that night by someone's unwitting intervention; perhaps that tramp was hanging around. I should say, too, that if anyone *could* have hidden those bodies successfully, in defiance of an organized search of the district, Amber was the most likely chap. If he was guilty of all that, then it would have been characteristic of the fellow to have murdered Laval while Willie kept doggo outside the building, and then come and tell you the tale he did just now.'

The Super nodded slowly.

'Amber's a strong character,' he admitted. 'If what you suggest is true, or even if it isn't, we shan't be able to shake Willie after the briefing he gave him in front of us. I may 'ave made a big mistake just now, Major, havin' them in together. What do *you* think about it all, Henry?' he asked.

Henry Baxter shook his head.

'Amber was a commando, wasn't he,' he supplied, obviously thinking of the recent brutal murder of Laval.

Valentine laughed impatiently.

'So was I, Baxter. Laval was trained in a similar school, too. Look here, Super, it's all very well tackling Baxter and me. You haven't committed yourself yet about Amber and Willie Oaker.'

'Me,' the Super smiled, 'I'm just listenin' — and changin' my mind.' He consulted his watch. 'Take Henry downstairs, Major, and give him lunch. Send Hughie Grant up here on your way. I'd better see him alone, I reckon.'

He was still sitting behind the desk when the landlord of the Welsh Harp came in. Hughie Grant was trembling and literally green with fright as he took the seat Mike Amber had vacated.

'Now listen, Superintendent,' he began hysterically, 'I told you yesterday all it was within my power to tell. It's bad enough leaving the missus to cope with the bar at a time like this — '

'I'm looking for a tramp,' the Super told him abruptly. 'Mike Amber said you were the best person to ask about 'im, seein' 'e patronizes your place.'

The landlord looked so relieved that he seemed on the point of bursting into tears.

'A tramp, sir! You mean that French chap with long black hair and horrible yellow teeth? Why didn't you say so yesterday?'

'I want to know everything you can tell me about him, Grant.'

'My God, sir,' Hughie cried, as the thought struck him for the first time, 'do you suspect *him* of the murders?'

'Just answer my question, will you?'

Grant did his best; he was eager to help, and he certainly seemed to have a remarkable memory. He recalled that the tramp had called first at the Welsh Harp during the rush hour, between nine and ten at night, a week before the disappearance of Nadine Price. He had ordered a pint of beer and sat down against the wall at one end of the bar. He had stayed until closing-time. Like most tramps, the landlord continued, he had kept himself to himself, discouraging the friendly approaches of other customers, but had listened keenly to the conversations around him. He had paid his second visit to the pub at approximately the same time two nights later; and he had come again, rather earlier, on the night of 'the disappearances and the suicide'. He had not shown himself there again until 'about a fortnight ago'. Hughie Grant added that he had not seen him since.

No, he had had no conversation with the man. So far as he knew no one in the locality knew anything about him. Yes, he agreed, this was rather unusual; tramps were not infrequent in the district, and his customers usually saw them begging, or shopping, or camping out, and talked about them in the bar, which was not the case with the one in question.

The Super fired a succession of questions which elicited the following answers: The tramp's black hair was certainly the longest Grant had ever seen on the head of a man. His skin was bronzed and dirty 'like a gipsy's'. He had badly needed a shave each time he had seen him. There had certainly been 'an unnatural sort of brightness' about his eyes. Amber and the hunchback had tried to buy him a drink and get into conversation with him one night, but without success.

'What night was that?' the Super persisted, in relation to the last statement.

Grant looked embarrassed and shook his head.

'I can't recall which night,' he mumbled.

The Super leaned forward on his elbows and fixed his victim with an aggressive glare.

'Now, Grant,' he rasped, 'you're goin' to tell me what you were too scared to tell me in your pub yesterday afternoon. It's somethin' about Mike Amber or Willie Oaker, ain't it?' He waited while the frightened landlord stared back at him in silence, and went on, 'Perhaps it'll loosen you up if I tell you Mike Amber

346

'as already confessed to 'aving dug that grave.'

Hughie Grant looked startled, incredulous and relieved in turn. And he loosened up.

'Then I've nothing to tell that'd be news to you, Superintendent, honest,' he said earnestly. 'It was the night Mike and Willie tried making friends with the tramp. I remember now, I did hear Mike warning him to keep clear of Colwin Woods because his lordship 'd been particular down on tramps since one of 'em started a serious fire some years ago in the forest back of Larne. I remember grinning to myself because Mike didn't tell him in my hearing it was himsel' would be after him if he didn't heed his warning.'

He paused and gave the Super a long, almost appealing look before continuing:

'It was after closing-time, and I was clearing the bar when I passed Willie and Mike, and overheard Willie — he was rather tight — say not to forget the spade for the grave. I was that taken aback I stopped with a mind to take

Willie up on what he'd said exactly. What stopped me was Mike. He'd gone all red and was threatening Willie with his fist. But then, just as suddenly, he got a grip on himself and put an arm round Willie's shoulders and took him off to the street.

'I told my missus about it over supper. She only laughed and said I must have mis-heard Willie. But next day, when the grave was discovered, and Miss Radford's spade — '

'I see. You're sure of your date, are you? This was the night of the disappearances and the suicide?'

'Yes, sir,' Grant said huskily. 'But I thought you told me he'd confessed — !'

'That's right. By the way, who discovered the grave?'

'Joe Early it was. He fell over the spade nearby on his way to The Retreat, getting it ready for Major Valentine he was, that morning. The spade was lying across the path through the woods.'

'Was it,' the Super said with an unpleasant smile. 'Well, that's the end of the inquisition, Grant, except for one question that slipped my mind just now — about that tramp. What newspaper did he read?'

Grant stared.

'I didn't mention no newspaper,' he protested. 'But as a matter of fact he always had one. Used to hide behind it and pretend to read while he listened-in to whatever talk there was.'

'What newspaper was it?'

'The local rag. *The Border Times*. Each time he came. You can't mistake the bad print and the great pages, even if you don't happen to see the title. I remember wonderin' whether it wasn't the same issue each time, brought to hide behind and keep folks from intrudin' on his privacy like.'

'Thank you, Grant. That's all for now. You can go back and relieve your missus. But let me know quick if this chap turns up in your bar during the next day or two. And set his tankard aside so we can grab his fingerprints.'

'I'll remember, sir,' the anxious landlord promised as he got up from his chair. 'You don't really think he'll turn up

349

again, do you? Not if he's mixed up in — ?'

The Super shrugged. A moment later, as the door closed, his blank expression changed to a scowl.

'That's torn it,' he growled.

21

The Super was still sitting behind the desk, staring in front of him unseeingly, when Henry Baxter returned to the room.

'Would you like me to bring your lunch to you here, Mr. Greene,' Henry offered. 'There's some jolly decent cold chicken, and — '

'Henry,' the Super interrupted, as though he had not heard him, 'are you any good at simple arithmetic? What do two and two add up to?'

Henry smiled tolerantly.

'They still make four, sir.'

The Super lapsed into a worried frown.

'That's what I thought, Henry. Well,' he went on, 'here's a not so simple problem about Laval's murderer: According to Amber, he didn't leave the building during the material time. According to Constable Taft, he didn't enter the bar. According to me he didn't hide in any of the rooms on the ground floor or in the cellars. According to you, he didn't hide in any of the rooms above the ground floor. So what did happen to him?'

Henry said: 'I can't help feeling that Amber is either a liar, sir, or else he made extravagant and reckless statements in order to impress you favourably. After all, it was pitch dark outside when he and Willie Oaker were sitting on the steps of the summer house, and — '

'I don't agree with you,' the Super retorted. 'I've seen the view from that summer house, and I remembered them doors exactly when Amber was talkin'. Furthermore, he gave a very good reason for being observant. And finally, son, 'e's intelligent enough to know that, if he was guiltily mixed up in this business, it would have been more in 'is interests to have encouraged me in the belief that the murderer *did* leave the building.' He paused and added quietly but firmly, 'I think Constable Taft was mistaken.'

Henry looked incredulous.

'You mean the murderer returned to the bar before Major Valentine tackled Taft?'

'I mean precisely that,' the Super nodded, 'and I'm goin' to prove it. In other words, I'm goin' to prove that two and two make four. Now here's a titbit that doesn't look so good for Mike Amber on the face of it.' He related the incident between Willie Oaker and Mike Amber which the landlord of the Welsh Harp had witnessed in the bar at closing time, and added, 'So Amber seems to have lied when he told us he dug that grave three days before it was discovered.'

'Then he probably lied about other things as well,' Henry cried with a certain malicious satisfaction.

'We shall see,' the Super promised. 'Now about that chicken. Is Mam'selle Everard very busy right now?'

'I shouldn't think so, sir. Major Valentine was finishing when I left him at lunch just now; he'll be taking his coffee in the lounge. That leaves only you for mam'selle to serve.'

'Then send her up here,' the Super said, pushing himself out of his chair.

When Lucille Everard entered the room five minutes later, the Super was standing with his back to the open fireplace.

'There's a book lying open on that desk, mam'selle, that will interest you,' he told her pleasantly.

She walked to the desk and bent over the album of Gabriel Laval's women. It was lying open at the nude study of herself. Her back was towards the Super as she stared at it, but he saw her neck reddening.

'What would you give me for that picture, mam'selle?' he asked.

She turned and gave him a level, defiant look.

'Nothing,' she snapped. 'I was paid a quite satisfactory price when I posed for it.'

The Super walked to the desk, tore out the picture and tore it into small pieces. He saw surprise supplant the hostility in the Frenchwoman's eyes; and this was what he wanted.

'I found another book in this room,' he told her when he had returned to the fireplace. 'A diary in Nadine Price's handwriting, all about the goings-on at

Threeways. Does that ring a bell for you, mam'selle?'

'No,' she replied promptly.

'Laval kept Nadine there as his wife. Janet was the maid. There were week-end parties at which dope was taken.'

'I told you,' she said, 'the name mean nothing to me. Threeways that is. But Laval kept his several activities in very separate compartments, if you understan'. I was just in one.' She seemed really trying to be helpful for the first time; probably, the Super reflected dubiously, because she wanted something out of him.

'Take another look at the album, mam'selle,' he invited. 'The picture where it's open now is a picture of two women. One of them's Janet. Can you identify the other woman as Nadine Price?'

She bent over the album again, straightened up and shook her head.

'I never saw this other woman at the flat,' she said. 'Janet come many times, I assume as a messenger between Laval and this Nadine.'

'The association seems to have terminated abruptly. Did you get any idea, perhaps through Janet, that they had quarrelled?'

'I got no ideas about Nadine at all, Superintendent. Janet nevair talk to me either.'

'I see. Would you like to see if you can recognize any other women in that album?'

'No,' she said bluntly, 'because I should not admit it if I did recognize someone. I don't want to make enemies for nothing.'

The Super sighed resignedly.

'Well, that will be all for now. Take Mr. Baxter to the kitchen, please, and give 'im a tray of lunch for me. Just chicken and biscuits-and-cheese; no sweets or coffee. I think you'll find 'im waitin' discreetly outside this room. Tell him to send Major Valentine up here to me, while you're doin' the tray.'

When Major Valentine entered the room he found the Super behind the desk again, with Nadine 'Laval's' Dorset diary in his hands. He pointed to a chair on the other side of the desk and pushed the volume towards the major as he sat down.

Valentine, when he had seen the printed writing and scrawl on the first page, stared questioningly at the Super. The latter told what he knew about the diary and its implications.

'You'll see where a page was torn out at the end, Major. That looks to me like our Nadine wrote about somebody and then didn't want 'is name in the diary. At a guess, I'd say the association between Nadine and Laval stopped very sudden like. The reason *may* 'ave been that the game 'ad got too risky. What I like to think, however, is that Nadine fell badly for another man and cleared off with him. I want to find out who 'e was and where they went together.'

'Surely,' Valentine protested, 'you won't find that out very easily, Super. Those sort of people don't leave a forwarding address as a rule, do they?'

'You'd be surprised, Major, how much curious folk *do* find out about people who don't usually leave a forwarding address. Anyway, I'd rather send a private individual than a copper on this job. Someone who can make tactful inquiries at this place in Dorset, about the couple who called themselves the Lavals, and their maid, and their parties, and what you might call their terminations as far as Boxsted people were concerned.'

Valentine still looked dubious.

'Rather a long time ago, wasn't it?'

'Ten, twelve years ain't so long to some people, particularly country people, Major. Would you care to motor down to Boxsted and see what you can do?'

'*Me?*' Valentine looked quite taken aback. 'I . . . I'm not sure I'd be much good at that sort of thing — '

'Will you go and find out, Major? I think you're the ideal man for the job, and since you offered your help . . . '

Valentine accepted the commission. He wanted to take the diary and read it, to brief himself more adequately for the job, but the Super shook his head.

'Afraid I got to read it carefully myself, Major. Maybe I'll find some more useful clues to something or other.'

'I'll get off at once and pick up a

few things from my house,' the major promised. 'You'd like me to telephone if I hit on anything that may be useful?'

'Yes, if it's urgent,' the Super nodded. 'Otherwise just get back 'ere as soon as you can. And thank you very much for takin' the job on, Major.'

As the door closed, the Super pulled the telephone towards him, dialled 'o', asked for Trunks, and then for a London number. It was Whitehall 1212. He had just concluded an important conversation with Chief Detective-Inspector Holland, one of his intimates at Scotland Yard, when Henry Baxter came in with his lunch on a tray.

'Ah, this looks good, smells good too,' the Super said with relish. 'Right, Henry. I've sent Major Valentine down to Dorset to try and find out what he can about the people who lived at Threeways during part of the war. Now I've got a less interestin' job for you, son. I want you to search these grounds for a very small bottle, or other sort of container, that smells of turpentine. It's just a hunch of mine that Laval's murderer may have thrown away such a container soon after the murder last night.'

'Very good, sir. Colonel Fielding has just returned, by the way, and I left Inspector Griffiths, telling him about Janet's suicide. Do you want to see him, Mr. Greene?'

'Not before this cold chicken,' the Super said firmly.

A hard look darkened his florid face as the door closed behind Henry and he picked up a knife and fork. The murder of Laval had forced its way back to the forefront of his mind; and for the first time he had a suspect. It was, as he had remarked mysteriously to Henry, a matter of simple arithmetic . . .

22

The Super had just finished his lunch when Colonel Fielding joined him. The chief constable looked more harassed than ever, if that were possible.

'I hope to heaven,' he said fervently as he sat down in the chair Major Valentine had occupied on the other side of the desk, 'there won't be any more violent deaths here. Griffiths has just told me about the barmaid; they've just taken the body away. I hope that Frenchwoman doesn't try anything of the sort, Greene — '

The Super laughed reassuringly.

'Not mam'selle, Colonel. Not on your life she won't. Well, we've made quite a bit of progress since you went off to your 'eadquarters. Did you get them pictures of Charlton off like I said?'

Fielding nodded. He had sent one to Cumberland, he explained, by a private 'plane belonging to a friend of his.

'It ought to be in Carlisle early this afternoon.'

'Fine, Colonel. The sooner that question can be answered one way or the other, the better.' He proceeded to show the chief constable his various finds in that room and Janet's; and he had just finished his report when there was a knock on the door.

It was Lucille Everard in search of his tray. But she looked taken aback when she saw the Super's companion, and he was quick to guess the reason.

'You've thought of something else you want to tell me, mam'selle,' he suggested. 'You can do that in front of Colonel Fielding, you know. He's in charge here, not me.'

Lucille Everard took a moment to make up her mind — as deliberately as she did everything. Then she shrugged and said, with the tray in her hands:

'I think perhaps I may tell you why Janet took poison this morning, gentlemen. Ever since Threeways, Laval keep an eye on Janet because the poor child know too much about that dope business, and he make sure she not give him away. Laval put the fear of God into her. He tell her he is not the real boss of the dope racket; that the real boss is a terrible person, who knows all about her, and would certainly kill her if anything happen to himself, Laval. There is no such person,' she stated emphatically, 'but Janet fear the unknown even more than she fear Laval. That was why she was so terrified this morning, when you threaten to question her and perhaps force her to talk. She die because she cannot live any longer with this great fear. She kill herself also, I think, because she fear something might 'appen to her baby to force her to be silent.'

It was badly put, but clear enough to the Super and Colonel Fielding.

'I thought it was something like that,' the former remarked sadly in self-reproach. 'I should have kept a closer watch on the poor girl. So you tell us, mam'selle, there is no such person as the boss Laval spoke of to Janet.'

'Yes, I am certain. I know all along Laval was bluffing her to make doubly sure of her silence.'

'Then,' the Super reflected grimly, 'the murder of Laval had nothing to do with Laval's some-time dope activities; *was* Laval still mixed up in the racket?'

Mam'selle shrugged, to indicate she had said all she intended saying, and went off with the tray. Fielding stared helplessly at the Super as the door closed.

'Then we're as much in the dark as ever,' he said, bitterly, 'except that the murder definitely had something to do with the defacing of that oil painting?'

The Super shook his head.

'I think the murderer wants us to believe what you've just said, Colonel,' he replied, darkly.

'Do you think this chap Amber — ?'

'What I think about the murderer of Laval,' said the Super, 'is that he was back in that bar when Major Valentine found Taft and told him of the crime. And there we must leave it for the time bein'. Now, if you'll excuse me, Colonel, I'm going to treat myself to a hot bath, and a nap on that palatial divan bed over there.'

It was four o'clock that afternoon when Henry Baxter wakened the Super to show him the small glass phial he had found — not in the actual grounds, but below them, on the edge of the water. It was empty but had certainly contained turpentine a short time ago.

'I'd say someone tried to get rid of it in the river, sir,' Henry suggested, 'and all but succeeded. But I still can't think why you had to have two containers for turpentine, sir.'

The Super chuckled as he lifted himself off the bed and went back to his chair behind the massive desk.

'Can't you, son? Well, here's the sensational explanation: Laval's murderer wanted us to believe that Laval had defaced that oil painting, when he did nothing of the kind. So when he'd killed Laval he sprinkled turps from this small glass phial on to the Frenchman's waistcoat. Now do you see why there wasn't no turps on Laval's chef's clothes?' He grinned. 'The cleverest of 'em make mistakes, son, and this seems to 'ave been one of 'is.'

Henry's pale face was positively distorted with bewilderment.

'So Laval had to die because he could have told who had destroyed that painting?'

'That's 'ow it looks, don't it?'

Henry shook his head.

'It doesn't make sense to me, sir,' he confessed. 'After all, there were scores of people here who could have identified the original of that portrait — '

'Yes, son, but the murderer destroyed it believin' it was the only existin' portrait of Robert Charlton, and it was desperately important to 'im that we shouldn't print that picture in the papers.'

'Because, then, it was desperately important to the murderer we shouldn't find out more than we knew about Robert Charlton — and perhaps Nadine Price, too. Both of them being dead already and hardly recognizable.'

'Yes.'

Henry sighed.

'Well, what are you waiting for, sir?

Why don't you print Charlton's picture in the papers; and that picture of Nadine Price you found in that album, as well?'

'Because,' the Super answered patiently, opening the suitcase that Henry had brought into his room, and taking out a hairbrush to tidy his sparse grey thatch, 'because I want the murderer to go on actin' on the belief that that picture no longer exists . . . until I'm ready for 'im.'

'You speak,' Henry accused him with a faint smile, 'as though you don't think it will be long before you *are*, sir.'

'No, it won't be long, Henry, it won't be long. There's one particular gap in the story of Charlton and Nadine that we got to fill in; and then we shall know automatically, you might say, who the murderer is.'

'The murderer of Nadine, Charlton and Laval?'

'In other words,' the Super said, ' 'X' the unknown quantity. Now,' he went on, sitting down behind the desk, 'I'm going to send you on a journey in that posh car of yours. A journey to Bristol.

367

Take another look at this diary Nadine kept when she was runnin' Threeways with Laval, Henry. I want you to buy a book similar to this; you ought to find one easy enough in Bristol. Then I want you to go to this address I've written on this bit of paper, and collect the chap who lives there and bring 'im 'ere as quick as you can. Jim Piper's 'is name. He's retired now, like me; but in 'is time 'e was the cleverest crook of 'is class. I've sent 'im a wire already over the 'phone, so he'll expect you and be all ready. If Jim asks precisely why I want 'im 'ere tell 'im the truth: you don't know, see?'

★ ★ ★

It was just before seven o'clock that evening when the Super received the wrist watch that had been taken from the body of Nadine Price, a forensic report on the sacking and rope found with the bodies, and the shreds of fibre he had found on the tree near the grave. This report proved his conviction that Willie Oaker *had* encountered the body of Nadine Price hanging from that tree on the night when the bodies of Nadine and Charlton had been put in the open grave and a false bottom laid to it.

With this report there came also the police surgeon's *post mortem* reports on the two bodies. Both Nadine and Charlton had been strangled by someone with powerful hands; someone who, the doctor suggested, had probably strangled before.

The wristlet watch was identical to Laval's watch; and the poison chamber in the wristlet — as the Super thought of it confidently — was empty. 'As it 'as been empty,' the Super growled to himself, 'since the night of Evelyn Radford's death from cyanide . . . '

★ ★ ★

At eight o'clock that evening the Super presided at a conference in Laval's room — his lair as he referred to it with relish — which was attended by Colonel Fielding, Inspector Griffiths and Sergeant Evans.

'So this is where we are right now,' the Super summed up with a confidence that the chief constable seemed to feel more frightening than reassuring: 'Nadine and Charlton came to Larne and Colwin primarily, if not entirely, to hide from an individual we've been referring to as 'X'.' Conscious of the occasion, and his own importance to it, the Super dropped hardly a single aspirate during his speech. 'We also know about 'X' that he arrived here on the evening of their disappearance; that he made his presence known to Nadine; that in panic she telephoned Charlton, packed her bag and met him later that night, determined to clear out.

'My conviction is, as I've stated already, that Miss Evelyn Radford caught them together and learned too much for their liking; that one or both of them decided they couldn't afford to leave her behind here alive; and that she was murdered forthwith in the way I've made known to you gentlemen already.

'What happened then is a matter for conjecture, of course, but my theory is this: 'X' arrived on the scene in time to prevent the flight of Nadine and Charlton. My guess is he strangled Charlton at the cottage while Nadine was attending to Miss Radford; and he dealt with Nadine when she returned to the cottage.

'And this,' he continued, with a twinkle for the chief constable, 'is where we do seem to come up against coincidence. Amber had either dug that grave already, or he dug it that night. 'X' probably didn't know of its existence! My contention is he drove to Colwin that evening in a car which he hid somewhere convenient to the cottage. He took the bodies of his victims away with him in that car. And he took their luggage, too, to create the impression they'd both cleared out of the district that night under their own steam.

'Now, a corpse is the most difficult thing in the world to get rid of satisfactorily, and 'X' knew it. To say nothing of two corpses. My guess is he was still considering that considerable problem when he read in a newspaper about that open grave in Colwin Woods, and Nadine's hat therein, and the police search for evidence of foul play. That grave, gentlemen, must've seemed to 'X' like a gift from the gods; for he realized that that grave — once the fruitless search in the district was over — was the safest place in the country for getting rid of his corpses. So he used that gift, daringly if you like; and if it hadn't been for me, perhaps, them bodies would never have been found.'

Colonel Fielding protested:

'I grant you that, Super. But surely this 'X' was running fantastic risks by bringing those bodies back to this district, seething with suspicion as it was still; back to the very grave?'

'I don't agree,' the Super retorted. ' 'X' is a very daring man, but by no means reckless; and that grave was an opportunity only a bold, confident man could avail himself of.'

'But I still say the risks were fantastic for an utter stranger to the district to take.'

The Super shook his head stubbornly.

' 'X' wasn't an utter stranger to the district, sir. He knew, for one thing, all about Willie Oaker's habit of sleepin' in them woods. He knew about Willie's stories of the naked woman in luminy black; and that knowledge inspired him to scare Willie out of them woods the night he put them bodies and a false bottom in that grave — with the 'disappearin' corpse' of Nadine Price, which he dressed in the black swim rigout, briefly, for the occasion. Moreover, the fact of his doing it that night implies that he knew the grave was going to be filled in early next morning by the ideal chap for the job, in the circumstances: Major Valentine's short-sighted gardener-handyman.'

The chief constable said:

'You've mentioned this French tramp, in relation to Major Valentine's encounter with him, and his visits to the Welsh Harp. Do you seriously consider him as 'X' — or an accomplice of his?'

'Not an accomplice, sir. I think he *was* 'X'. Very much disguised, of course. Hughie Grant's testimony this morning pretty well convinced me. That long hair;

unshaven; never talkin' at all if he could help it, and then in a hoarse voice and broken English; and listenin' thirteen to the dozen while hiding behind a local newspaper that would also, incidentally, have kept him up-to-date on the people and territory that concerned him so vitally. Not to mention his yellow-stained teeth, and unnaturally-bright eyes that doubtless had drops in them to make 'em that way.

'However . . . this is where we start walkin' in the fog, gentlemen, and I don't mind admittin' it. Yesterday afternoon Henry Baxter and I brought back here with us that oilpaintin' of Robert Charlton. 'X' discovered what it was; and because it was vitally important to him that we didn't get further into the background of Charlton and Nadine Price than we had, he destroyed that picture. And he murdered Laval because Laval could have told us what he'd done.'

'Then,' the chief constable cut in urgently again, ' 'X' was pretty familiar with this establishment as well as its proprietor. Those red rubber gloves from the kitchen, that hotel towel he used . . . ?'

'Yes,' the Super agreed, ' 'X' was familiar enough with the establishment and Laval. He certainly borrowed that dagger from Laval's office to do the murder with.'

'And after the murder, in spite of Constable Taft's emphatic evidence to the contrary, 'X' managed to get back to the bar without being noticed?'

'Yes, Colonel.'

'But *how*, man?'

The Super smiled.

'That's a nasty little fog patch, isn't it, sir? Never mind, it'll clear.'

'So 'X's' name will be found on the list of customers Sergeant Evans made later on in the bar?'

'It's there all right, Colonel.'

'And you believe,' the chief constable accused him bluntly, 'you know who he is?'

'I think I do, sir; but I'm not going to commit myself until I can prove it.'

'How do you propose doing that?'

'Just ploddin' on, Colonel, and bein' patient.'

'Again as to the relationship between Laval and his murderer: Laval can have had no suspicion that 'X' was connected with the disappearances of Charlton and Nadine Price, and Miss Radford's death?'

'Laval knew who he was,' the Super replied darkly, 'he didn't know *what* 'e was — not even when he died.'

'But Laval must have known 'X' had despoiled that oilpainting,' Fielding tackled him incredulously. 'You said yourself . . . '

The Super made an impatient clucking sound with his tongue.

'I should 'ave chosen my words more carefully, Colonel, if I said that. My impression is that I said Laval was murdered to prevent 'im telling us that 'X' had done that job on the paintin'.'

'Then he *must* have known!'

'Dear me,' the Super said, 'am I still obtuse or whatever the word is, Colonel? Laval was murdered, perhaps, to prevent 'im *findin' out* about that

376

painting despoilment and *then* tellin' us.'

Colonel Fielding pulled out a handkerchief and wiped his forehead.

'If that's the lot, then,' he said, 'we'd better get down to that cold dinner Man'selle Everard promised us. I could do with a drink, too.'

'That's the lot,' the Super said as they got up from their chairs, 'with the exception of something for you, Sergeant Evans. I want a close watch kept on the movements of Mike Amber and Willie Oaker and Hughie Grant, too. And the same applies to the first chap Nadine Price was engaged to 'ere — Denis Pugh.'

'Denis Pugh!' the chief constable exclaimed. 'I had no idea you suspected — ?'

'If you don't mind,' the Super wound up, shepherding his companions towards the door, 'I'll have something to eat and drink up here on a tray — as soon as Mam'selle Lucille can manage it. I'm expectin' some telephone calls.'

★ ★ ★

The first call came through half an hour later — from Chief Inspector Holland whom the Super had spoken to at Scotland Yard that afternoon. Holland's cheery tenor voice reported he was on the job the Super had given him.

The second call came through at half-past nine. The caller was Inspector Grantham, also of Scotland Yard, and he was speaking from the Peacock Club, Soho.

'I think I've got your man, though he hasn't shown up yet,' Grantham reported. 'The Assistant Commissioner said I was to report direct to you. Billy Jenkins — 'Jinky' is his nickname, as you probably know — is a shareholder in this club and usually shows up around ten o'clock. Laval is known here, and known to Jinky.'

'Billy Jenkins!' the Super cried delightedly. 'He's the private 'tec who works almost exclusively for the underworld, as they call it, ain't he? Well, make the picture as grim as you can, Bert; and get him 'ere if you can, as quick as you can.'

'I'll manage him,' Grantham promised.

The third call came from Major Valentine, to report his arrival in Boxsted, and his address as the Crown Hotel there.

'I'm not very hopeful, Super,' he confessed. 'This place was crowded with troops, and refugees from the towns, in the war years; and my tentative inquiries haven't got me far up to now. But I've located Threeways, and I'll do what I can in the morning.'

'Cheer up, Major,' the Super replied. 'If Threeways was the sort of show I think it was, you ought to find *someone* with an interesting story to tell.'

At half-past ten Inspector Grantham telephoned again from the Peacock Club.

'Jinky's here,' he said, 'and I've had a yarn with him. He's rather scared of the Laval business, whatever it is, and concerned for his own skin. He doesn't want an escort, and is ready to find his own way up there in a pretty powerful car he's got. Be all right to send him solo, will it? He says he ought to make it by two o'clock in the morning . . . '

'Do me fine,' the Super replied warmly.

'I shall be in circulation when he gets here, son. You go home to bed.'

★ ★ ★

At three o'clock in the morning Bill Jenkins was seated with the Super, facing him across Laval's huge desk. He was a rabbit-faced, elegantly-dressed little man of indefinable age; and, encouraged by frequent drops of spirit from a bottle on the desk, he was eager to talk.

'It's my job to know everybody, good and bad,' he said, 'and I've known Laval since well before the war. His frequent visits to this country then were whispered about as being connected with dope peddling — which is why I gave him a wide berth professionally, if you get what I mean. Yep, I heard about Threeways, his joint in Dorset; and I heard enough not to be curious. I knew that tart Nadine; she was a night-club hostess when Laval found her and took her into partnership. He was quite daffy about her for a time; but after that, as I understood, it was purely business.

380

'Then, sudden like, she dropped him and disappeared; and that was also the end of Threeways so far as Laval was concerned. After the war Laval vanished from his old haunts; got married and turned respectable *if* you could believe what you heard. Then, when this scandal here broke into the newspapers, Laval telephoned me. It was the first I'd heard of him for years. He was in a blue funk; told me Nadine had been working for him here, and had cleared out in the night. He was scared stiff, believe me; she'd got something on him, apparently, to do with their partnership days. He offered me a figure to keep an eye open in the Soho district, and give him the word the instant she showed up. That's where I come into this, Superintendent, and that's all I do come into it. I never got so much as a sniff of Nadine, but Laval kept on ringing me periodically at the Peacock Club.' He made a gesture of finality. 'That's me come clean, see.'

The Super showed him the photograph of Janet and Nadine from Laval's album. Jinky identified Nadine Price at once.

'Yes,' he said, smiling unpleasantly, 'that's Nadine that was. But don't ask me for her history; you've got all I've got to give. She was a dame who knew how to keep her mouth shut all right. She'd got all it takes all right, believe me; there wasn't a man could resist her if she wanted him.'

The Super nodded as he retrieved the photograph.

'You said she dropped Laval suddenly and disappeared. Do you know why — or with whom?'

Jinky answered cautiously: 'I only know what I heard. Second or third, probably fourth hand. The story was she'd fallen for a man; fallen flat. I should say this chap had all it takes, too, for a girl like Nadine to have had it that bad. I'd say she'd found a man who could satisfy her at last.'

'You never saw this man?'

Jinky frowned.

'I won't say that. The last time she came to the Peacock Club, just before she disappeared, she was with a chap in Army uniform — a real handsome guy — and someone who knew her pointed him out to me with a hint he was IT for her. I never saw him again though — '

The Super pulled out his wallet and produced one of his prints of the oil portrait of Robert Charlton.

Jinky glanced at it, drew a quick breath and stared at him.

'That's him,' he said. 'My gawd, Superintendent, where did you get that from after all this time? What's been happening down here?'

'That man,' the Super told him, 'is Robert Charlton who disappeared from here the same night as Nadine Price.'

Jinky whistled.

'Cripes! So she had it as bad as that! It must be ten, eleven years since I saw them together.'

The Super put away the print in his wallet.

'Do you happen to know whether Laval really turned respectable when he got married?'

The little man shrugged.

'I wouldn't know. All I know is he was scared pink when he telephoned me about Nadine doing a bunk from here.'

Janet — the name and her picture — meant nothing at all to Jinky.

'Well,' the Super said, rising finally after further fruitless questioning, 'that's what I wanted from you, Jinky, my son; just all you could tell me about Laval and Nadine and this chap Charlton. Finish that bottle, and I'll find you a room for the rest of the night.'

But Jinky wanted only his car and his freedom. Half an hour later he was speeding back to London; and the Super was soundly asleep on Laval's great bed.

It was after six o'clock that morning when Henry Baxter arrived with Jim Piper from Bristol. The constable on duty in the hall told them the Super would see them in his room when he woke at eight o'clock.

Jim Piper — a foxy little man with a yellow beard and a squint — wanted only a drink and a bed just then. Henry supplied both before he retired to his own pillow.

At eight o'clock the Super roused Henry, collected a sleepy-eyed Jim Piper, and carted him off to his lair.

'You go back to sleep,' the Super ordered Henry, when the latter had produced the leather-covered book he had purchased in Bristol.

When Henry returned to the Super at ten o'clock he found him alone. Henry never saw Jim Piper again . . .

23

At half-past ten a Cumberland call came through on the 'phone. The caller introduced himself to the Super as Inspector Packer; he was speaking from police headquarters at Penrith.

'It took us a bit of time, sir,' he reported, 'for there've been a lot of changes in this part of the world since 1939. However, we found an old lady who worked as maid in the Radford household. She idolized Miss Radford, detested her brother. She didn't think much of the estate manager, Stanley Weaver, either, though she admits Miss Radford was very much in love with him. The answer you want about Weaver, sir, is Yes. This old lady identified the picture as him, without a doubt; hardly looks a day older, she says. She also remembers that Miss Radford had one letter from him to her knowledge, soon after he'd been sacked and cleared out.

The war was on, and he had joined up. Our informant thinks he was a commando or something . . . '

The Super looked across the room at Henry Baxter, as he put down the receiver.

'That's another gap filled, son,' he said. 'Robert Charlton was the Stanley Weaver Miss Radford fell in love with in Cumberland.'

At 11.35 there was a call from Inspector Holland.

'Three calls so far, Super,' he reported. 'Now we're having a bite of lunch. I think you ought to know about the third call..'

The Super listened, his blue eyes gleaming like polished steel, for upwards of ten minutes. Then, violently, he interrupted:

'*Paignton*, you say? Paignton in Devon? Blimey, if that don't do the trick then I *am* Little Boy Lost in this case. Those two men? Yes, that maid certainly gave you vivid descriptions. She must 'ave a marvellous memory; but then, these domestics do 'ave . . . Yes, I'm pretty sure I know both men. Stick at it, Frank, and let's 'ave everything as it comes.'

He waved Henry out of the way as he made for the door. Henry saw him open the door of the room immediately opposite and disappear inside, closing it carefully after him. When he returned to Laval's room five minutes later, he was looking grim.

'It won't be long, Henry,' he said, and Henry thought he looked rather tired as he slumped behind the desk. 'A lot depends now on what we 'ear from Major Valentine,' he muttered half to himself as he produced his packet of cigarettes.

Major Valentine called from Dorset at half-past twelve, and the Super's face fell as he listened:

'I'm afraid it's not much of a go here, Super.' Valentine sounded tired and discouraged. 'I've found one old lady who lives near Threeways and remembers the Lavals and their parties vaguely; but she's deaf and an invalid, her memory is chiefly concerned with the noise they made at Threeways — which she associates, anyway, with a patriotic cause. I can't find anyone else in the vicinity who remembers the Lavals at all. It's the war gap, and subsequent changes . . . I warned you, Super, I wouldn't be very good at this sort of thing.' He asked, when the Super said nothing, 'Any developments your end?'

'We're gettin' somewhere, wherever that is,' the Super replied. 'Look, Major, don't give up! Keep tryin' for the rest of the day! If you still get nowhere, make an early start for home tomorrow morning.'

He rang off and for a long five minutes sat huddled on his chair, staring at the telephone. Then he picked up the receiver and dialed 'o' and, *via* inquiries, put through a long-distance call. It took him a considerable time to get connected with the person he wanted; and the conversation that ensued was a long and difficult one. During the course of it the Super said:

'Try and get hold of someone who knew her personally . . . Yes, that would be better than ever, perhaps. Approximate dates will do. I got one picture but I'd give a lot to get another from . . . What? I see. No, whenever you're ready I'm ready at this number. Right . . . '

He rang off, frowning, and muttered to himself:

'Paignton . . . wonder if it's worth while . . . '

At that moment the chief constable knocked sharply on the door and came in.

'I'm going back to my office for a while, Super, unless you want me here any longer. Routine business goes on, you know.'

The Super gave him a level look.

'A lot has to happen yet, Colonel,' he said, 'but most of it will be on this 'phone. I'd say I'd be ready for another conference at noon tomorrow. No reason why you shouldn't sleep at 'ome tonight.'

Colonel Fielding smiled anxiously.

'No more violent deaths in the meantime, I hope?'

It was partly a question; the Super took it as such and spoke very gravely:

'I can't promise nothin'. A good deal depends on Major Valentine, at Boxsted, and at the moment 'e don't seem to be doin' very well.'

Colonel Fielding gave him a searching look.

'You seem to set a great deal of store on Boxsted,' he said. 'All those years ago . . . ?'

'Everything,' the Super replied, ' 'as to have a beginning. The Nadine-Charlton partnership seems to 'ave begun all them years ago, Colonel.'

'Yes. Well.' Fielding sighed. 'By the way, that odd-looking . . . er . . . guest of yours from Bristol came downstairs half an hour ago and gave me your note. I've sent him back to Bristol in a police car. You're being very mysterious, Super — '

'I'm taking risks, sir,' the Super returned aggressively, 'that entitle me to be mysterious. I'm taking risks you wouldn't dare look at.' He grinned maliciously. 'That's the big advantage of not being an official policeman. But don't worry, Colonel. You'll get the results.'

The chief constable smiled grimly.

'Results! You're right there, Super,' he agreed warmly. 'Well, until tomorrow. You know where to find me in the meantime.'

Five minutes later the Super picked up the telephone and asked to speak to Inspector Griffiths. He was put through immediately by the constable on duty at the telephone.

'Listen, Inspector,' he said urgently, 'you remember them particulars you took from Lucille Everard about herself? I told you to do nothin' about 'em for the moment. Well, now! Shut yourself in the private office and give them particulars to the Yard. I want a check-up made as a matter of top priority.'

The Super looked at Henry as he replaced the receiver. Henry said:

'You've taken a long time checking up on the Frenchwoman, haven't you, sir?'

'I have, son.' The Super seemed smugly pleased with himself. 'A dark horse is sometimes more useful that way. Lucille Everard had been pretty useful that way. But I don't want no loose ends when I close this case; and it won't be long now, as I told you. In the meantime, there's lunch. I think we might eat together down in the dining-room. I ain't even seen the newspapers yet, to find out what's been goin' on 'ere.'

The Super enjoyed his lunch *and* the newspapers; and he took no more notice of the Frenchwoman who waited on Henry and himself than if she had not existed.

After lunch he suggested a game of billiards, and spent the whole afternoon letting Henry beat him.

He had their tea brought up to Laval's room, and said when Lucille had departed after bringing their tray:

'It doesn't suit me very well, son, this waitin'.'

'It didn't appear to suit your game this afternoon,' Henry smiled. 'You know, it would be terrifically exciting to share everything that's in that wise old head of yours, Mr. Greene.'

The Super grunted.

'It'd be so excitin' you'd drop dead, Henry.'

He unlocked a drawer of the desk and took out the leather-covered book Henry had brought back from Bristol. He opened this, studied the first writing page for a long moment, and locked away the book again.

Then he relaxed, stretching out his legs under the desk, folding his podgy hands across his stomach, and closing his eyes. It was ten minutes later when Henry managed to persuade him to sample the tea and toast . . .

By half-past five he was stretched out again behind the desk, and seemingly asleep. But when the telephone rang at 6.15 he sat up as though a bee had stung his posterior, and grabbed the receiver.

The voice of Inspector Holland came to him:

'Your man has gone, Super.'

'*Gone!*' the Super barked. 'When?'

'Fifteen minutes ago. Gone for good, apparently.'

The Super relaxed, as though the last news had relieved him.

'Good. Now let's have the whole thing over again, Frank, and don't miss out as much as a comma.'

Shorthand was one of the Super's many accomplishments. He took down Holland's report verbatim. He had filled fourteen of the small pages of the memo pad in front of him by the time Holland had finished.

'That's fine, Frank,' he said, with forced enthusiasm. 'I'll want it in writing in due course, naturally, but this'll do for now. No, you go home to bed.'

He jammed the receiver back on to its rest.

'Now, Henry,' he said, 'I got to transcribe this short'and and write a long report of my own. You'd better push off and make an early night of it. I — '

The telephone rang again. He grabbed it.

'Yes? Well, you've been quick, me lad! . . . One of your constables *married* the girl, eh? Bring 'im on the line and make it snappy . . . Yes . . . Yes . . . Yes . . . '

There was a long period of listening, and, finally, the Super said:

'Thank *you*, son. I only wish I 'ad a

picture for you, but what you've given me's good enough for now. There *weren't* no pictures; that's the main thing. You be back in the mornin' early in case you're wanted. Goodnight.'

He rang off and appealed to Henry with his hands. He looked suddenly completely worn out.

'Henry,' he said, indicating the papers on his desk, 'be a good scout and keep the door of this room shut behind you, until I ring in the mornin' that I'm ready. I got one 'ell of a lot of work to do; simple arithmetic it is, and some not so simple; but I got to check up on everything and . . . 'Op it, Henry,' he ordered. 'Come back and meet the murderer. But don't come until I ring in the mornin' . . . '

24

It was noon next day before the Super answered repeated knockings on his door — except with a growl to keep out. A succession of telephone calls had been coming through for him. Only one originated from himself, and that was a secret between himself and the constable in charge of the small hotel telephone board.

When he opened the door at last, at the appointed hour, he looked weary beyond words, and older than he had ever done.

The first of the little gathering outside the door of Laval's room to enter it was Major Valentine.

'Greene,' he protested, 'I got back here two hours ago. Why couldn't you have seen me — ?'

'Sit down, Major,' the Super admonished him. 'That chair in front of Laval's big desk. You 'adn't got anything to report.'

'No,' Valentine protested, 'but still — '

Colonel Fielding stalked into the room and planted himself in the chair Valentine had occupied during Amber's testimony . . . how long ago was that? Inspector Griffiths followed, and stood by the fireplace. Henry did the same, not sure, until the Super waved him inside, whether he was wanted or not.

Sergeant Evans was out in the corridor too, but the Super shut the door on him, telling him to mount guard. Then the Super wandered back to the chair behind Laval's great desk and sighed resignedly, and looked at his three companions in turn. It seemed a small assembly for so large and ornate a room.

'Superintendent Greene,' the chief constable began rather stiffly, 'you've been keeping us waiting a long time. I think, perhaps, you may still be wanting this report on Lucille Everard. I don't know whether the presence of Major Valentine makes any difference, but, for what it's worth, this — '

'Major Valentine,' the Super said, mustering himself on his chair, 'makes all the difference. That's why I've got him here across the desk from me. Major Valentine can open these proceedings by tellin' us what 'e turned up at Boxsted yesterday about Threeways, during the occupation by the Lavals durin' the war.'

Valentine looked taken aback by the Super's attitude.

'I tried to get to you two hours ago, Super,' he protested, 'when I got back from Boxsted. I'm afraid I drew a blank. I told you on the telephone that — '

'What you didn't tell me,' the Super rasped, staring at the ceiling, 'was that you interviewed an elderly maid in the 'ouse next door to Threeways. A maid who,' and he began to forget his dropped aspirates again, 'was there when Nadine and Laval were in occupation during the war. During them parties, remember? This maid told you a lot about them goings on. But, at the end of the war, she happened to spend a holiday in Paignton, Devon. And there, by accident, she encountered Nadine again.' He paused to blow an aggressive snort through his nose. 'Nadine was with two men in uniform. One was the chap we know as Robert Charlton. The other *was you*. This maid was all upset because Nadine looked through her when she wanted to be recognized. So she made some inquiries. Nadine had a house rented in Paignton. Charlton was known there as her brother. You was known there, during her stay, as her *fiancé*.'

There was a deathly pause. Valentine stared blankly at the Super. Then he said hoarsely:

'What's the meaning of this, Super? I . . . I don't understand.'

'I mean,' the Super said, 'that you didn't report this interview with that maid in the house next door to Threeways, when you telephoned me from Boxsted. You said you'd got nothin' . . . '

'But . . . damn it, man!' Valentine cried wildly. 'I didn't leave Boxsted until early this morning — '

'You left Boxsted,' the Super replied, 'about six o'clock last evening. And you got that information from that maid hours before that. You see, Major, I had a Yard man followin' you from the moment you left your hotel — the name of which you obligingly gave me — until you left Boxsted yesterday evening. You got back here at ten this morning, eh? Why did it take you all them hours to do a four-hour trip?'

He opened a drawer in the desk in front of him and took out the book Henry had brought from Bristol. He opened it in front of Major Valentine. The first page contained this beginning in handwriting the major could not have mistaken:

A diary of
activities in Paignton,
By
Nadine 'Price'
from the advent of Major Valentine
until . . . .

Major Valentine stared at the page for a long, timeless moment. But he was still in control of himself as he drew back and stared at the Super.

'I don't get you . . . ' he said thickly.

The Super pulled out of the drawer in front of him the photograph of Janet and Nadine Price, from Laval's album, and laid it in front of the major.

'Take a look at that,' he invited, with a gentleness that, for the life of him, he could not keep from his voice. 'One of those women was Janet the barmaid here, Major, as you will see for yourself. The other is a picture of the woman you . . . believed to be your wife.'

Valentine stiffened in his chair. He seemed to age ten years in as many seconds; to become a shadow of himself, as he stared at the Super.

'Go *on*!' he said breathlessly at length; and it was in that moment that Henry Baxter saw how sick a man he was. 'Go *on*, Super . . . ?'

The Super glared at the picture of the two women as though he hated it as much as Valentine, apparently, feared it.

'Major Valentine,' he said very gently, 'I have just shown you a picture of Nadine. You didn't believe one existed. I have also — in spite of the fact that you murdered Laval — several snapshots of that oil-painting of Robert Charlton which you destroyed in my room in this hotel. I took them before dinner that evening; before you got to the painting while Laval provided you with an 'alibi' before you murdered him . . . '

He looked at the major almost appealingly.

'Do you want me to go on?' he demanded. 'Do you want me to read from that second diary of Nadine's that began with Paignton . . . ?'

Valentine covered his face with his hands for a brief moment, and then he dropped them. His face was grey and old.

'No,' he said, 'you win. I'd rather . . . get it over with here, Super, if it's possible. Only,' he added, falling limp on his chair, 'I suppose it isn't possible . . . '

25

Courage was all around him as Major Valentine drew himself upright in his chair and faced that unofficial court martial. He was superb, albeit a murderer many times over. He was also, as he pointed out apologetically, a dying man beyond the reach of any court. He was a man unto himself . . .

'Very well, gentlemen,' he began, 'I give in. I have to, anyway.' He had a sympathetic smile for the Super. 'He's got all the cards in his hands, and they're considerable cards . . .

'I met Robert Charlton, as I knew him by name, in the war. He was in Commandos. He had great charm as a man. He . . . saved my life on one of our raids. That meant a great deal to me. It meant nothing,' he added bitterly, 'to him. I realize that now. Perhaps you know that my father died at Dunkirk. We are a proud family.

Nevertheless, Charlton meant so much to me that I spent a leave, during the war, at Paignton — with Charlton and the woman he introduced as his sister.

'I did not know, gentlemen, that they were man and wife. I did not know what Nadine had been. I fell hell for leather for Nadine, and, accepting Charlton for what he appeared to be — they were living as brother and sister at Paignton at the time — I married her.

'It was an impulsive thing. One does that sort of thing in the war. My father had just been killed, so I didn't hesitate. I married her. And,' he went on vehemently, 'my child was born. My child and hers!'

He paused, gathering himself.

'After the war — and don't worry, Super, dates don't matter much in this! — I took my wife to my mother and my home in Scotland. I made Robert Charlton — that, of course, was the name they went under then — my farm manager. We were very happy. My mother, who is an invalid, was as much enamoured with Nadine and her 'brother' as myself, and accepted them. Ultimately, I appointed Charlton manager of the whole estate . . .

'Then, quite suddenly — can we cut out the incidentals? — I made two discoveries. One was that Charlton was swindling me. The other was . . . well, I discovered them in each other's arms, and they made no bones about it. They were not brother and sister but man and wife!

'The point of all this, of course,' he went on bitterly, 'was that my son — the son I had had by Nadine, the son who was accepted by my mother and everyone else who mattered — was a bastard. They made no bones about it. They used my son, then a lovely boy, as the means of blackmail. The truth would have killed my mother, dishonoured our family, and destroyed the boy I loved as my son and heir.'

Valentine stopped to get a grip on himself.

'I cleared them out. Then, gentlemen, I began to realize what I was up against.

They started to blackmail me. I paid up because of my son — my son and heir,' he cried passionately, 'whom my mother and I loved. The son those two swine could have destroyed along with my family name and honour. And how they knew it! This, indeed, was their diabolical plot from the beginning!

'But I . . . well, another factor intervened just then to alter my sense of perspective. A specialist told me I had a few months only to live; that I was dying of cancer . . . And perhaps my subsequent perspective is based on a cancer of the mind . . . '

He looked straight at the Super, whose head was bent.

'I had to make a decision, Greene, and I made it. I decided that the only way to save my son, my mother, and my family, was to murder Nadine and Charlton — and the whole story of my son's shameful birth. I decided to follow them and destroy them, and give my son honour and happiness, and my family its rightful place in history.

'So I paid their blackmail for the time

being. I kept track of them unknown to them. I followed them here to Larne and Colwin. Their purpose here, Super, should be obvious to you by now. Nadine was making an exhibition of herself on purpose to bolster up the price of the final settlement they would have *said* they would accept from me. So you see, the more notorious she could make herself here — in the absence of a picture anyone could publish, which was, of course, our common concern — the higher the price she could have demanded of me.

'A final settlement!' He laughed derisively. 'I realized the impossibility of that. I realized . . . ' He paused, wiping his face with his hand. 'I . . . was used to murder, gentlemen. I had murdered for the cause of freedom. I was prepared to murder, assuredly, for the cause of my son, my mother, my family name, and the happiness of all concerned — when the victims were the most despicable creatures imaginable. I was risking nothing, gentlemen, when my own life was petering out as it was . . . and is . . .

'So,' he braced himself again, 'I traced them here and plotted their destruction. I had a half-way house at which I stayed on my visits here, Super, as that French tramp I talked to you about. I learned the lie of the land, the habits of everyone, and in due course I murdered them . . .

'I didn't know about that grave,' he went on, now in an almost conversational tone, as though the subject had ceased to have any real personal interest. 'I read about it, realized it was an ideal place in which to get rid of the bodies. I had nothing to do with the death of Miss Evelyn Radford, the night I killed those two in Charlton's cottage, because I did not realize what Nadine was after when she left Charlton alone in their cottage after their panic-stricken conversation . . . I was too busy strangling Charlton.

'I . . . I am sorry, gentlemen,' he wound up, again on that pathetic note of apology, 'if I am not comprehensive in this story. I killed for my son, my mother, my family, as I would kill again for them . . . because that boy *is my son*. Even though his mother was . . . that woman . . . '

He sat very upright in his chair as he concluded:

'Yes, Super, I dare say you've been right about everything your uncanny brain has dug out of this. Those two photographs you have in your possession are my undoing. But . . . wasn't it rather a dirty trick to have sent one of your policemen to have followed me in Boxsted, and have checked up on my interviews, and have told you . . . what I kept back?'

The Super looked ugly as he leaned over the desk and put his hand on the 'Paignton' diary of Nadine Price's.

'That isn't the only dirty trick I played on you, Major,' he said harshly. 'Here's another.'

He turned over the first page of the diary. The second page of the book that Henry Baxter had brought from Bristol was blank. Major Valentine recoiled from the revelation. The Super snarled:

'Major Valentine, that page is a forgery.

I got it done myself. It's nasty, isn't it? So is three murders . . . of any human beings, and for any reason at all. And you darned nearly got away with those!'

26

The Super was muttering away to himself. He was tired out, almost oblivious of his companions; like an old man going over the lessons he had learned in a long experience:

'You know, Valentine . . . two and two make four. You was the only one who'd seen that oil-painting . . . What was your alibi worth afterwards? . . . It all depended on Laval, and Laval was murdered . . . See what I mean? If Laval had given you time to have got up to that room and have got back . . . Then Laval was dead and couldn't contradict himself . . . And you were the only one who could have done the murder, in a jiffy, and have got back to me, and then down into the bar . . . *unnoticed* . . .

'You know,' he went on, suddenly conversational, and looking at Valentine, 'that's where two and two make four, and the answer is only four. You were the only *possible* one, Major . . . barring somebody was hidin' on the roof, or Amber was lyin', or Henry was slippin' up — which the lad never did yet to my knowledge . . .

'But before then,' he said, as though emphasizing a point, 'you'd made a big mistake. A really big mistake. I checked up on it, not knowin' what I was doin', the morning after the murder of Laval, when I was checkin' up on them telephone calls of yours. The one came through from Scotland that night all right; but I also checked up on the one you said you had *from* Scotland that evening, before you came over 'ere to dinner. Remember it, Major? It was a matter of sheer routine with me. But it paid dividends. You said, after dinner, as 'ow that estate manager of yours in Scotland had telephoned *you* after we'd left you that afternoon; you complained that a chap couldn't get away from such chaps. He'd telephoned you, you said; but when I checked up on that call I found the call was *from* you *to* Scotland. That little difference, Major, between the words 'from' and 'to' and the frills you added on to it all . . .

'No.' He wagged his head reprovingly. 'That put me on to you. It made me question your alibi over the murder and, before then, the despoilin' of that oil-paintin'. It made me see, Major, that you could have persuaded Laval into coverin' you while you was supposed to be in 'is office after dinner, takin' that call from Scotland, while your pal in Scotland was holdin' on — '

'For God's sake,' Valentine intervened, almost hysterically, 'since you've got it, then say it! I pinched those gloves from his kitchen; I pinched one of his towels; I destroyed that oil-painting; and Laval was covering me all the time — while I told my pal in Scotland to hold the line. Don't bring *him* into it. I told Laval, frankly, that I wanted to look at the parcel Henry Baxter had brought in; I promised to explain to him later; I hinted it might have to do with something that concerned him; and, having a guilty conscience — '

'All right, Major,' the Super continued,

more gently than ever, 'you faked that alibi for yourself, knowing that you had to kill Laval to confirm it — because it was so important to you to destroy the picture of Robert Charlton.'

'Yes, damn it all, because of his connection with Nadine!'

The Super sighed.

'Nadine,' he said. 'The cause of it all. Well once I had seen how that alibi might've been a fake, Major, the rest fell into place. You were very keen on spottin' me when I got to the hotel, under the common name that belongs to me. The next afternoon, remember, you hung on until three-thirty to see what Henry and me'd been up to since breakfast, and then came to look for us. You was very interested in that brown-paper parcel of Henry's. And that uncomfortable 'ouse wasn't 'ardly the place for a man of your wealth; not the way you was livin' without a maid. Then I startled you several times; you wasn't very convincin' when you saw that oil-paintin' and turned pale, you know, and took quite a time before you 'remembered' havin' seen Charlton on the river path by your garden; and, on top of everthing, it was pretty odd, though you was forthright, your bein' with your gardener when he was detailed for the job of fillin' in that grave — '

'*Shut up!*' There is a limit to all things, and Valentine had reached *his* limit. 'All right, Superintendent Greene, I've admitted my crimes, haven't I? In a moment, you'll be telling me it was *brave* of me to have told you about the French tramp, my disguised self . . . '

The Super stared at Valentine dolefully.

'About your build, Major,' he said. 'You gave me that yourself. Yes, it *was* brave of you, when Amber was in this room, to 'ave planted yourself in front of him and, virtually, 'ave dared him to connect that character with yourself. You succeeded in what you was after. 'E likened the Frenchy's build with 'is own . . . which is the same thing.'

He slammed the flat of his hand on the desk and got to his feet.

'Colonel Fielding,' he said, 'I commend Major Valentine to you as the murderer

416

of three people. I don't give a damn
what sort of people they were. Murder
is murder, and Valentine is guilty on 'is
own confession.'

He walked around the desk to Henry
Baxter.

'Come on, son,' he said. 'I've 'ad
enough of my job, even in retirement.
Let's get out of this.'

He turned to Colonel Fielding.

'If it means anything,' he said, 'I gave
orders for your men to watch Amber,
Oaker and Pugh, to keep their attention
off Major Valentine. You can tell Amber
I understand his conversation with Willie
Oaker on the night before the grave was
closed in; they were plannin' to put the
spade on that path through the woods
and *make* someone discover the grave
they'd dug two nights before then.'

He looked over his shoulder at Major
Valentine.

'Two Victoria Crosses in a row, Major,'
he said sadly. 'And then you have to get
all out of perspective like this, for a son
who won't, please God, ever know a war.
It's all wrong, you know. Murder I mean.

All right in a war . . . maybe that's the trouble. In the meantime, Henry and me 'ave got to look after that baby of Janet's . . . '

He went away, shaking his head.

THE END

A LANCE FOR THE DEVIL
Robert Charles

The funeral service of Pope Paul VI was to be held in the great plaza before St. Peter's Cathedral in Rome, and was to be the scene of the most monstrous mass assassination of political leaders the world had ever known. Only Counter-Terror could prevent it.

IN THAT RICH EARTH
Alan Sewart

How long does it take for a human body to decay until only the bones remain? When Detective Sergeant Harry Chamberlane received news of a body, he raised exactly that question. But whose was the body? Who was to blame for the death and in what circumstances?

MURDER AS USUAL
Hugh Pentecost

A psychotic girl shot and killed Mac Crenshaw, who had come to the New England town with the advance party for Senator Farraday. Private detective David Cotter agreed that the girl was probably just a pawn in a complex game — but who had sent her on the assignment?

THE MARGIN
Ian Stuart

It is rumoured that Walkers Brewery has been selling arms to the South African army, and Graham Lorimer is asked to investigate. He meets the beautiful Shelley van Rynveld, who is dedicated to ending apartheid. When a Walkers employee is killed in a hit-and-run accident, his wife tells Graham that he's been seeing Shelly van Rynveld . . .

TOO LATE FOR THE FUNERAL
Roger Ormerod

Carol Turner, seventeen, and a mystery, is very close to a murder, and she has in her possession a weapon that could prove a number of things. But it is Elsa Mallin who suffers most before the truth of Carol Turner releases her.

NIGHT OF THE FAIR
Jay Baker

The gun was the last of the things for which Harry Judd had fought and now it was in the hands of his worst enemy, aimed at the boy he had tried to help. This was the night in which the past had to be faced again and finally understood.

PAY-OFF IN SWITZERLAND
Bill Knox

'Hot' British currency was being smuggled to Switzerland to be laundered, hidden in a safari-style convoy heading across Europe. Jonathan Gaunt, external auditor for the Queen's and Lord Treasurer's Remembrancer, went along with the safari, posing as a tourist, to get any lead he could. But sudden death trailed the convoy every kilometer to Lake Geneva.

SALVAGE JOB
Bill Knox

A storm has left the oil tanker S. S. *Craig Michael* stranded and almost blocking the only channel to the bay at Cabo Esco. Sent to investigate, marine insurance inspector Laird discovers that the Portuguese bay is hiding a powder keg of international proportions.

BOMB SCARE — FLIGHT 147
Peter Chambers

Smog delayed Flight 147, and so prevented a bomb exploding in mid-air. Walter Keane found that during the crisis he had been robbed of his jewel bag, and Mark Preston was hired to locate it without involving the police. When a murder was committed, Preston knew the stake had grown.

STAMBOUL INTRIGUE
Robert Charles

Greece and Turkey were on the brink of war, and the conflict could spell the beginning of the end for the Western defence pact of N.A.T.O. When the rumour of a plot to speed this possibility reached Counter-espionage in Whitehall, Simon Larren and Adrian Cleyton were despatched to Turkey . . .

CRACK IN THE SIDEWALK
Basil Copper

After brilliant scientist Professor Hopcroft is knocked down and killed by a car, L.A. private investigator Mike Faraday discovers that his death was murder and that differing groups are engaged in a power struggle for The Zetland Method. As Mike tries to discover what The Zetland Method is, corpses and hair-breadth escapes come thick and fast . . .

DEATH OF A MARINE
Charles Leader

When Mike M'Call found the mutilated corpse of a marine in an alleyway in Singapore, a thousand-strong marine battalion was hell-bent on revenge for their murdered comrade — and the next target for the tong gang of paid killers appeared to be M'Call himself . . .

ANYONE CAN MURDER
Freda Bream

Hubert Carson, the editorial Manager of the Herald Newspaper in Auckland, is found dead in his office. Carson's fellow employees knew that the unpopular chief reporter, Clive Yarwood, wanted Carson's job — but did he want it badly enough to kill for it?

CART BEFORE THE HEARSE
Roger Ormerod

Sometimes a case comes up backwards. When Ernest Connelly said 'I have killed . . . ', he did not name the victim. So Dave Mallin and George Coe find themselves attempting to discover a body to fit the crime.

SALESMAN OF DEATH
Charles Leader

For Mike M'Call, selling guns in Detroit proves a dangerous business — from the moment of his arrival in the middle of a racial riot, to the final clash of arms between two rival groups of militant extremists.

THE FOURTH SHADOW
Robert Charles

Simon Larren merely had to ensure that the visiting President of Maraquilla remained alive during a goodwill tour of the British Crown Colony of San Quito. But there were complications. Finally, there was a Communist-inspired bid for illegal independence from British rule, backed by the evil of voodoo.

SCAVENGERS AT WAR
Charles Leader

Colonel Piet Van Velsen needed an experienced officer for his mercenary commando, and Mike M'Call became a reluctant soldier. The Latin American Republic was torn apart by revolutionary guerrilla groups — but why were the ruthless Congo veterans unleashed on a province where no guerrilla threat existed?